Praise for *Silent Scream*

"Alex is at it again! This fun, riveting *Armchair Anthropologist* sequel is even better than the first! This time, the setting is Norway, with ample and sometimes hilarious gestures to Nordic Noir. Varzi's writing is sharp, funny, and filled with brilliant observations about neurological difference, cultural patterns, and the timeless human passions that fuel artistic creativity. Varzi invites us into the lively and curious imagination of her main character, expanding our minds along with her every step and blunder."

— Sherine F. Hamdy, Professor, Department of Anthropology, University of California, Irvine

"Roxanne Varzi's latest Anthropology Whodunnit combines theoretical sophistication and ethnographic sensitivity with sublime storytelling skills. The outcome is the most erudite mystery novel since Eco's "In the Name of the Rose." Reading Varzi's thrilling new mystery almost makes me wish for more murders in Oslo."

— Thorgeir Kolshus, Head of Department, Department of Social Anthropology, University of Oslo, Norway

"I always look forward to seeing a new mystery novel from Dr Varzi. I love how her mind works!"

— Dr. Fernette Eide, neurologist and co-author of the *Dyslexic Advantage*

"Ingenious, intriguing and atmospheric."

— Olga Wojta, author of the *Miss Blaine's Perfect* mystery series.

Praise for *Death in a Nutshell*

"A very unique story .... while you are reading a story about a murder, the author is also educating the reader in between chapters with her Field Notes. "
— Cozy Mystery Book Review

More than a breezy murder mystery – a real page-turner. Varzi tackles the history of visual anthropology and photography, the ethics of war photojournalism, paleontology, the use of dioramas – all the while keeping up the suspense.
— Camp Anthropology

Praise for *Warring Souls*

Inside and outside the pulse of war in Iran, close up and far away, Roxanne Varzi weaves her spell; two parts anthropology, one part poetry and film theory, three parts a soaring imagination and a big heart. A tour de force.
— *Michael Taussig, Columbia University*

How to study culture on a national scale, and present the results effectively, have long bedeviled anthropologists...no small achievement.
— *Patricia J. Higgins, American Anthropologist*

A multi-dimensional picture of Iranian youth. In playing the role of observer, participant and academic, Varzi reveals the psychological, philosophical and political facets of the crisis, thereby setting the stage for comprehensive reform.
— *Rose Carmen Goldberg, Journal of International Affairs*

[A]n extraordinary book written on many levels by an anthropologist who acts sometimes as a psychologist and some-

times as a sociologist. And when the described reality sounds too harsh for the reader, she balances it with a poetic prose narration.
— *Peter Chelkowski, NYU*

This painstaking study of an emergent Islamic secularism struggling to grow in the space between wars has a terrible poignancy at the present time.
— *Vron Ware, Signs*

Praise for *Last Scene Underground*

Literary romance and ethnography are joined in perfect dialogue in *Last Scene Underground*. Roxanne Varzi has written a rare, powerful book that is both a whirlwind story of how it feels to be young and idealistic during the time of the Green Movement, and a pointed reckoning with the state of censorship in Iran today.
— *Nahid Rachlin, author of Persian Girls*

This beautifully written book captures the predicament of every Iranian artist who is conflicted between one's own creative imagination, personal and social responsibilities, and political reality.
— *Shirin Neshat, Artist*

Amazing and wonderful! Roxanne Varzi brings together her own Iranian heritage, excellent ethnographic research, and deep insights—all in a gripping read.
— *Mary Elaine Hegland, author of Days of Revolution: Political Unrest in an Iranian Village*

Writing with an inspiring combination of creativity and criticality, Roxanne Varzi has crafted an exceptionally memorable portrait of Iran, bringing both Tehran and its young people to life.
— *John L. Jackson, Jr., Provost, University of Pennsylvania*

This surfeit is what remains after an ethnographer has paid dues to
the science of empirical social knowledge. What is left is not quite
hard data, but nonetheless an invaluable remainder of insight,
affect, conversation, and emotion; an entire sensorium, which even
if the ethnographer wants to, will not let her go.
— *Ather Zia, 3:AM Magazine*

# Silent Scream

## *A Nordic non-Noir*

Roxanne Varzi

BOUNCING
BOX
PRESS

An Armchair Anthropologist Murder Mystery

*Armchair Anthropologist where anthropology meets art --
powered by #dyslexicthinking*

*In an era of fake news and science denial, a little anthropology goes
a long way.*

Cover art designed by Kasra Paydavousi
All Artwork Copyright © 2025 Kasra Paydavousi

First Edition
Library of Congress Control Number: 2025919692
Varzi, Roxanne 1971
Silent Scream: A Nordic non-Noir / by Roxanne Varzi—1 st ed.
p. cm.
ISBN 9798988684411
[1. Murder Mystery—Anthropology—Oslo—Norway—Neurodiversity —Sound Studies—Dyslexia—ADHD—Amateur Sleuth—Climate Change—[Fic]-

*For Rumi, who will always be his own character.*

*The world is not what it pretends to be. All intellectual activity is fundamentally about exploring what is hidden out there, beneath the treacherous and distorting surface.*
Thomas Hylland Eriksen

*And if detective stories are escape literature, and why shouldn't they be, the reader can escape to sunny skies and blue water as well as to crime in the confines of an armchair.*
Agatha Christie, *Death on the Nile*

# Chapter 1

## *Killer Rhythm*

**B**obbing headsets flickering red, green, and blue lights illuminated Kulturkirken Jakob's silent disco night like a holiday show gone wild. The DJ at the green turntable spinning EDM dominated the disco, followed by red lights blinking to house music, and blue lights blissing out to Abba and Cher. Sporadically a stray out of tune A cappella voice bounced off the walls as dancers slammed into each other, swinging hips, shimmying shoulders and throwing arms up in the air.

Alex slipped off her headphones and savored the sensation of standing still in the silence while the crowd continued to dance away. She studied the dancers, trying to sense the beat. Was rhythm to be heard to sense, or could you, *Feel it in the air?* She wondered, humming, *Rhythm is a Dancer, it's a sole companion...*

She replaced her headset and set her channel to blue. A man changed channels each time Alex did: green to blue, blue to red, back to green. She smiled at him from a distance as they slipped into a shared rhythm. Another man, flashing green, shimmied up to Alex despite her blue light. They danced together in clashing beats. Sweat wet his brow and curly brown hair. He wiped his long bangs from his forehead with the back of his hand, and she recognized him from her first *Silent Singles* event -- the *Silent*

*Read*, at the library, where sitting across from one another, they periodically peeked up at each other from behind their books, communing in silence, careful not to break the rules. Tonight, the other *Silent Singles* club members were out of sight and would be none the wiser if these two slipped off their headsets to speak. Talking was a titillating possibility. Alex bit her lip and moved in closer. Her face was at his chest. She could feel the heat rising off his body; smell his spicy aftershave, whisper and be heard. She slipped off her headphones just as he slipped away.

"Hey, Hei," she called after him in English and Norwegian, her voice swallowed by the unselfconscious din of out-of-tune Eurovision karaoke on steroids.

She struggled after him through a seabed of swaying limbs and emerged unscathed and alone at the deserted knave of the church where the buzzing beat of heavy breathing and stomping feet receded. He was gone. Had slipping out not been an invitation to follow? Why play hide and seek?

She looked around: four walls and no doors. *Only ghosts slip through walls*, she shivered. She wiped her fogged tortoise glasses on her sweaty t-shirt, put them on and spotted a stairwell: admissible, or forbidden? Forgivable. She ventured down the stairs, nearly knocking her head on a low hanging beam.

"Hello?" she called out. Was this a game?

An open door led to a musty, empty coat room filled with dripping raincoats and wet umbrellas. She brushed her hand along the moist coats. They swung lightly from the racks unencumbered by heavy bodies. Another door, to the right of the stairwell, led to a bathroom. A New Yorker never passed up an empty restroom. She slipped in and re-applied her new Perfect Plum Pout lipstick – a splurge on her student budget, but too perfect a contrast to her auburn hair to pass-up. She wiped her glasses again and applied a fresh layer of blue mascara to her tired hazel eyes. The warm glow of mood lighting accentuated her ethnic ambiguity, gifted by her possibly Asian father.

Alex left the ladies' room and peeked into the men's room. No sign of her mystery man. No sign of anyone.

She returned upstairs and to the back of the church. The low lighting lent a warm tenor to the silence, enveloping her in a comfortable cozy feeling the Norwegians called *koselig*.

A dark mural of the nativity, barely perceptible in the low light, hung above a half-circle of empty kneelers. Alex was not religious but practiced both a respect for all belief and an innate call to participant observation. She kneeled, imagining a lingering scent of incense.

Baby Jesus at a disco. *Eder er i dag en frelser født* – Alex's translation app spat out: *Today is unto you a savior born.* Mary pinched her baby's blanket by the corner like a filthy object, as if she were revealing something unsavory. Alex typed her fieldnotes: *Savior, savory. Her newborn child. She should be holding him, cuddling him and cooing.* Alex was an anthropologist, and Oslo was her field.

A hush slipped through the church between songs like a lost prayer. The next song began reanimating the distant figures. Stray voices bounced off unaffected walls. Alex slipped her headphones back on and heard Ane Brun's *Take Hold of Me.* She stood to rejoin the party; she loved Ane Brun whom she saw perform at the Oslo Opera House. Ane's long, lovely arms whirled about her like a windmill wrapped in red chiffon. Her bright red satin lips summoned spirits with song. Alex touched her lips, *My lipstick!*

She rushed down the stairs to the bathroom, colliding headlong into a tall, handsome stranger. He wore a black knit hat and sported an indigo tattoo on his right arm. The tattoo was his least distinctive feature.

"Sorry," Alex apologized.

"Why?" His smile was broad and forgiving. His singsong Norwegian English made a statement sound like a question, and sad news sound happy.

"Why?" Alex asked.

A low, urgent grunting came from the basement.

"They found a nicer way to communicate," he winked at her. He had long blond lashes and barely perceptible freckles. She blushed and covered her ears with her headphones.

He leaned in, lifted her headphone and whispered, "Anders." The scruff on his cheek brushed hers and awakened an unexpected tingle of pleasure.

"Alex," she breathed.

"Let's go, Alex." Anders took her hand as *Pump up the Jam* came on the blue station.

Alex bounced back to the dance floor with Anders. He spun her, dipped her and returned her to his arms. She tried but failed to read his tattoo. Reading was not her strong suit.

The next song came on and Alex yanked off her headset.

"What is it?" Anders asked, removing his headset.

"Earworm," Alex answered.

"Let's get some air. There's a smoking exit downstairs. Pleasant view of the river," he said and gently took her headset.

"Yeah," Alex agreed.


"What happened to the lights?" Alex asked at the darkened stairwell.

"It's a timer?" Anders suggested.

He placed his hands on her shoulders and guided her down the dark stairs, a careful step at a time. Years of midnight bathroom trips without her glasses meant she could feel her way blindfolded anywhere. While she did not need Anders to guide her -- she wanted him to.

As her foot landed on the last stair, she felt a finger brush her ankle. She jumped back and screamed. Anders caught her from falling over the body slumped across the bottom of the stairs.

Alex flashed her phone light and Anders squatted down next to the man and asked if he was hurt.

"He must have hit his head on the beam. I came close earlier," Alex said.

"Out cold," Anders said.

"He grabbed my foot," Alex said.

"Or you brushed his hand," Anders suggested. He took the man's wrist in his hand. "Pulse is weak. Call—" Anders started.

"Calling the paramedics," a man said as he ran down the stairs. "I'm the night manager. We, I heard a scream."

"I'm a doctor," a woman following him said. She was buttoning up her shirt.

"That was fast," Alex remarked.

The doctor ignored Alex and addressed Anders in Norwegian. She came alongside the man and took his wrist. She tilted her head to listen for life.

"He's most likely drunk," the night manager chimed in.

"His breathing is rapid," the doctor grimaced as she placed her head on his cheek.

"Yet, he's so still. Still breathing?" Alex asked.

"Yes. I suggest you do the same," the woman said curtly. "Loud breathing is a sign of panic."

Anders rubbed Alex's hand, "In and out." He demonstrated a deep breath. "It's OK, we Norwegians like our drink, nothing to freak out about. He'll be fine. Follow my breath." He held her gaze and demonstrated a slow breath. "You have pretty eyes," he stated.

Alex held his gaze as they breathed together, wondering if Anders was a yoga instructor, or if all Norwegians were champion breathers – due to icy water dips once a year? She heard it was a new year's ritual. Her mind was racing.

"Let's turn him," the doctor directed Anders, in English, otherwise ignoring Alex. "On my count," she said. "One, two, three." They flipped him, and the doctor pulled off his wool cap.

Alex gasped.

"What is it?" Anders asked Alex. He lightly touched her hand.

"We are in a group together. I. We. I saw him earlier," Alex said, *He danced in my direction and disappeared* ... Alex studied him and said, "He was leaving and changed his mind -- or was he stopped?"

"Stopped?" The woman asked, pronouncing a sharp T at the end of the word.

"One arm is sleeveless. He was putting on his coat to leave when ... someone or something interrupted him," Alex suggested.

"And did what?" The night manager absently wiped lipstick from his cheek. Alex noted it was the same bright pink color as the doctor's smudged lipstick. She wore a wedding band; he did not.

"Knocked him to the ground," Anders answered.

"Or an epileptic episode," the doctor inferred. Her headphones hung around her neck like a stethoscope. "I'm going to meet the paramedics," she said standing.

"I'll make sure they know where to come," the manager said, and scurried off after her.

"I thought you were here alone," Anders looked up at Alex.

"I was. I am," Alex stuttered, "We attend events together, in silence."

"Why?" Anders asked.

"Why?" Alex asked, kneeling next to him.

"Why silence?"

"Not sure. We never spoke."

"Right," Anders replied. He put his cheek to the man's cheek.

"I thought it would be an easy way to make friends without speaking Norwegian."

"Everyone in Oslo speaks English," Anders pointed out. "We learn it in high school."

"It's less the language barrier, and more the social barrier. You find friend groups in kindergarten and stick together. I mean ... language is important," Alex blurted impulsively.

"I spoke with you," Anders reminded her.

"I shouldn't generalize. I didn't mean to offend... It's been ... I did try to learn Norwegian. Ask the passive-aggressive green owl. Duo hates me. I'm not great at languages. Sorry, I get verbose when I'm nervous."

"It's OK. There's no reason to be nervous," Anders said gently, "He's just drunk or something. You've never seen a drunk man?" Anders laughed.

"Is he dead?" Alex pointed to the man whose hand suddenly fell to his side.

"Dead? He's unresponsive," Ander's assured her. He rubbed her shoulders.

"Poor man," Alex said, and scooched away from Anders and closer to the man. She had seen a dying man and ...

"No name?" Anders asked.

"Not one I learned."

"So, you know him, but you don't know him?" Anders asked.

"More or less," Alex whispered. "I should know his name. A name is the same in any language," Alex said, her gaze off in the distance.

"What is it?" Anders followed her gaze.

"Nothing, the candle on the table," she said, "I'm tempted to light it." Candles were a Norwegian hack to instantly create hygge --coziness. The basement's vibe was the opposite of hygge – a darkness no candle could light. Anders tried anyway.

Alex knew he was doing everything he could to make her feel comfortable. It was the man lying unresponsive on the floor who needed comforting. Alex leaned over him and opened his jacket.

"What are you doing?" Anders ran back and put his hand on hers to stop her.

"Helping him breathe. He looks hot."

"The doctor wants him to stay warm," Anders said, kneeling beside her, "He could be in shock."

Alex ignored Anders and peeled away the man's half-worn coat. She put her hand on his heart.

"Alex?" Anders gently touched her elbow. She held her hand firmly to the man's chest and muttered, *no not again.*

"In and out," Anders instructed her to breathe.

"The murderer?"

"Murderer?" Anders said. "Not in Norway."

"You are aware of the overwhelmingly lucrative Nordic noir industry?" Alex asked.

"In and out," Anders stroked her back.

"The killer was in and out?" Alex looked up at Anders but did not remove her hand.

"Alex, what is it? Why do you insist someone tried to kill him, this is not the U.S," he said.

Alex raised her hand like lady Macbeth revealing her blood-soaked palm.


The paramedics arrived and pronounced him dead at the scene, after which the police arrived and sequestered the party. They took brief witness statements and released the stream of disco goers back into the night. Everyone but Alex and Anders, who were asked to stay behind for further questioning.

"You were in attendance, ja?" the officer asked Alex. She had taken Alex away to a quiet corner, sleekly separating her from Anders.

"In attendance?" Alex clarified, in case something was lost in translation. *Of course I was in attendance, I stumbled on the body,* she wanted to shout. Was the officer asking if she was attending? As in a question she had been asked on repeat her whole life: "Are you paying attention?"

*What did it mean to attend to? Attentio, active direction of the mind. Was attention auditory, to be in audience? Was it about hearing, listening? Teachers asked whether she was listening, when they really wanted to know if she was paying attention. Will hearing without paying attention form a memory of what was heard? If a tree falls... We must listen. Hearing is not enough. Listening demands attention. Hearing does not.*

"Miss?" The officer demanded, cool as a cucumber. Unlike American cops who packed jalapeño level heat, Alex did not spot a single gun. What she did see was a police officer hug a freaked-out disco-goer, while Alex was politely invited not to leave Oslo, making her proverbial police hug more of a chokehold.

"Enjoy Norway for now," the officer said as she re-tied her blond ponytail.

Alex started toward the stairs, desperate and relieved to leave, when another officer stopped her.

"You. Come with me," he said and took her to the door of the lady's room.

"You were here?" The officer asked, pointing to the bathroom, now cordoned with yellow police tape.

"Yes, I told you in my statement," Alex's heart beat rapidly. Alex, who tended to overshare, had told the police her every move. "Yes, I was in the bathroom earlier, before all this." Alex desperately wanted to curl up on the old church pew along the wall outside the lady's room. "I sat at the kneelers. I danced. I told you." Alex reminded her. She wished she had a paper bag to breathe into. She wished Anders were with her.

"Come in here, please," the officer instructed her and lifted the tape so she could duck under.

"Explain?" The officer pointed to a primitive stick figure drawn in red crayon on the mirror.

"It's a petroglyph," Alex answered like the good student she sometimes was. The Norwegian police would recognize a petroglyph when they saw one. The stick figures graced boulders and stone surfaces all over Norway. Alex once mistook one as child's play and, to the horror of the locals, stepped on it. Norwegians did not construct iron-clad fences around their antiquities. They trusted people to act respectfully.

"Miss?" the police coaxed her back to the task at hand.

"There's one in Ekeberg Park," Alex offered. The sculpture park was a short tram ride or twenty-minute walk from Alex's apartment. Everything in Oslo was within walking distance if you were Norwegian. Alex's mind raced.

"Yep," The police officer sighed.

"I'm not that kind of anthropologist," Alex stammered, "I study contemporary civilization," Alex explained. Earlier, when giving her statement, she had explained that she was in Norway conducting research for her anthropology PhD. She did not clarify what kind of anthropology, and now she was being used as an archeological expert.

"People always confuse social cultural anthropology with archeology. I study contemporary civilization, the Anthropocene, you know, people alive now. Archeologists on the other hand, they—"

"We are studying a dead person, alive an hour ago," the officer cut in curtly. "So, if you could please answer the question."

"Sorry, I missed the question."

"Have you seen this before?"

"No. I can confirm I've never seen it."

"Look closer," the officer demanded. "Do you recognize anything?"

Alex approached the washbasin and looked into the mirror. The figure staring back at her was drawn with Alex's new, expensive, organic Perfect Plum Pout lipstick.

# Fieldnotes From the Frosty Fjord

*The anthropologist arrives, and the spirits depart.* Joseph Campbell

Do I go home and appease the spirits -- or choose a different profession?

Sound: a collision of molecules. Chance: a collision of events. Anthropology: Alex on a collision course.

Dear Will,

You owe me a hundred bucks. You bet I wouldn't leave NYC and here I am in Oslo. As you insist that we communicate via letter, and as I am limited in my ability to write, it's either a letter to you or fieldnotes. Tonight, you win. Convincing a dyslexic to engage in a communication art so doomed to failure is quite a feat. You had me at Wordsworth: the world is, indeed, too much with us. I disagree Will a relationship doesn't dim when ~~lovers~~ friends talk every day. The quotidian is integral to ~~romantic~~ relationships. ~~Are we in a "relationship?"~~ I would relish hearing your voice, about your day, ~~every day~~. Every mundane detail. About the wolves and your friends (some of whom are wolves, literally and pejoratively). Tell me what you're reading, cooking, thinking. ~~I love the sound of~~

~~your voice, the resonance of certainty, the pitch of care and concern.~~

I have a race car brain with crap brakes. Coffee can slow me down, but not tonight. Not like I planned to sleep tonight, I hoped to be dictating fast and furious fieldwork notes ~~or having fast and furious~~ ... Kit's texting, I miss her. She's been so busy with her new job, ~~and I'm so busy failing~~

KIT

> Disco night, hello? No news = good news? Meet any new friends?

ALEX

> Glowing skin, bouncy curls, big smile, cat eye liner – nice profile picture! It's less assistant professor and more dating app – what's up?

KIT

> Evading the question won't work. You're hiding something, or someone. Meet anyone?

ALEX

> Yup. He's showering.

*Wrong answer, she's calling.*

KIT

> Alex???? Answer!!! WhatsApp shows you're online!!!

*Kit's stellar at reading technology and even better at reading me.*

ALEX

> April Fools! No man in the shower.

KIT

> You're not funny. It's March 31st in California. How was the disco?

ALEX

> Research.

KIT

As if you're up writing fieldnotes. What big
ethnographic discovery is keeping you up so late?

ALEX

...

~~Dead body.~~
*She'd freak out and be on the next plane. A grown-ass woman
does not need rescuing. This can't be happening again.*

Adorno's idea of music's collective spirit -- it's all
ideology and good vibes

~~until someone gets killed.~~

Every sound says we.

KIT

And your "We?"

ALEX

My wee (as in tiny) social life, or my wee (as in tiny)
ethnographic life? They crashed on the dancefloor
in a spectacular collision tonight.

KIT

You collide with anyone human, drama queen?

*Kit is immune to distraction.*

KIT

What happened to that hottie from the Silent
Read?

ALEX

I saw him for a hot minute and then... I lost him.

How's this for a research question: can silence
and sound co-exist?

KIT

How's this for a better question: can Alex and a man co-exist? Are you sure you didn't try to lose him?

ALEX

Not fair. He's distancing me with his letter only rule. Talk about fear of intimacy.

KIT

The Disco hottie? I thought it was a silent meet-up, you never mentioned letters.

ALEX

Will. I meant Will.

KIT

Letters are so intimate. You chose to leave Bozeman.

*And still, the city's ghosts follow me...*

ALEX

Need Sleep. Night, Night XO

# Chapter 2

## *Silent Spring*

A warm spring glow kissed and woke the Botanical Garden from its winter nap. Then like a cruel, cold April Fool's Day joke, a bitter blanket of snow slammed it back to sleep. Still, tiny, tenacious sprouts of green stretched from slumbering bulbs underground and bumped along the limbs of barren trees below the dusting of snow.

The Victorian Water Lily House yawned a puff of steam as Alex opened the door. She sneezed.

"Hei," Liv startled her.

"Didn't hear you," Alex said. Liv listened to music while she worked. The louder, the better.

"You look like you've seen a ghost," Liv said.

"Can't see anything else." Alex wiped her fogged-up glasses on her wet puffer jacket, which did not help.

Liv handed her a tissue. "Sit," Liv said. "Warm-up."

Alex met Liv, a botanist at the University Botanical Gardens, on her first day at the gardens when she stumbled into the Lily House looking for a place to warm-up and found Liv at work on her lily project. They fell into a daily teatime, when Alex took a break from her recording project and Liv from her Lilies. Liv was Alex's sole Norwegian friend, but not, Liv insisted, Alex's "native informant," as she was not a "typical" Norwegian due to five years living and working in London's Kew Gardens. She had a posh London accent, a sleek black bob (dyed) and an ever-so-slightly different outlook on life from the "average Norwegian." Trained in anthropology, Alex would not posit the existence of an "average Norwegian."

"It's beautiful outside. A winter wonderland," Alex marveled.

"Nature's little April Fools' prank is not amusing for those of us she has tortured all winter," Liv stated.

"It charms things to life. I half expected Ibsen's statue to shrug the snow dusting off his bronze shoulders and strut about," Alex said.

Liv chortled. "You missed the freezing cold part of the year when days are as short as a coffee break."

"Come on, tell me you don't love the pigeon tracks, or the fluffy white line along the tram cable or the little mound of snow on a trashcan lid."

"Snow's perfect symmetry does not excuse its excess. It has overstayed its welcome," Liv said with finality. "Never mind the snow. How was your night out? Death at the disco?" Liv poured tea from her thermos and handed a cup to Alex.

"You've heard?" Alex was disappointed. She wanted to break the big news. Liv told exceptional stories of finding venomous spiders curled up in prize roses at Kew Gardens, finding love in a first kiss atop a glacier under the Northern lights; finding peace, kayaking among icebergs. Alex's Oslo life was long walks recording sound, and long hot showers to warm-up after -- nothing to write home about. She finally had a story to tell Liv, and someone had beat her to it.

"Who told you?" Alex asked.

"Word gets around," Liv said. "Oslo's a village."

"Were Botanical Garden folks there?" Alex asked. She hadn't recognized anyone.

"No, my neighbor's daughter's friend broke the news to the whole neighborhood."

"How is this such big news? Aren't people always getting offed in Oslo?" Alex quipped. *Offed in Oslo*, great title for her ethnography, thought Alex.

"Ha, ha," Liv said. "Oslo is the safest Noir scene in the world." Liv was a fan of Jo Nesbo's thrillers and took the occasional meal at Schroeder's Restaurant where a table was dedicated to Nesbo's fictional detective, Harry Hole. Alex called Nesbo's writing "too violent" -- an accusation Liv took personally. Nesbo was a Norwegian national treasure.

"You heard about the prehistoric symbol on the bathroom mirror?" Alex asked.

"Symbol?" Liv asked. She shook off her lab coat and sat down next to Alex. Liv rarely broke from work to chat. In this she was a hundred percent Norwegian. "What kind?"

"No idea, but drumroll: it was drawn with my lipstick."

"What?" She inched away. "You lent the killer your lipstick?" Liv asked. "You met the killer?"

"No! I was alone. I left my lipstick on the sink in the bathroom and--"

"Inconvenient," Liv said.

"Exactly how the police put it. You're more Norwegian than you think. American police would not find this *inconvenient*," Alex said.

"No?"

They'd find it *suspicious*, thought Alex. Inconvenient was an understatement.

"How did they know it was your lipstick?" Liv asked, setting down her thermos to pull off her heavy wool sweater. Beads of sweat dotted her forehead. The greenhouse felt hotter than usual.

"I told them in my statement. I left my lipstick behind in the bathroom. I was going back downstairs to retrieve it, when," Alex skipped over meeting Anders, "I got distracted."

"Of course you did." Liv said and poured Alex more tea. "Alex, you may have met the killer in the bathroom. Did you see anyone?"

"No. The police also asked -- they kept my lipstick."

"Did you want it back?" Liv made a sour face.

"No. But …I don't know, I would have liked to chuck it in the trash myself. It's intimate –it touched my lips."

"It's evidence in a crime. Yeah." Liv sucked in a sharp breath as Norwegians did when they drew a conclusion. "Strange. And the killer touched it. Your DNA and the murderer's," Liv sipped her tea. She was pensive, which was not unusual in a Norwegian conversation, but not with Liv. "Are you a suspect?" Liv asked carefully.

"What? They can't think--" Alex started.

"Well, I mean, aren't you? Having been there. And …your lipstick. And, yeah, weird." Liv sucked in air, a sign the matter was settled. She set down her teacup, picked up her lily pad rehabilitation kit and stood to leave.

Alex put her head between her knees.

"Alex?" Liv asked.

"The heat is making me woozy. I was up all night. Need a minute…" The moldy scent of stagnation, and the realization of her new reality made her nauseous.

"I'm sorry, I did not mean to suggest you're a suspect, but it must have occurred to you. Surely, they're keeping an eye on you."

"They didn't say," Alex answered.

"I'll be next door if anyone comes," Liv said and left.

"Why would anyone—" Alex started, but Liv was gone. She laid down across the wooden bench and fell asleep.


Alex woke to a rapid knock on the door. She sat-up confused, drenched in sweat and unsure where she was.

"Liv?" Alex called over the loud music.

When Liv didn't respond, Alex went to answer the door, expecting the usual harried mother looking for a lost child. She was instead met by two police officers. She impulsively shut the door and just as quickly opened it.

"Sorry, I…" Alex stammered.

"Ms. Olsen?" they asked in unison.

"Is she expecting you?" Alex asked. They stepped inside without answering and Alex led them to the Lily rehab room, which was demarcated not by a wall, or a door, but by a large plastic tarp. She folded the tarp back and ushered them in.

"Thank you," the officer said curtly, indicating Alex could leave.

Alex retreated behind the tarp.

"Liv Olsen," she heard Liv introduce herself.

*Good luck deciphering parallel meaning in tones and decibels,* tone might give away meaning eavesdropping in any other language, but not Norwegian, thought Alex. Norwegian was sung as much as spoken, making Duolingo lessons in standard Norwegian Bokmal useless training for eavesdropping on real Osloites whose tone and pitch changed on every syllable. Norwegian sounded like a secret handshake in song. They could be having a party, for all Alex knew.

When the police left, Alex slipped into the rehabilitation nursery and found Liv staring out the foggy window.

"What did they want?" Alex asked, biting her nails, a habit she gave up in sixth grade.

"A list of employees with access to the seed depository."

"Why?"

"They are investigating casuarina seeds."

"What are those?"

"Coastal she-oak. Native to Australia and Melanesia."

"The police are interested in seeds?"

"They were slipped into the ears of the victim."

"*The* victim? The disco murder?" Alex swallowed; she was parched.

"Yes," Liv said, studying Alex.

"Do we have those trees in the gardens?"

"That's what they wanted to know."

"And?"

"No," Liv shook her head, "Nothing's going to seed anyway, it's barely spring. But we *may* have the seeds." Liv puffed her cheeks and released the air.

"Without the trees?" Alex wiped her forehead.

"Svalbard has a seed vault," Liv said.

"A what?" Alex asked. "Where? Main building?"

"Svalbard is in the arctic. The permafrost keeps the temperatures at freezing which preserves the seeds. In the event of a world disaster, we have all the world's seeds ready to plant and to rebuild."

"Cool. I'll keep it in mind next time I plant a garden," Alex said.

"It's a top security concrete bunker, not a tourist shop."

"Why did the police ask you? Why not go to Svalbard?" Alex asked.

"We also have a seed library," Liv answered.

"Oh," Alex said. "Also in a bunker?"

"No. But secure. You can't waltz in and take a seed. You need access."

"Was there a break-in at the seed library?" Alex asked. Sweat was dripping into her eyes.

"No, which is why the police wanted to know who has access to the seeds."

"And?" Alex asked.

"Anyone with a Natural History Museum employee swipe card: botanists, paleontologists, curators, cleaners, visiting researchers." Liv's gaze rested on Alex.

"Me?"

"All of us. They are at the office now for a full list of swipe card users."

Alex felt for her swipe card in her back pocket. Her wet winter underlayer was plastered to her skin. She would freeze when she stepped outside. She wanted to flee.

"Have you ever studied Melanesia?" Liv asked. She poured them each a cup of tea from her thermos.

"Melanesia?" Alex looked at Liv and accepted the tea, though she would have preferred water.

"Apparently, the seeds are used in a ritual in the Pacific Islands," Liv explained.

"The police are researching a ritual?" Alex asked, swallowing. "Why would I study Melanesia?"

"You're an anthropologist. She took a sip of tea, and studied Alex, "All eyes are on the anthropologist. Don't you all study primitive culture? Wasn't Margaret Mead's fieldsite in Melanesia?" Liv asked, she was fiddling with her iPhone, priming a tune.

Alex was not in the mood to unpack "primitive," or to provide a geography lesson.

The music came on forcefully, too loud.

"The natives are misbehaving," Alex shouted over the music, knowing Liv couldn't hear her.

# Fieldnotes: Killing Time

*The sun was gone but had left its footprint in the sky. It was the time of sitting on porches beside the road. It was time to hear things and talk. These sitters had been tongueless, earless, eyeless conveniences all day long. Mules and other brutes have occupied their skins. But now, the sun and the bossman were gone, so the skins felt powerful and human. They became lords of sound and lesser things. They passed nations through their mouths.* Zora Neale Hurston, *Their Eyes Were Watching God*

Hei Will,

What a tease! The sun flirts with Oslo and then disappears behind a veil of clouds.

I am killing time. Weird expression, killing time – time kills itself without any help from us. It keeps ticking on. It's "wasting" time if we do nothing other than produce our next breath. Max Weber's *Protestant Ethic and the Spirit of Capitalism* is less social theory and more self-help manual for Americans. No need for religion to drill the Protestant productivity ethic into our American souls -- Kindergarten suffices. The Norwegians, who are far wealthier (due to sheer dumb luck and geography), define a productive life as one well spent enjoying nature, friends, family, cooking, eating, drinking, reading.

I'm so behind. Stuck and stumped in a subzero Scandinavian country staring at a blank page as white and taunting as the freshly fallen snow mocking my every attempt at making a trace ... across icy Oslo, across an empty page. A new chapter, and -- ~~another dead body.~~ Up the engorged Akerselva River without a paddle. ~~Out of curiosity, as you're a math guy, what are the statistics of stumbling on dead bodies while doing fieldwork, keeping in mind I am a social-cultural anthropologist (studying living culture) and not an archeologist? The chances should be low, right?~~

Statistics suck. Life is random, but not meaningless. Why me? There's an algorithm for "random." Numbers are not my thing. Prince Haakon, Norway's heir to the throne, has dyscalculia. He too knows the tyranny of time and numbers. As you have yet to mail me a letter, I'll re-read my earlier texts from Kit. Loneliness causes repetitive gestures.

ALEX

Kit?

KIT

Thought you were sleeping.

ALEX

I can't sleep. What are you doing?

KIT

Prepping tomorrow's lecture. Big mistake bloating my syllabus with books I want to read "one day" -- now I'm cramming the same material as my grad students.

ALEX

Whoops.

KIT

Yeah, whoops. What's keeping you up?

ALEX

No one taught us what to do in the field. What am I supposed to be doing?

KIT

And you need to solve this now? Isn't it 4 am in Norway?

ALEX

Can't sleep until I do.

KIT

Participant observation – go participate and observe.

ALEX

Yeah, see where that got me…

KIT

Where?

ALEX

Nothing, roleplay Professor Whiner, please.

KIT

Yeah, I love pretending to have tenure and freewill.

ALEX

You will. In his last email Professor Whiner wrote: Anthropologists write ethnographies, Alexandra, what's all this nonsense about ethnographic sound projects? We finally accepted the diorama as a valid form of ethnographic output and now you propose a soundwalk? Everybody else is getting tap water and you want bottled water, Alexandra?

KIT

Your response?

ALEX

Ethnographies use too much paper; the forests are crying; the trees are dying.

KIT

For God's sake, digitize it.

ALEX

Kit – character! Whiner needs help creating a PowerPoint; he's the last person to suggest digitizing anything.

KIT

Pray tell, Alexandra, what new discovery or innovation will you make in the field?

ALEX

Museum exhibits on climate science fail to hold people's attention. Replacing the scientific mumbo jumbo printed in ten-point font and pinned to trees along a narrow path with sound and stories is a more effective way to educate the public. Sound, according to Adorno, elicits an emotional response, and an emotional response leads to learning, advocating and caring.

KIT

Doesn't Adorno condemn music for providing solace to the "impotent and deluded face of the progressive freezing of the world under the pressures of rationalization."

ALEX

Nothing gets past you. He especially hated Wagner who, "justifies the persistent irrationality of the world." Music animates feelings and allows thoughts the freedom to wonder and innovate. Imagine?!

KIT

How will you measure emotional response, Alexandra?

ALEX

Do people leave the exhibit with a passion to save our planet? What will they do next? Did you know music's emotional elements cannot be notated. Volume and intensity and the way a piece is played, including the imperfections, are what elicit emotion. Tenor imparts emotional depth. The question is: how do we attain and then retain or sustain people's attention? Is attention a bird, captive in a cage, or free to come and go?

KIT

Exit interviews?

ALEX

Always the practical one.

KIT

Alexandra, this is how you speak with your
advisor? And your Fieldsite?

ALEX

Oslo Botanical Gardens, the interpretive pathways.

KIT

Given your dollhouse/diorama/nutshell fiasco in
Bozeman, why should we approve this sound
silliness?

ALEX

Really, Kit? Whiner approved my sound project.

KIT

Defend it anyway. You'll be on the job market soon
enough. Your defense does not end with the PhD.

ALEX

Now I'm just depressed.

KIT

You are giving up too fast, Alexandra, answer the
question. Advocate for yourself. Explain how
ADHD and dyslexia have left you parched. It takes
more, and different water for your system. What's
the big deal? We must make it possible for
everyone to meet their potential and do amazing
things – for you it takes Evian. So, say yes, I need
Evian! When I got the African American women in
the sciences award and wanted to turn it down
because it felt like a door prize, you were the one
who reminded me there's no place for self-
consciousness in this game. You told me to treat it
like a key to the club. You said what matters is
what I do once I'm let in. Take your own advice,
Alex.

ALEX

You'll make a great advisor.

KIT

Flattery will get you nowhere Alexandra, 😊 You go girl!

ALEX

Whiner would never utter such a phrase. Stop breaking character.

KIT

I deviated.

ALEX

I'm the deviant, no one listens to me.

KIT

A random Norwegian believed in you. Go channel the Scandi fortitude. Just no Norwegian Noir! Last thing you need is another dead body LOL. 😰 You'd get booted faster than you could say primitive.

ALEX

Need motive.

KIT

Huh?

ALEX

Motivation. Dictation error. You know this is it. My last chance to prove myself, right?

KIT

No such thing as last chances.

*Tell that to the dead man at the disco.*

# Chapter 3

## *Silent Sinking*

Alex waited for a passerby to swipe her into the 9th floor. She was late. Norwegians were never late. *Surely, Norway has students with ADHD,* Alex huffed, as she considered alternative ways to enter the impenetrable department. A keypad's promising blue light blinked at her unphased as she waved at it, punched it and pushed it. A sticker of a stick figure fleeing a fire by way of the stairs, suggested there may be stairs somewhere. An initial scan revealed nothing but four walls and an elevator.

Finally, a tall man with longish white or blond hair and the tell-tale Norwegian 5 o'clock stubble, wearing faded jeans, a white T-shirt and Orange Suede Vans, appeared on the other side of the glass doors.

"Al-ex?" the man asked, or stated, in a Norwegian sing-song tenor as he opened the door with his swipe card.

"Yes. I'm here to meet Professor Storesund."

"Well, here he is," he pointed at himself. "Call me Thorvald."

Thorvald looked nothing like his faculty picture, where his hair was short, spiked and light blond or white. Norwegian hair color was proving to be seasonal.

The scent of fresh brewed coffee and pear soap grew stronger as they walked down a narrow hallway of offices that led to a large light-filled meeting room. A south facing picture window framed the hills, treetops and rooftops leading down to the Oslo Fjord.

"Wow," Alex breathed.

"Yep." No shame in gratitude. "Coffee? Fruit? Nuts?" He enticed her further into the sleek communal room.

"Are you having a party?" Alex asked.

"No. Why?" He asked.

"That's some fruit bowl," Alex wasn't referring to the beautiful fruit, but the sleek midcentury modern wooden bowl.

"Monday, we have fruit," he explained.

"Oh," Alex said, "And people think Columbia University is posh."

Thorvald chuckled agreeably. "Yes, I've been."

"Then you know we don't have fruit at Columbia. Red wine, million-year-old red brick and antiquated attitude," Alex said. She chose an apple and accepted a cup of coffee.

"My office has more privacy," Thorvald nodded toward the exit, a sign to follow him down the narrow hallway to the last door. Where he invited her in and kicked the door shut. Male professors in the States never closed the door when alone with a female student. This spoke to the gravity and secrecy of the situation. Or female students could trust their professors to behave in Norway.

"So, you're here about a murder?" He rubbed his hands together, and she half expected him to twist an imaginary Hercule Poirot mustache.

"I..." Alex started. She requested this meeting on the premise of her sound project. He was known for his work on ritual music in Tuvalu. She did not mention murder in her email.

"Toss me the bike helmet," he instructed her, pointing to the couch. "Take a seat."

He hung the helmet and sat at his office desk. He swiveled to face her and rolled his chair nearer. He was overly affable and athletic for a retired senior academic. Anyone who fought their way to work on a bicycle through an Oslo winter would be athletic, and as spring was right around the corner, most Norwegians were affable.

"Tuvalu is sinking?" Alex began.

Thorvald laughed. "Right after your email requesting a meeting about a sinking Melanesian Island, the police called to ask about Melanesian seeds. Now, I'm no detective, yeah, but, well, ...coincidence."

He emphasized *coincidence* as if *that* was the suspicious part.

"You were friends?" Thorvald asked.

"With whom?" Alex asked.

"The victim. Police said he was an American. Roger Walsh," he said. His dark green eyes were laser focused and unnerving. She looked away, which she heard indicated truth. Liars looked you right in the eye – defiant and over-confident.

"American?" Alex repeated and swallowed hard. Feeling guilty for no reason was a side-effect of years in special ed. The minute you needed anything extra you were guilty of costing more time, energy, money. "News to me," Alex answered evenly. How did a retired anthropology professor have insider information?

"Did *you* know him?" Alex asked.

"The police have asked me to help with their inquiries. Due to the seeds." He squinted at her and nibbled his cuticles.

"Right," Alex said.

"You sure you didn't know him?" Thorvald smiled warmly, but with a fixed gaze. Alex wondered if he was trained by MI5, or whatever the Norwegian equivalent was.

"No, I mean," she muttered.

"What is it?" He sounded concerned. She needed his help. Her Columbia professor vouched for him, said he was trustworthy, and she trusted Paige. In a genealogy of kinship, a chain of trust, one trusted those who were trusted by the people one trusted. Was this too many generations of trust? She eyed his whiteboard; she needed to draw a kinship chart. She could see their value.

"You've heard the story of the seeds?" Thorvald asked.

"No," Alex answered.

He rolled back to his computer and typed in his password. Alex joined him at his desk. She peered over his shoulder at a picture of a beautiful pine tree on a remote island.

"Tuvalu," he said.

"You miss it..." Alex commented.

He looked at her, "I do."

"Is it truly disappearing?"

"Swallowed by the sea," he said solemnly.

"Is the tree, or are the seeds, particular to Tuvalu?" Alex tried properly pronouncing the Melanesian Island's name. She knew it only as a disappearing dot on the map. "Why would anyone put seeds in someone's ears?" she wondered aloud.

"Well, since you could easily google it, and get it wrong, there's no harm in telling you." Thorvald swiveled his chair to look at her. "When placed inside the ears of a mother, the seeds, aided by the swooshing of trees, block the sound of a crying infant," Thorvald explained.

"To help new parents sleep?" Alex guessed.

"No. They are placed in the ears of the dead mother to block the cry of her infant so that her soul won't linger. No mother could leave a crying infant," He frowned.

"That's very sad."

"It happens. Women die in childbirth, especially in places with poor medical care. And so, we create rituals."

"But why him? He surely did not give birth. Is it a metaphor?" Alex asked.

"Hmm. Good question." Thorvald rubbed his chin.

"Could it be witchcraft?" Alex asked. "Is magic a normal line of police inquiry? Why inquire about magic in Melanesia?"

"Not technically Melanesia. We Norwegians are culturally sensitive and respectful of ritual," Thorvald said.

"So much so that the police would entertain witchcraft?"

"Does witchcraft scare you?" Thorvald studied her.

"No. Malice does. What keeps me up at night are people not in control of their emotions; unbridled anger, drug-induced behavior." Alex said.

"That's quite a list. You've given it thought."

"I live in New York City."

"Then you know you have listed things you cannot control. No use losing sleep over things we cannot control." He advised.

Alex wondered what worries formed the sleepless shadows under Thorvald's eyes. What was keeping him up at night? The possibility that one of his students was the killer.

"The University of Oslo is a popular place to study Anthropology of the Pacific. You've given hundreds of lectures to students, and the public?" Alex noted, thinking of the substantial roll call of students/suspects.

"I don't teach witchcraft," he laughed.

"You must teach about it, no? Did you teach it to anyone in particular?" Alex asked.

"Who wouldn't want to play around in Margaret Mead's fieldsite?"

"The police assume a female Columbia anthropology student – me-- would be an ideal mini-Margaret Mead," Alex said, thinking, *As if.*

Thorvald leaned back in his chair, folded his hands in prayer and pursed his lips. "You're a natural detective."

"Aren't all anthropologists?" Alex asked.

# Chapter 4

## Screeching Trams

Alex dove through the rapidly closing tram doors at Storgata and into the crush of commuters, landing in a swarm of teens making a beeline through the flower market to McDonalds. She stood still as they passed, lest they sting. She was on a mission to capture the high-pitched start of an older tram.

An approaching tram with the smooth contours and matte paint finish of the vintage Alex was after would in a matter of minutes arrive, release its passengers, board the new ones and be off with a high-pitched screech. Alex thread her way through the crowd to the edge of the sidewalk, reached her arm out like a human selfie stick, and pointed her phone toward the oncoming tram to capture her establishing shot.

The train arrived and was unloading the passengers as Alex furiously fumbled with her sound recording app, intently concentrating on setting sound levels when she felt someone slam into her and push her to ground.

She hit the pavement palms down and inches from an approaching tram. She saw for the first time the trams were coming and going on a diagonal. She conceded the value of geometry. The more pressing question was whether someone pushed her into, or out of the way of the oncoming tram?

She craned her head like a cat to look up at a tourist admonishing her for being in the middle of the tracks.

"You're lucky you didn't fall on your knees or your hip or your head," the woman addressed Alex in English, "You're lucky an old Norwegian lady swiftly pushed you out of the way," she added.

Alex rubbed her arms thinking the tourist was selling the older Norwegian woman short. Old lady or not, she punched above her weight, and unlike the tourist, did not stick around to admonish Alex or wait for her to thank her. The Norwegian went about her day. Alex collected her phone and what was left of her dignity.

"Alex?"

Alex stood and turned to see Mandi Singer, a member of her Columbia cohort smiling down at her. A smile Alex distrusted.

"I thought that was you, hard to tell with the tram whizzing by," Mandi said. "Need help?" she held out her hand.

"What are you doing in Oslo?" asked Alex, refusing her hand.

"All roads lead to Oslo. I'm here for a conifer climate conference. Question is what are *you* doing in Oslo?"

"I'm in the field," Alex answered without elaborating.


The last time Alex saw or rather, heard Mandi was in Butler library's ladies' room. Mandi walked in with a friend, ladened down with books, chatting away, oblivious to Alex, who, in no mood to say hello, stayed hidden in a stall, hoping they'd soon leave. Instead, they stood at the mirror re-applying make-up, (unnecessary for writing and researching) while giggling and gossiping. The old building's lofty ceilings, marble floors and wooden doors provided perfect eavesdropping acoustics.

"Janaki got a Fulbright. Remember how bad her proposal was in our grant writing workshop? They'll give a Fulbright to anyone," Mandi said.

"True story - didn't you get one?"

They laughed.

"Well, not *anyone*. Alex didn't get any research funding," Mandi noted.

Alex stared down at the shiny marble floor and held her breath.

"Are you surprised?"

"She's so peppy for someone on the cusp of being thrown out." Mandi remarked. Alex swallowed hard.

"Statistics show one member of every cohort drops out, so we should be thankful Alex is in our cohort!" The women laughed.

"Get this, Whiner is letting her do a sound project instead of a dissertation."

"No way. Whiner's her advisor? He isn't exactly *Mr. Experimentation*. Why would Whiner sanction that?"

"Could be a disability thing – she has autism or something."

"My cousin has autism, and he can write. She has a reading problem. Reading and writing are related, no? If you can't read letters, you can't write them, right?"

"How did she get into a PhD program if she's illiterate?" Mandi asked.

Alex's tears released the minute the door swung shut behind them.

"Fulbright?" Mandi asked, bringing Alex back to Storgata.

"No," Alex said, "Fulbright funding is too little for Oslo."

"It's super pricey, right?" Mandi eyed Alex's thrift store hat – a striped wool beanie with a pompom. "Haven't they like socialized everything -- medicine education. I just bought sunscreen at the pharmacy, and they like asked me if I was local. They do local and non-local prices. Seems discriminatory."

"Less discriminatory than giving you no sunscreen. You don't pay into the system, so why should you get the subsidy? If you break a leg here, they won't send you home with a bill as long as your arm."

"You always were funny," Mandi chuckled. "And different. So, what are you doing risking your life in the middle of the street? Looking for clues?" Mandi joked, "Seriously, don't count on me saving you, I don't have your murder mystery solving skills, so if something untoward happened to you, you couldn't rely on me." Mandi joked.

*Wouldn't count on it*, Alex thought. The whole department knew about the mystery she solved while doing fieldwork in Bozeman. Though the more titillating part of the story for her cohort was the fact that she had failed to produce any research data in Bozeman and abandoned her project.

"Yeah, danger seems to follow me everywhere," Alex said, holding Mandy's gaze. "So cool running into you. Enjoy Oslo," Alex said, and turned to leave before Mandi could reply.


Alex skirted the Oslo Domkirke, crossed the street to the train station, and then over to the Opera House, where she turned right and away from her apartment. She walked toward Sørenga and took a sharp right onto a wide dock frequented by skateboarders and pot smokers. She sat on a bench overlooking the Fjord and wiped a tear from her eye. She wished she weren't so bothered by fellow graduate students. She wanted to measure self-worth internally and without the input of outside opinion. She wasn't quite there yet. She once overheard her mother tell Professor Lillian, "Alex may never go to a school like Columbia. But it's irrelevant. She does not measure herself by other people's standards, which means she's free to do new, creative and important projects. The same dyslexia that holds her back from Spelling Bee Gold medals and 4.0 GPAs and Ivy League possibilities has gifted her with being herself."

She would *act as if* and try to believe in herself if only for the two strong women who loved, mentored and imparted to her every ounce of strength, love and goodwill they could before leaving this world too soon.

# Fieldnotes: Not So Silent Night

*We are all by definition experts in our own experience. The job of philosophers should be to study the space between the sense perceptions that bombard us and the mental pictures we fashion of things as we believe them to be.* Charles King *Gods of the Upper Air*

*Silent Singles* was Roger's idea. He started the group. Why silence? Did he come to Scandinavia for silence? They say: in Scandinavia silence is not awkward; it's a national treasure.

Noise is a distraction. Noise is sound out of place: excess, excessive, unformed, undefined -- superfluous.

Like weeds: plants out of place.

Like me in Oslo: anthropologist out of place.

Dearest Friend,

Norwegian Anthropologist, Thomas Hylland Eriksen found notation liberates music from the performer and makes it possible to store music independently of people, so, an individual player can learn a piece of music without personal contact with another performer. But it only transmits what can be written. Music, like speech, has an indefinite residue that cannot be transmitted through text. Notation freezes a song into a particular performance rather than allowing it to be a living, breathing, changing song. And because pitch and speed, which emit emotion, were noted, the feeling of the music also stayed static. Imagine a feeling sailing through the ages on a musical note.

"Ever since Pythagoras revolutionized the mathematical structure of music by composing the world's first algorithm, musicians have been deliberately breaking the buildup of patterns or triumphantly completing them in order to orchestrate an emotional response — the sorrow of unmet hope, the elated relief of its redemption." Maria Popova, *The Marginalian*. Sorrow of unmet hope: me and math. Did you know we have a finite number of heartbeats? For us, the beat goes on, while Roger did not get to drum out every one of his beats. Are we aware of our first and last beat? Our first and last breath? Numbers are only part of our story; the other part is emotion, awareness, attention.

What I love about micro-rhythms is even when they break with convention (whether lagging behind or beating ahead), performers play them with consistency *acting as if* they are correct. Like samba -- stumbling and sloppy but consistent and unique. Notation, like any alphabet, is a tyranny of exclusion. Playing by ear, reading by ear is a creative act. What we consider musically correct is a convention, pure cultural conditioning, and the meat of anthropological inquiry. What does it mean to be in tune? Socially, neurologically, musically, academically, politically...and why must we be in tune? Harmony considered in tune in one culture may be well out of tune in another. I'm out of tune in Norway.

Imperfection is my happy place. Beauty is in the places where perfection is resisted: Persian rug weavers who purposely leave a flaw to communicate only God is perfect; micro-rhythms like samba and swing dance us into imperfection and beauty. Too much precision sounds cold and emotionless, in short -- machine music. Producers of electronic music added inaccuracies to heighten emotion but failed. Humans cannot play perfectly. The greatest drummers in the world cannot "beat" a computer performance. I love this. It's one more argument for why AI cannot beat us at being human. AI will lag in beat even as it tries to forge ahead of us in tempo because it aspires to perfection. We are most human in our imperfections. Which is why the world needs neurodivergent people like me with dyslexia. Eugenics was an apocalyptic attempt to forge our image in the face of a computer. Eugenics and computers -- human inventions that aspired to create a system of supremacy. We "atypical," "neurodivergent," "imperfect by contemporary cultural norms," forged in an age of insincerity, will excel in this new AI future.

# Chapter 5

----

## *The Silent Scream*

Bjørvika, once a freight ship dock with blocks and blocks of metal containers filled with foreign goods, was transformed into a steel, glass and concrete city of high-rise apartments running alongside the railroad tracks. It boasted a new commodity, marked by a barcode patterned into the new high-rises that sold a design for living as well as a destination. Ships slid in and out of the Fjord; tram lines moved up and down the Operagata; trains, came and went from Oslo Central Station. Bjørvika was a place to pause in as much as to pass through.

At its center -- the Oslo Opera House - a white Italian marble iceberg floated on the edge of the Fjord, inviting pedestrians to scale the slanted marble roof to operatic heights. There, gulls paused to consider the short flight to tiny clumps of forest on not-so-distant islands. Timed right, human and bird might peer down the skylight at the roof's center to see 1,400 people (when at capacity) sipping champagne in the lobby between arias.

Around the corner, the Munch Museum, bent toward the weak light like a desperate and stubborn weed. From Alex's viewfinder the Museum looked like a large gray barnacle, clinging to the dock and jutting out at the Fjord like a crooked middle finger.

"Hei!"

Alex turned abruptly to see Anders coming up behind her. "Didn't mean to startle you," he apologized.

"You scared off the bird I was trying to photograph," Alex said, trying to play cool.

"The one perched way up there?" Anders asked. "Wait..." Anders pointed to a bird flapping toward the dock. "There, take your shot."

"Nice scarf -- Norwegian design?" Alex commented on the heavy cotton shawl wrapped around Anders neck.

"I was at the sauna." Anders removed the towel from around his neck.

"Sauna?" Alex asked.

Anders pointed to a colony of floating wood cabins moored along the edge of the dock where a woman in a bikini was showering.

"In this weather?" Alex shivered. Would all her fieldsites involve freezing water and a dead body?

"It's perfect sauna weather," Anders said.

A sheen of fresh ice wrapped the water like cellophane. Alex frowned.

"We dip for a second," he assured her.

"You dip?" Alex asked.

"Or dive," he pointed to wooden diving towers in the distance. Alex thought they were sculptures. "Sørenga is bursting in the summer with sunbathers. The city lays ropes for swim lanes," Anders added.

"It's winter," Alex stated.

"Spring technically. Which in Norway is kind of summer. In winter swimmers wear wet suits. The serious swimmers wear their birthday suits."

"I'm afraid of dark water," Alex admitted.

"So, the frigid temperature does not deter you?" Anders laughed.

"It doesn't entice me either. I blame *Charlie and the Chocolate Factory*."

"Whatever for?"

"For the terrifying, claustrophobic scene of a child lost in a sea of dark chocolate. It's real nightmare material."

"Roald Dahl was Norwegian."

"That explains it. I thought he was English."

"With Norwegian ancestry. He spent summers with relatives in Norway. *Charlie and the Chocolate Factory* was inspired by the Freia Factory, right around the corner," Anders pointed toward the train station.

"Are you trying to freak me out?" Alex asked.

"What brings you here? It's nice running into you again, I was hoping you might call," Anders said.

"I'm waiting for the museum to open," Alex paused, deciding whether to tell him the truth. She studied his warm smile and remembered the way he helped her breath and said, "Today is the *Silent Scream*. I want to see who shows up. You know, look for clues."

"About the guy's death?"

"His murder, yes. Want to join me?" Alex asked.

She heard it best not to come on too strong with Norwegian men, lest she scare them off. But to hell with a feminism that precludes men from befriending women.

"Will this lead to anything?" Anders asked.

"I... have a boyfriend, sort of," Alex blurted out.

"Cool. I meant us lurking at the museum. Lying in wait of a murderer." Anders clarified.

Alex's cheeks burned. "Right," she answered, "Who knows. Desperate times, desperate measures. The sooner this murderer is caught, the sooner I can leave Oslo," she was saying.

"And get home to your sort of boyfriend," Anders smiled.

Alex turned from Ander's unnerving gaze toward the door.

"And when someone from *Silent Singles* shows-up, what exactly do we do?" Anders inquired.

"We'll ask about Roger. Someone must have known him," Alex explained.

"Roger?"

"Yes. He was American."

"Why would they want to talk to us? Or anyone, for that matter," Anders asked, reminding her she was dealing with Norwegians.

"Right. We can observe them," Alex suggested.

"On the sly -- as you Americans say. And what...notice if they try to kill anyone?" Anders laughed.

"You think this is funny?"

"We can't question strangers," Anders pointed out.

"Why not?" Alex asked, and added, "Oh because you're Norwegian."

"And Americans will question anyone?"

"I'm an anthropologist."

"Sounds like anthropology is an excuse to be nosy," Anders replied.

"Yup."

"And how do we talk in a silent club?" Anders raised the ante.

"We ask them if they killed Roger. Don't Norwegians get right to the point?" Alex joked.

"We're polite."

For Norwegians, speaking with strangers was functional and utilitarian, like: *What time is the train?* which a Norwegian would never need to ask. On the other hand, if one asked, *How are you?* the answer would not be the superficial American, *OK.* A Norwegian would disclose precisely how they were doing.

"Are you saying asking someone if they are a murderer is not polite in Norwegian society?" Alex raised her eyebrows. "Did *you* kill Roger?" her voice was shaky.

"No. I've never met the man."

"We need to look at his kinship chart, who knew him and how. We'll do a genealogy. We'll treat this place like a village. When anthropologists showed up in villages they would start with the chief." Alex explained.

"Who by all counts is dead," Anders pointed out.

"Right. If Roger was the chief, who was his successor?"

"It's not exactly an inheritance worth killing for," Anders chuckled. "Did you kill him to become the head of this group?" Anders asked.

"I had no idea he was the organizer. I found the group online and never spoke with anyone. I barely remember their faces."

"So maybe we skip the kinship chart?" Anders smirked.

"But this could be about kin – a silent dalliance. An illegitimate child is a great motive for murder." Alex thought aloud. She imagined a dead infant whispering in a mother's ear. If the Casuarina seeds blocked a dead infants cry to prevent a ghost from lingering, and they fell out of Roger's ears, then would his ghost linger?

"Not in Norway," Anders said.

"Huh?"

"Illegitimacy."

"Oh, right. Why not?" Alex asked.

"Norwegians have children out of wedlock all the time," Anders winked at Alex, "illegitimacy isn't a motive for murder here. Was he in a relationship?" Anders studied her carefully.

"How would I know? Besides, he was American. It's a motive for murder back home," Alex added.

"You're the expert." Anders squeezed her shoulder. "Did he hit on you?" Anders asked.

"We danced."


Tinted windows dulled the scant natural light and protected visitors and artwork from the relentless Norwegian summer sun. In winter they matched gray winter sky.

"Munch is doing wheelies in his grave." Alex said as they stepped onto the escalator.

"Wheelies?"

"He painted color and light and intimate, vibrant spaces. This is more mausoleum than museum – and this escalator is like riding up the skeleton of a flayed fish." Alex held her nose for emphasis.

"Color it is. All the way to the top." Anders took her to the exhibition of Edvard Munch's early work.

"Munch was a native of Kristiania – the old name for Oslo. He was a symbolist and an expressionist. Nature was his religion – very Norwegian," Anders explained.

"You Norwegians are way more religious than you admit. He reminds me of William Blake. Only Blake did woodblock, rather than brass, and he wrote poetry."

"Come," Anders took Alex's elbow and led her to a casement full of Munch's notebooks.

"He was a poet?" Alex said, examining Munch's notebooks. "Who knew?"

"Everyone in Norway," Anders said.

"Gorgeous," Alex pointed to *The Kiss,* which was all but ignored, glanced at, and passed by the cruise ship tourists on their way to find *The Scream.* "It's quite a commentary on our culture," Alex said.

"What, a kiss?"

"Immortalizing *The Scream* and ignoring *The Kiss.*"

"A kiss is common," Anders suggested.

"Don't know about you, but I don't get kissed like *that* every day. If anything, we take love for granted." Alex glanced at him.

"Yeah," he studied the painting and added, "Munch was better at mental distress than at love."

"Imagine mental distress being your legacy and creating the world's most famous meme for pain and in 1893, no less. What did he do to deserve that?"

"Quite a lot. Visit Åsgårdstrand, and you'll see what I mean." Anders said.

"We heard Roger's last scream," Alex said.

"It wasn't a scream per se," Anders reminded her.

"Well, I thought..." Alex blushed.

"Yeah, me too," Anders said.

"There's literally no one here," Alex noted.

"No cruise ships this week. The museum is empty when the ships aren't in."

"Norwegians are on time, and it's late. Is there another Munch Museum?" She looked at her watch.

"Yes."

"Really? In the same city?" Alex said following Anders outside.

"Do you have a bike?"

"No?"

"No problem, we will walk," he said, and set out rapidly toward Operagata.

"Can we take the tram?"

"No, it's faster to walk. If we go over the pedestrian bridge and cross the train station, then it's just up the hill."

Everything in Oslo was *just up the hill*. They crossed the pedestrian bridge over the train tracks and landed in a neighborhood lined with halal butchers and Indian sweet shops with trays of gooey honey laden sweets laid out in the windows like precious jewels. Alex noted the same penchant for formal wear as in her chichi hood, only here the dresses were ankle length, the sleeves wrist length, and were accompanied by glittery hijabs.

"Do you own a suit?" Alex asked Anders.

"Yes, every Norwegian man has one. We wear them on national day unless we wear a traditional costume. Confirmation, other people's confirmations."

"Confirmation? I thought you were secular."

"Everyone is confirmed at 16. Secular folks get confirmed at the city hall and religious folks are confirmed in their churches. It's a big deal."

"Right," Alex said. "So, you all like ritual?"

"We need something to celebrate when one month looks like the next. Don't you?"

"We are a very diverse population; Americans celebrate a variety of things."

"Yes, but everything is closed on Christmas. Not so secular."

"You have a good point." Alex agreed.

They were approaching a beautiful glass pavilion.

"A café?" Alex pointed to empty patio chairs in front of the glass pavilion.

"Yes, it belongs to the Munch Museum."

"Isn't it confusing calling it the Munch Museum?"

"It's the old Munch Museum. It's a gallery space ... and it's closed," Anders paused and put his hands on his hips and looked around.

Alex dropped into a forward bend and released her lower back.

"Had I known we were going for a hike, I'd have left my camera behind."

"Shall we pause before going to the next museum?" Anders asked and took her backpack. He slung it over his shoulder and directed her onward.

"Next museum?" Alex gasped.

"The national museum is where the actual *Scream* is. Shall we check it out?"

"Absolutely," Alex looked at her watch, "Let's go, *Silent Scream* ends soon."

"So, we jump on the bus."


Anders's knees knocked Alex's as the bus started and stopped along to Aker Brygge. Every time their knees touched, she went a little wobbly. She had not expected to see him again, let alone spend the day with him, especially so soon after the death at the disco. Oslo really was a village.


They disembarked the bus, and Anders swiftly took Alex's hand, "Run!" he exclaimed.

Alex ran, wondering if she should duck or hide instead. Were they in pursuit or being chased?

"Wow - serendipity."

"Huh?" Alex asked.

"Look up in the window," Anders panted as he pointed to a small window at the top of the Nobel Building. "We made it just in time," he smiled at her.

Alex squinted. Was it a sniper? A man with black gloves was holding something delicate.

The city hall bells chimed John Lennon's *Give Peace a Chance* and the man in the window released a white dove which soared about the Fjord to the delight of the small crowd. *Would these people give peace a chance?* Alex wondered.

"Which of the many wars is this about?" Alex asked.

"The dove is freed every Friday," Anders said. "Come on, museum is around the corner."


The lobby of the National Museum was dark and cavernous, and emitted the heavy gravitas that cement and marble lent to important buildings.

"So, this is where all the tourists were hiding," Alex said, "A murderer among them?"

"A cruise came in. They disembark long enough to gawk at *The Scream* before returning aboard in time for the next highlight on their tour. A volcano or glacier or something," Anders surmised.

*The Scream* was easy to find, given the steady stream of tourists headed there, but impossible to see. Like the *Mona Lisa* in the Louvre, it was smothered by hundreds of on lookers and selfie sticks.

"Do you recognize anyone here?" Anders raised his voice over the din.

"Are you kidding? Everyone looks the same – capris pants, jeans, polo shirts, iPhones and yet, nobody looks familiar," Alex sighed heavily. She was being swallowed by the crowd as one would be taken by a riptide. Anders held out his hand. She accepted it and he pulled her to safety.

"What do you know about trolls?" he asked.

"Nothing."

"Ah, and you call yourself an anthropologist," he said, leading her out of the exhibit.

"You're thinking of folklorists," Alex said, "I'm a cultural anthropologist," she insisted, following him through the lobby to a second set of stairs. At the landing he took a right to a hallway Alex would never have found on her own.

"This is cultural," Anders announced as they entered a dark, empty exhibit lit by a string of fairy lights. Soft music accentuated the fairytale forest. It reminded her of the wolf diorama in Bozeman's natural history museum, with the fake snow and sweet-smelling fir branches like a forest after a rainstorm. Only here at the center of the exhibit, was no wolf but a giant puppet of a one-eyed troll.

"Did you know trolls share an eye?" Anders asked.

"Really? Is it a metaphor -- seeing the world through a single vision or something?"

"They have a hole in their forehead," Anders pointed out.

"Why?"

"For the shared eye. They pass the eye around and stick it in the hole when they want to see," Anders explained.

"They must have a heightened sense of smell and hearing," Alex remarked.

"Yes. They excel at sniffing out Christian blood," Anders said.

"Does it have a particular scent?" Alex mused. "And what about sound?"

"You must be psychic. Sound is integral."

"It's my research area; I ask everyone about sound," Alex admitted.

"An anthropologist researching sound is like saying you're researching air."

"Lots of anthropologists do research air."

"Yeah, but what about it in particular?" Anders asked.

"Pollution, climate change, asthma."

"I meant what about sound, sound pollution?" Ander asked.

"Not sure. Just started -- I'm using sound to relay scientific information in a more accessible way for the public."

"Like audiobooks and audio guides?"

"Yeah, put like that, it's a no-brainer. But, believe me, not in my field. I'm doing more than an audio version of a scientific text; I'm translating data into a story -- making it visible, like translating science into art."

"Why Norway?"

"Because you have trolls."

"Church bells scare them."

"I rarely hear church bells here."

"There aren't any churches in Bjørvika. It was an industrial area. Though you might hear the ghost screams from the asylum over where the shipping crates are now. Below Ekeberg park. Munch's sister was there."

Alex shivered.

"Thunder too... Trolls hate the sound of thunder."

"You know this because you've asked them?" Alex raised an eyebrow.

"Funny. Church bells and thunder are the sounds of a pissed off God. You don't want to piss off Thor."

"No, of course not," Alex answered. "Speaking of pissing off authoritarians, we didn't exactly tell the police the details of our meeting on the stairs," Alex said carefully. She watched Anders' reaction.

"We told them we were there together?" he said or asked, she never knew which when a Norwegian was speaking.

"Coming from different directions. They assumed we were always together."

"They never asked," said Anders.

Norway in a nutshell — only give information asked for.

"Only in Norway would police trust us to verify each other's alibis. We validated each other like we would a generic parking ticket." Where was Anders "parked" before we met on the stairs —

ascending or descending --levers pulled by an unseen force, Alex wondered.

"Shall we continue this over a coffee? I don't think anyone else is going to show up today," Anders concluded.

"No!" Alex answered empathically, thinking of Conan O'Brien's interview with a Norwegian sex therapist who told him Norwegians preferred to have sex with a possible romantic interest before having coffee together. *An anthropologist should not take cultural cues, let alone relationship advice from a comedian.*

"Tea it is," Anders insisted.

"Tell me more about Munch?" Alex asked.

"You want to know about his disastrous love life?" Anders clarified.

Alex nodded.

"Everything you need to know is in Åsgårdstrand," Anders told her.

"You're right, diminishing returns," Alex exhaled in resignation.

"Love?" Anders asked.

"The museum. No point in hanging out any longer," Alex said. "And thank you for the dove," she added. "That was really cool."

Anders smiled and said, "There is one last exhibit to see. Come with me," Anders took her hand, and she knew she'd follow him anywhere. *No.* She whispered. *It's just a crush;* she lied to herself.

He led her into a low-lit exhibition with bare walls.

"Where are the paintings?" Alex asked.

"You make your own," he said as they entered a hive of activity around the brass-plate-table tops.

"What is this?"

"Brass etchings of Munch's most famous works," he said and handed her a crayon and a blank piece of paper. "Go ahead," he encouraged her to make a rubbing.

Alex placed her paper over *The Kiss.*

"Imagine a world where *The Kiss* was his lasting meme," Alex said.

"It's interesting what prevails." Anders said and placed his hand over Alex's.

Together they rubbed the red crayon back and forth until there emerged an image of a couple wrapped in a kiss.

# Fieldnotes: Fearful Fjord

Kjaere Will,

The sun sinks taking her blues, greens, yellows and oranges and leaving the fjord engulfed in black -- a large, dark, endless body of water. My greatest fear. Fieldwork is delving in, participating and saying yes to every invitation, local custom and activity. And here, I turned down the only invitation I've been offered due to a dark water phobia. Why on earth would anyone voluntarily ride through a dark sewage tube in a kayak? It takes less than five minutes to go from under the grimy Grønlund T-bane stop, under and across Operagata, along the edge of the Munch Museum, and out to the mouth of the Fjord. Five minutes is all it would take to give me a heart attack. The underside of ships – which are beyond spooky, especially viewed, you guessed it, in the dark -- are less terrifying than that tunnel. It must have fabulous sound, and kayakers emerge laughing – which neither convinces nor reassures me.

Kit thinks it's a past life fear. My terror is assuredly from this life, when I witnessed Augustus Gloop, like narcissus himself, peer into a deep, dark, chocolate lake, and fall, not for his own image, but for the promise of endless chocolate, from whence he never returned. It's no coincidence that Roald Dahl's inspiration for

*Charlie and the Chocolate Factory*, the Freia Chocolate factory, is mere blocks from this terrifying tunnel. The warning Roald Dahl imparted to young children everywhere about greed and gluttony and satiating cravings at all costs, left me, not short of a sweet tooth (Freia is delectable), but in mortal fear of dark bodies of water. As a serious chocoholic I've been a regular visitor to the Freia store, having been, until now, utterly unaware of its dark history in the annals of petrifying children. Should have guessed. Norway is, after all, the land of trolls and beings that go bump in the dark, dark night.

Oslo is my immersion therapy. Nightly walks along the black ribbon of water from the Munch Museum to the opera, to the fortress have fortified me. The twinkling lights on the water and soothing steam from saunas now comfort me. Even the ghosts are typical Norwegians who keep to themselves.

Dahl saw the world backwards, sideways and upside down. His teacher insisted she had never seen anyone so consistently write words meaning the exact opposite of what was intended. His dyslexia became a talent in the BFG (Big Friendly Giant) where helicopters are *belly poppers*, and skin and bones are *skin and groans*. Speaking is "squiggly" for the BFG, for whom word retrieval is a challenge. I get it. I'll see and say a word in my head and hear it come out wrong. Yesterday I yelled to a tourist in English to watch their child whose balance on the playscape was "vicarious." I meant to say precarious. As it came out, I knew it was the wrong word. I used to say human beans which may explain my ~~propensity~~ proclivity for anthropology. Dahl played deliberately with his dyslexia. In the *Vicar of Nibbles Wicke* The vicar (unbeknownst to him) said words backwards, creating silly sermons and unintended comedy. We dyslexics aren't always rewarded with good laughs for our creative use of neologisms. Dahl used his squaggles to fight back. Like his character Mathilda, Dahl surely possessed an exceptional IQ, otherwise his dyslexia would have been an exceptional struggle rather than an exceptional gift.

It's hard for me to get what I see three dimensionally in my brain down on paper. Or to translate thoughts into a linear sequence when they don't appear in my head that way. Helen Taylor says we are defining our unique problem-solving machine as a disability. We assume difficulty with writing is a deficit and yet, as she points out, writing is a recent invention. Imagine if someone's bad at computer programming, we don't label it a neurobiological disorder. She has a good point. That said, I write to you, daily, despite the difficulty. And you, for whom it comes so naturally, have not sent me a single word in return. I spend my days dangling one foot in the fjord, waiting to pull it out or jump all in. It matters not Will whether I am knee deep or up to my neck -- the Fjord waters run deep: hope is lost in its depths, waiting to be fished and retrieved with one word: hello will do.

# Chapter 6

## *Silent Suffering*

M unch's mustard colored summer cabin sat atop the small hill overlooking Åsgårdstrand's small seaside promenade which ran alongside the wharf like a satin ribbon cutting a cool clean line through the sunny day. He bought the cabin at the height of his success, when he most craved the tranquility of youthful summers spent here as a boy.

Alex peeked inside an adjoining red barn where replicas of Munch's paintings were stacked against walls. Easels and jars of paint added to the reenactment of Munch's workspace.

"This is the outdoor studio," a woman, the docent told Alex, "The cabin is small, so it's good you're the only visitor. It's off-season," she informed Alex.

Only five people fit at a time," she said as she unlocked the door to the adjacent cabin.

Alex stepped inside and smiled. She was alone in Munch's bedroom.

"Ah, this is where the magic happened," Alex said looking at the long twin bed

The docent assumed she was referring to the small writing table and an easel, when in truth Alex was imagining what it would be like to have been Munch's lover. Alex wondered if her desire for a long dead, unhinged man, who either shot himself, his lover, or her husband was evidence of slipping sanity?

Aside from a telephone, which was a rarity in Norway back then, he possessed no other creature comforts than this single bed, the writing table, a guest room, also with a single bed, and the sparse accouterments of daily life: a toothbrush placed in a childhood mug above a washbasin, a kettle, and two hot plates.

Alex stepped into the guest bedroom where she was enveloped by a sense of sadness and loneliness.

"What are those?" she asked pointing at an array of tiny holes. "They're too big for thumbtack punctures."

"Bullet holes," the docent answered, "It's quite a story. A witness saw Munch's lover arrive, enter the cabin and close the door. Soon after, a man arrived – her husband. Shots were heard, the husband and wife left, and Munch lost his thumb. Perhaps not in that order."

"Is timing everything?" Alex wondered. "Did he shoot himself? Was it an accident? Did the husband shoot at Munch, or God forbid, his own wife?" Alex asked.

"All we know is: one night Munch's lover arrived and, sometime later her husband arrived. Shots were fired. Shots were heard. Munch lost a finger. Aside from the bullet holes and the missing finger, nobody knows what transpired inside the cabin. The man left with his wife. The end."

"Aren't you Norwegians meant to be understated when it comes to love?" Alex ventured.

The docent laughed.

"Had Munch offered her coffee before sex, he could have ascertained her marital status and mental state. You know, determine whether she or her husband were homicidally insane," Alex said, "Coffee and a chat would have gone a long way to saving his finger."

"It was Munch's gun. He owned and shot it," the docent offered.

"At himself?"

"I imagine someone tried to stop him, hence the lost finger."

"Talking can solve so much," Alex said, thinking Roger might still be alive had he been chattier. Was his death about love? Roger lost more than a thumb. He was pierced right through the heart; a puncture wound painted with pain. The murderer's pain was further exhibited on the bathroom mirror with Alex's plum pout lipstick -- a chance tool wielded by an angry, vengeful, slighted lover. Roger's murder was not an apathetic act. Kit claimed apathy, and not hate, was the opposite of love. Whoever murdered Roger was not apathetic. They had strong feelings – untypical of a Norwegian. Though bottled feelings, thought Alex, lead to all sorts of mayhem. One needed to look no further than Nordic noir.

"Munch suffered scandal, blasphemy, rejection, the early death of his mother and sister, lovers who left, alcoholism that stayed, despite attempts to go dry with doctors and at sanatoriums," the docent informed Alex.

"No wonder his legacy is the most infamous meme for pain and agony."

"Hmmm. The agony of desire: to be seen, heard, wanted, loved and admired. He was human. There were people whose attention he desired, like playwright Henrik Ibsen, for example. And those whose attention he detested, like the police who shut down his show due to indecency in Berlin, and again in Oslo. The negative attention brought him the positive attention he desired in the form of Ibsen who, on sniffing scandal, waltzed into the Grand Hotel Café where Munch was a regular to request a private viewing of Munch's show, telling Munch, 'The more enemies you make the more friends you make. Scandal attracts the attention of people who value what you are doing,'" said the docent.

"Ah, the inception of scandal marketing. Munch's gunshot reminds me of a Janet Cardiff diorama. It's of a cozy suburban home surrounded by low lit streetlamps and perky shrubs. Curtains drawn, doors closed – the sole signs of life are the sound of a couple fighting. A gunshot. And Silence. On a loop: meaning the order of events depends on when you arrive at the scene. The light felt different in the silence following the gunshot, and different in the silence foregrounding the fight. The sound was on a loop; the light was not. The silence was peaceful on approach, and mournful on leaving – it was all the same track," Alex marveled.

Cardiff created a doppler effect of light and imagination. Time is everything. Time adjusts a scene's aperture even when everything else remains unchanged. Time changes *before* into *after*: love into hate, care into apathy. Time is a micro-rhythm, a twitch.

"Life is only on a loop in our imagination. Is love and who we love, about timing? Munch arrested time in the scars of love's loss, dotted along a wall he lived with day in and out."

*Was it love, or obsession? And where was the line?* Alex wondered.

"Hmm," the docent agreed. "I'll wait outside, if you want a few more minutes alone?"

"Yes, please." Alex folded her hands in gratitude.

When the docent left, Alex went straight to the wall with the bullet holes. She moved her finger along Munch's wall, like reading text, one finger moving under the words as her eyes tracked letter to letter. In Munch's wall she read despondence, heartbreak. The micro rhythm of a reverberating gunshot, a morse code, a map of mourning, tapping along a wall like braille from one century to the next. Edvard Munch's wall was a canvas of loss. In the old days they called dyslexia "word blind." They tried teaching Alex braille when she couldn't read. They failed. And yet, *this* she could read. She was reading with a different sense, the kind one might need in the jungle, in a place where all was obscured, and where she would have to feel her way to the answers. If anything, for her own safety.

Alex peeked into Munch's outdoor studio to thank the docent.

Scream – jealousy – death room – death struggle – loving women – kiss – woman and men among forest tree trunks – three women – vampire – were lined up along the wall.

"Paintings from his *Life Frieze* show," the docent explained.

"Who's she?" Alex pointed to a dark woman standing shadow-like against the tree-trunk.

"A nun or the naked woman's shadow -- sorrow, and death. The naked woman has a zest for life."

"And her?" Alex pointed to a pale, cheerful woman walking out toward the ocean.

"She walks toward eternity; she is the woman of longing. Together, they are the *Three Women*. They inspired Ibsen."

"And him? Who's he? Alex pointed to a man among the trees.

"Ah, the pained man amidst the tree trunks. Funny you should ask, as he was the inspiration for the anti-hero of Ibsen's last play, *When we Dead Awaken*, a story of a sculptor whose masterpiece, *Resurrection*, is split up – just like Munch's frieze."

*Plagiarism, inspiration, coincidence? Mysteries are not solved by coincidences but are informed by them. They are a well-told story.* Thought Alex. She thanked the docent and took her advice to walk the high road back to the center of town, to experience the quaint wood houses facing the sea -- the same ones Munch passed on his way into the small town for provisions or to meet friends.

Sporadic signage appeared in front of a house or scene Munch had painted with a snapshot of the painting and its date. The houses were little changed since Munch's time: a new coat of paint, shutters open or closed; mermaid weathervane rusted or replaced, clotheslines new, but hanging on the same axis and blowing in the same sea breeze that banged the shutters, spun the mermaid, and dried the clothes as they had in Munch's time.

This was very much a community. Munch died alone yet was not inherently a loner. He died single and childless, yet with a trove of friends. He kept a guest room and owned the only phone in town, and one of the few in Norway. His friends in Oslo gathered at a telephone exchange once a week to receive his call.

Without seeing his wall, Alex would never have known Munch's worst scar. A scar that outlived the fleshy stump of his lost thumb. Without the bullet holes it would be left to an astute observer to notice his maimed thumb and wonder if it was more than a cooking, wood chopping, quotidian accident. He wanted future witnesses to his pain. The choice to preserve the morbid souvenir of his lover's last visit was deliberate. The desire to live with the bullet holes day in and out was a form of penance. Munch, of all people, could have painted over it. Yet, who knew better than Munch that a re-painted canvas retains a trace of the underpainting.

<h1 style="text-align:center">Chapter 7</h1>

<h2 style="text-align:center">Silent Sauna</h2>

Alex spun around listening for the source of incessant buzzing. *The door?*

She peered into her intercom. Her first visitor. She was unsure how to use the contraption. She pressed a button, and a foggy figure emerged on the screen.

"Liv?" Alex pressed the key symbol, and buzzed her in.

Liv entered and handed Alex a flat cardboard box.

"It's Saturday," Liv announced, unsheathing the frozen disc.

Alex hung Liv's puffer jacket and bike helmet and led her into the sitting room *cum* kitchen.

"How can the healthiest people in the world, and this is an actual record, eat frozen pizza once a week?" Alex asked.

"Because we walk and bike everywhere. And eat lots of fish," Liv said. She set the oven dial and slipped the pizza onto a tray.

"How ... did you do that?" Alex stared at her oven in disbelief.

"Slip a pizza on a tray?" Liv asked, amused.

"Turn on the oven. Hours of YouTube videos later and I still can't figure it out."

"How do you cook?" Liv asked.

"I don't. I'm besties with Mr. Falafel by the Grønlund T-bane entrance."

Liv shook her head.

"Good timing. I was about to put on a Bergman film," Alex announced.

"Would rather slit my wrists," Liv protested, "Save the sorrow for the Swedes."

"To what do I owe this pleasure?" Alex asked.

"A murder suspect gone incommunicado. I came to make sure you weren't offed, or under house arrest. You said to come anytime," Liv reminded her.

"Yeah, a month ago," Alex agreed.

"Was your offer rescinded?" Liv asked.

"No, it's unexpected."

"Nice and roomy. We call this an open American floor plan. This place cost a pretty penny." Liv spun around and whistled.

"My funder sold her farm in Bergen and bought this."

"Bergen to Bjørvika."

"Yup. She's at her cabin or mansion in the mountains -- or should I say *hytte?*"

"How did this arrangement come about?"

"One of my professors may have bedded her -- as he put it, in the eighties. No one shared the details; but I ended-up the lucky artist/anthropologist with the prize to make the education wing soundscape. I'm also using it as my dissertation project."

"I thought the gardens were getting government subsidies for an artist?"

"Yeah, me," Alex grinned.

"You're not Norwegian," Liv pointed out.

"So you all like reminding me," Alex frowned.

"How does your patron make her money?" Liv asked as she stepped outside onto the balcony.

"I thought you weren't supposed to ask how people make money in Norway."

"We can ask how, but not how much. Wow, you have a view of the Oslo Fjord, and the Munch Museum. You can walk to the saunas! This is crazy."

"Oh no!" Alex hit her forehead.

"What is it?" Liv asked.

"*Silent Sauna*. I totally forgot. It's in an hour."

"Which sauna?" Liv asked, "There are a dozen of them right outside your door," Liv swept her arms to demonstrate.

"It's moored near the opera house."

"Easy," Liv said. "Around the corner."

"I don't want to go alone."

"I'll come with you," Liv offered. "Do you have an extra suit?"

Alex hesitated. She planned to invite Anders but forgot to. She was keeping Anders to herself -- Liv was critical of Norwegian men, to say the least.

"I have an extra bikini. You'll come?" Alex asked.

"Sure, why not," Liv agreed.


An hour later, the women crossed the square to the Saunas wrapped in robes and carrying water bottles and towels.

They checked in with a harried sauna master, host and all-around custodian.

"We don't get much traffic at this time of the week, or this hour," he said.

Alex shrugged. She had asked Liv not to mention *Silent Sauna*.

"In here," Liv directed Alex to the lockers where they left their robes and flip flops. "You need the towel to sit on," Liv instructed Alex, "And leave your glasses, they'll get destroyed by the heat."

Liv pulled the heavy wooden door, and a blast of heat hit them in the face.

"You'll adjust," Liv said, pulling Alex into the inferno.

And she did. Minutes later, she was sitting on her damp towel in the $100°$ cedar box looking out onto the darkening waters of the Oslo Fjord, feeling serene and dehydrated.

"Ugh, pizza before sauna was not a good idea," Liv panted.

Alex chugged her water.

"Too much salt. Small sips, you'll get a tummy ache," Liv

instructed and took a delicate swig from her water bottle. "Salad is better for sauna nights. Is he in your group?" Liv referred to a tall, muscular man, in a black knit wool cap who walked in as if he owned the place. He took a ladle of water from the large wood bucket and threw it on the coals and placed a second log in the burner.

"I've never seen him before," Alex said.

"I don't see anyone else here tonight," Liv noted. "This is bliss," Liv exhaled. "It's been ages since I've been to a sauna."

The smell of sweat and sage permeated the fiery air and burnt the edges of Alex's nostrils.

"I feel like a fire breathing dragon," she flared her nostrils at Liv who rolled her eyes. Kit would have laughed, thought Alex.

*Swish, whack, swish.* The man beat himself with a bundle of sagebrush branches.

"I'd love to record the sing song of the whacking and swishing," Alex whispered to Liv.

"That would be frowned upon in the privacy of a public sauna," Liv said. "Your phone would melt anyway," Liv added.

The man shushed them, and they giggled.

"How dare he," Liv said. "He's not Norwegian."

"Is the sound necessary? Does it add more pain to his increasingly vigorous flagellations? Does he crave pain?" Alex wondered aloud.

"Do you ever stop researching?" Liv asked.

"No," Alex answered.

"He is too loud to be in your silent group?" Liv giggled.

"Are we meant to be silent?" Alex asked.

"It's not a sauna rule per se."

"No, he's not in the *Silent Singles.* I've never seen him before. Roger wore a similar hat."

"Black wool beanies are popular this winter, half of Oslo is wearing those," Liv said. "Who's Roger?"

"The murder victim. The American guy."

The color drained from Liv's face.

"What is it?"

"I was told a different name. I thought he was Norwegian," she said.

"You look overheated."

"Mm." Liv murmured and looked around, "By the way, Mr. Sagebrush over there beating himself to a pulp is the sole human here aside from the Sauna master."

"Thanks, I can't see anything." Alex reminded Liv, who insisted Alex leave her glasses in the locker.

"You'll thank me. Your lenses would be destroyed by the heat," Liv said.

"It is darn hot. The jury is out on whether this is restorative or destructive. My brain is melting."

"We must destroy to restore. Go take a dip," Liv instructed. "I need a few more minutes."


Alex wobbled out of the sauna via the locker-room, retrieved her glasses and stumbled to the outdoor shower.

Her skin tightened and her jaw locked under a luscious downpour of freezing water pumped directly from the Fjord.

In the distance a splash punctuated the silence as a brave soul dove into the freezing dark water. A body emerged, floating, face-up.

*Who would float on a frozen Fjord?* Alex wondered. She shivered. Norwegians! Liv? There were two exits from the sauna, which meant Liv may have gone directly to the waterside deck to cool off. Alex turned off the shower, wiped her glasses and looked out onto the water where the floating body was Mr. Sagebrush who darted in and out of the foggy Fjord like a dolphin. No sight of Liv. Surely she left the sauna – even a Norwegian would melt after this long, thought Alex. Her body craved heat again, maybe Liv's had too.

She entered the locker alcove and sensed a change in atmosphere. Was the lightbulb dimmer? Was it quieter? Less humid? Warmer? Mustier? The scent of eucalyptus was stronger as she approached the sauna's heavy wooden door. Mr. Sagebrush's branch sounded scratchier. He was swimming. Was Liv whacking herself with his branch? Alex pulled the door, anticipating a sting of burning air. But the door did not budge.

She pulled and pounded. The scratching on the other side intensified.

"Liv?" Alex shouted.

A muffled response came from the other side of the jammed door.

"Help!" Alex screamed. She pulled and kicked at the door to no avail.

A scrawny, young sauna master came running in and pushed Alex aside.

"We don't have locks on the door. It cannot be locked," he said.

"We need to get her out. She's been in there since we came here," Alex pleaded.

He frowned and pressed his palm to the door.

"It's really hot," he said and ran outside. He returned in no time with a woodchopping axe.

"Stand back," he demanded hoarsely and swung furiously at the door.

"I'm dialing 113!" Alex shouted.

The sauna master kept swinging.

"The window!" Alex yelled. Each sauna had a window out onto the fjord.

They ran outside and collided with Mr. Sagebrush climbing out of the water and onto the deck. Together they broke the glass in two strikes, climbed in, scooped Liv up and carried her out to safety. Alex dipped her towel into the frigid Fjord and wrung it over Liv's face and body.

"She's responsive," Alex shouted to the Sauna master who relayed the information to the EMT on the phone. Mr. Sagebrush massaged her arms and legs and forced her to sip water until the EMT arrived and took her away.

. . .

Alex dressed and left the sauna. She took the tram two stops to the urgent care where Liv was being held overnight for observation.

Liv was asleep in a narrow, private room with a single small uncomfortable chair that Alex took as her proper penance for putting Liv in danger. Alex scrunched her back and squirmed around until she was comfortable.

She watched Liv asleep, thinking it was the first time she was around Liv in silence. Was it the squirrels in Liv's head that caused her to listen to music all the time? People often work while listening to music or a podcast. Alex couldn't concentrate with noise. She couldn't imagine having voices in her head.

Alex heard a television and the evening news in Norwegian coming from the room next door. People banishing the voices, or the silence, the loneliness via the TV or radio. *We tire of our own thoughts.*

She watched Liv. Were her dreams loud? Dreams were memories being processed. Liv was frowning in her sleep. What unpleasant memory was nudging its way to the surface?

Do events we fail to pay attention to, but experience get registered, let alone stored? Alex took out her notebook and wrote:

*Daniel Leviton, the neurologist I am reading for my lit review, likens stored memories acquired when we are distracted to items dumped in a junk drawer. There goes the mystery and romance of repressed memories and their retrieval. Dreams could be fragments of memory -- our brains de-fragmenting. We are not Teslas and ring cameras or Freud's idea of a screen memory, indiscriminately recording the environment -- nor do we have a computer's filing system. My brain is like a junk drawer full of things like door wedges I either never saw or failed to remember seeing, a sound of the perpetrator sneaking in or out of the sauna. I never heard anything...or did I? It's not my faulty memory, but my lack of attention that is at fault.*

*Leviton says as we go looking for something in our big messy memory junk drawer, only the big, obvious things are found, like the death of a beloved pet, or the useless snippet of a nursery rhyme. Memories remain, but like a half-broken paperclip stuck to the underside of the drawer, they aren't easy to retrieve.*

Alex got up to wipe her glasses. She had not been able to thoroughly clean them since entering the sauna. And now, no matter how vigorously she washed and dried them, she was unable to wipe off the fine squiggly lines swimming in perfect lanes up and down her lenses. Nothing helped – not alcohol wipes, soap or water. Had she scratched them at the sauna? Alex never took physics due to her dyscalculia, but knew molecules expanded or contracted with extreme temperature fluctuations. Matter and molecules -- had heat destroyed her lenses? What else had it destroyed? Evidence? She frowned. Was it permanent? She would throw them in the freezer when she got home. And, more realistically, look for her back-up pair. Her student insurance did not cover another pair until the following year. She prayed her back-ups weren't too ancient. Given the state of this pair, she'd settle for seeing well enough. Another reason to leave Oslo. To give up and go home.

Liv woke briefly, glanced at the drip in her arm and rolled back on her side.

"Liv?" Alex asked tentatively.

"She needs rest. And talking is dehydrating." The nurse startled Alex.

"Didn't see you there," Alex said.

"You're welcome to stay, but no talking." She took Liv's pulse and left the room.

Alex opened her Notes app and wrote: *Mist is hell for people who wear glasses. Norway's weather is hell for me...it's either raining on my glasses, fogging them with cold or misting them in the Lily House. Wearing glasses is seeing the world through a foggy lens. My world is often smudged or fogged or dirty – a bright, crisp and clean world is a gift others take for granted.*

She then checked her email, opening and as quickly closing,

another missive from professor Whiner. Academia was slowly spitting her out. She could exhibit agency and jump ship. Professor Whiner was coming down hard. He was testing her, and she was failing. *Whiner the whiner* thought Alex.

"Hei, Hei," the nurse arrived, and gently nudged Liv awake. She handed her a cup of warm water and a straw.

"You have a visitor," she said and motioned to a familiar female police officer to enter the room.

"Great," Alex muttered under her breath.

"The sauna was compromised by a small wood wedge under the door," the officer informed Liv, but watched Alex, "Not an accident." Turning fully to Alex, the officer continued, "The sauna master says he saw you in the shower the whole time. Did you wedge a piece of wood in the door as you left? By accident?" The police asked Alex.

Alex's eyes teared-up.

"It wasn't her," Liv croaked. "I heard someone at the door five minutes after she left."

The police officer shook her head, "Are you sure?" she added something in Norwegian.

"Yes. And besides, Alex would never try to hurt me," Liv insisted in English.

"Who knew your sauna plans?" The police officer asked.

"No one," Alex answered quickly.

Liv shot Alex a look. Alex shook her head slightly. If the police connected the *Silent Singles* meet-up to the sauna incident, it would further implicate Alex in Roger's death.

"We met at the Botanical Gardens," the police officer reminded them, "Is this a coincidence?"

"This?" Liv feigned ignorance.

"Our meeting again soon after our last encounter. Three's a charm. Or is it coincidence? Silent disco, Botanical Garden and now here."

"Oslo's a village, I'm told," Alex said, plunging her hands into her pockets and then wondering if it made her look guilty.

"Accident or attempted murder?" She looked at Alex, "You have a swipe card for the Botanical Gardens?" Was this the Norwegian inflection or a question, Alex was not sure. Her money was on *statement* as they already knew about her swipe card.

"You are welcome to help, or we may take further measures in our investigation."

What did *further measures* mean? And did they mean "welcome" in the same way they said she was *welcome* to stay but could not leave? Was this clumsy English Norwegian style or did she need a lawyer? Norway was not a litigious society. Kit would say Alex was in deep Kimchi. Kit would be on the next plane to Oslo if she knew Alex was in deep kimchi, which would put Kit in deep Kimchi with her new job.

"This is my friend; she would not hurt me," Liv maintained.

The police officer took in a sharp breath.

"Why would she?" Liv asked.

"Did you see her take the seeds from the Botanical Garden? You need to tell us now for your own safety," the officer told Liv. "I did not see her take any seeds."

"Do not leave town," the officer reminded Alex.

"So you've already told me," Alex said brazenly.

The officer turned to Liv and took her hand, "Ønsker deg en rask bedring," she said in Norwegian and left.

Alex fell into the armchair next to Liv's bed and exhaled.

"Alex, why didn't you mention *Silent Singles?*" Liv's voice faltered.

"I don't trust them."

"We are not American, we trust the police here," Liv's voice was scratchy.

"Yeah, she squeezed your hand – odd, no?"

"No. It's compassionate, I'm in the hospital. They hug people in distress."

"So I've seen," Alex commented.

"No more *Silent Singles*, Alex. It is dangerous. Leave it to the police," Liv insisted.

"Why would anyone want to kill you? Why *you*?" Alex asked.

"Perhaps I saw the killer when they came for the seeds?" Liv suggested.

"Right," Alex said, her mind was racing.

"It was an accident," Liv insisted. Alex knew full well it was no accident.

# Fieldnotes: Attending

Sauna: a gap between mist and fire. A lick of mist to flame is enough to disperse heat and cool the fire. The optimal gap between mist and fire ensures the fire does not dry the mist as it cools the fire. Like Yellowstone fumaroles. My relationship with Will.

Mist.

Dry.

Seeds. Dry but alive. Death leading to life. *Petite mort.* A small death? Wordplay and metaphor won't get me out of the mess I'm in. What other evidence do I have to play with? Anthropologist Michael Taussig suggests we pay attention to people's dreams in the field: *The subconscious Alex tells us much about a cultural zeitgeist.*

In my dream, Professor Storesund's suspecting (or suspicious) eyes bore into me from a TV screen. He is discussing witchcraft and magic on the nightly news. Do I find him suspicious because he finds me suspicious? He's on the radio, in print, online, in his choir sweatshirt, in his academic blazer, waxing anthropological on everything from New Year's resolutions and the joy of singing to cannibalism. Hurra to Norwegians for listening to anthropologists. Americans don't ask anthropologists for an opinion, which is why we Americans are the forerunners of fake news. Thorvald cautioned me not to research the seeds on the internet. Was he saving me from misinformation or purposely misleading me? Double check everything and everyone, Alex. I looked up the casuarina seeds and found no reference to dead or crying infants. Divination, but not death. Was he derailing me? Distracting me? Is he a magician of the Western parlor trick sort who relies on distraction and misdirection?

Alex's FaceTime lit up with Kit, sparkling in a sequin tank and velvet blazer. Her short curly hair was crowned by a gold headband.

"What's the occasion?" Alex peered closer.

"Donors at the gallery. Sneak-peek. No time to run home and change after work."

"Dressed to kill," Alex said absently. And quickly added, "Is being homesick akin to failure in the field?"

"No, we all get homesick. You sound lonely," Kit suggested.

"Am I a fun toy one quickly bores of and sets aside?"

"Why would you say ... what's going on?" Kit frowned.

"Will is ghosting me."

"You're a Rubik's cube; men get frustrated when they can't figure you out. You are anything but boring."

"Stop toying with me."

Kit laughed, "See, you are more than a fun toy. You're smart and complicated and need a playmate who can play with smart and complicated toys."

"How do we know it's love and not a crush?" Alex asked, adding, "I'm more myself around him -- I bumble less."

"That's not being yourself," Kit chuckled.

"I'm more focused."

"Case in point."

"He laughs at my jokes. He's tender, careful -- aware. He pays attention."

"That's it," Kit said, "Love demands attention."

"Explains why I suck at it. Wait, are you suggesting that I'm attention seeking?"

"All humans crave loving attention. Love is giving somebody our full attention, time, space and patient care. It is to be in attendance. It's why we call people seeking medical care patients. Doctors attend to and with patients/patience. Attention is a gift. Attention takes time, and time is a gift. I thought Will was ghosting you?"

"He is. I've found a tall Viking. Only he's scrambling signals. I haven't a clue if he's interested."

"What are the signals?"

"Brushed my hand. Squeezed my shoulder. Catches my eye and I melt."

"Promising. What's the problem?"

"Norwegian men are feminists; they'll never make the first move."

"Hyper-aware of predatorial history?" Kit raised a perfectly plucked brow.

"Difficult to untangle."

"Feminist Vikings? First move is on you," Kit joked.

"No."

"That's the reality, Anthropologist."

# Chapter 8

## *Whistling Wind*

Damp but not raining. Quiet, but not desolate. Late enough to still pass for day in Oslo. *Perfect conditions* thought Alex, as she out to record the container docks on the other side of her apartment building in Bjørvika.

Alex paused at the top of the pedestrian/bike path that ran alongside the dock and a major freeway and recorded the roar of oncoming cars that flew out the mouth of the freeway tunnel like bats winging a dark cloud toward the city. She continued to walk. The sidewalk curved and climbed above the container docks where Alex hoped to record the sonic symphony of wind against metal. But instead, on arrival, she heard only sputtering trucks shifting gears, and bike bells aggressively shooing her out of the way.

With nothing more than sporadic, grainy sound, she gave up and returned down the path. At the bend before Bjørvika, she noticed an open gate leading to the length of landfill where ships on either side unloaded their wares. No sign told her to keep out, so Alex ventured in.

"A life-size Lego city!" she recorded into her phone. She switched to video and set her aspect ratio to cinematic mode to capture the majestic metal crates -- the size of two-story apartments, colored like Easter eggs. Alex risked losing her way and walked deeper into the labyrinth of metal. She was half-tempted to leave a trail, but did not want to litter, or look ridiculous. She thought of the stats on people who die because they don't want to look ridiculous -- at the top were women choking alone in their homes, too embarrassed to run outside and throw themselves in the path of aid. On the one hand, there was no one here to save Alex should it come to it. On the other hand, she would prefer to be alone. She sensed she was being followed, but every time she turned to check, it was too late to see whether it was a foot or a small animal scurrying behind the crate. Her heart beat faster. *Turn around and meet them, or move on and see if they follow?* She moved on. The wind whipped fiercely from every direction forcing her to lose her sonic bearings. It felt like someone was holding her ears and giving nearby predators – human or otherwise, an unfair advantage.

She paused between crates. It was the ideal condition for recording sound: no need for a filter or editing or to tiptoe or to hold her breath. Absolutely nothing -- not even a scream-- could be heard above the whistling and banging.

Alex walked the narrow alleys between crates, recording the whistle of wind meeting metal. The deeper she ventured into the maze of crates, the closer they were stacked together. Alex's claustrophobia won and she turned to look for a quick way out. As she attempted to retrace her steps, she realized she was lost. *Don't panic.* She looked to the murky sky for construction cranes, but the horizon was a uniform canvas of gray blocking anything above crate level. She needed perspective – to be higher – if she were to see anything.

The crates had ladders – sort of. A row of rods that may or may not be meant for climbing or holding her weight. She pocketed her phone and climbed a rung, and then another. When she was high enough, she turned slightly, holding tight to the wet and slippery metal and looked for construction cranes, her north star. The world appeared darker. She heard a drip, and then another. Uniform and musical. She was tempted to record one handed, desperate for found sound, unique sound. But this sonic story might well tell the sound of her demise. Her hands slipped. The drip changed tempo …faster and harder, the drip, drip, drip went from pianissimo to fortissimo roar. A roar and a bang. Thunder? She could not discern its direction. Surround sound in real time. The sky was pumping up the jam. She hoped the boom was thunder, and just as quickly prayed it was not. *Doppler, to or from? Away, far, near?* Her mind raced.

*Footsteps?* Thunder. Boom!! Rain poured down harder. Her hands slipped. She scraped her knuckles as she caught and held tight to the next rung. She slipped again nearly dislocating her shoulder. She was shaking and risked falling if she released her grip to grab the next rung down. Another boom startled Alex, but she held tight. The god of thunder was angry.

She squeezed her eyes shut. In the distance she heard sirens. They gave her hope and pause in equal measure. What if it was the police? She prayed for firefighters. She and the police were becoming too familiar, and without the hugs.

She saw the lights before she noted the red color. A firetruck turned toward her. *The parking lot!* She found direction, her bearings, hope. She slipped down the ladder and ran toward the flashing lights. She paused behind a crate and waited. Two firemen in scuba gear were lowered into the cold, dark water and disappeared beneath the dock. Had someone fallen in? All eyes were on the water as Alex ran past the truck and out of the parking lot toward the Operagata. The last thing she needed was to be found at another crime scene. Her fingerprints were all over the crates. Would her trace survive the rain?

# Chapter 9

## *Silent Read*

Oslo's Renzo Piano designed central library appeared like a Christmas tree ornament dangling in a design store. A sign demanded **Silence!** *Tell that to the molecules,* Alex whispered. Sound was everywhere. And so were the tourists. Books, not bombs, in a city where libraries and monuments to peace were tourist attractions. Tourists pretended to be pirates on a ship's crow's nest while viewing the spectacular view of the Oslo Fjord from the library windows, ignoring the teens who flirted above the fjord, while pretending to do their homework.

Was a demand for silence a demand not to distract other readers who needed to "hear" the words and pay attention? Alex wondered. She rarely read in silence. She was an ear reader and experienced literature through audiobooks.

Only weeks ago, she sat in a private reading room at the *Silent Read* where she and Roger threw flirty, furtive glances at one another across candles specially lit for the occasion. The rules dictated silence. Their eyes lifted from their books and belied a shared desire to talk -- or so Alex had thought -- until they met again at the *Silent Disco,* where the rule of silence could be transgressed but was not. At least not with her. Her desire to slink off to a private corner with him was not a shared desire. Were she and Will still a shared desire?

She was uncharacteristically early to meet Anders and his friend Peder, giving her time to wander the stacks. Alex loved books. Dyslexia did not preclude a love of liber, libre – books meant freedom – to explore, to be elsewhere, to be someone else, to think new thoughts. Entering a book in the privacy of her mind was the purest crush. Reading silently was to conduct a clandestine love affair in public. No one is privy to the secrets that pass between you and a book. No lipreader can edge in on this privacy. Was this why Will suggested letters? Letters outlasted phone conversations. Words live on in the squaggle and squiggles reanimated with a trained glance. This was the power of reading. A power Alex worked immensely hard at acquiring. Touch, smell, words: the crinkle of paper, the haunted silence and command of a caught breath is the perfect love affair. Their smell.

"Hei," Anders came up behind her and startled her. She dropped the book of Frost's letters. He picked it up and handed it to her, but not before checking out the title.

Beside him stood Peder wearing shiny silver hoop earrings, his long brown hair pulled back in a ponytail, high, wide forehead and thick teeth, like a horse, tall and scruffy-handsome, part pirate, part painter. He fit right into the crow's nest.

"Anders says you lent this American bloke a book, yeah?" Peder got right to the point.

"Yes," Alex confirmed the story she and Anders concocted to convince Peder to let them into Roger's apartment.

"It took forever to get a decent cleaning job. We Norwegians clean our own messes. Finally, this American guy hires me and boom, he gets killed. What are the bloody chances? And I'm back at the Nav."

"The Nav?" asked Alex.

"Didn't Anders tell you how we met again after all these years?"

"No," Alex said.

"The bloody unemployment office. You're an anthropologist, huh? You should study our celebrated social welfare system." Peder set down his backpack and wiped his forehead. Did he live rough? A rare smell of piss around someone asleep on a bench could mean he was passed out drunk after a party or was unhoused. It was hard to tell in Oslo where the wealthy dressed down, and the unemployed dressed up, making everyone dress alike. A stain on Peder's painters' pants that wasn't paint did not match the fact of his pristine white tube socks he surely wore right out of the store. His Birkenstocks were new.

"Unemployment office in Oslo? What's that like?" Alex asked. Anders shook his head, too late -- Peder took the bait.

"You can't imagine. Fluorescent lights: they make my head hurt. My butt hurts from sitting too long. It's moldy and smells like the bottom of somebody's old wet shoe."

"Do they help you find jobs?" Alex asked. Anders shook his head.

"Sometimes. And when they don't, it's our fault and they punish us by sending us to a jobseeker's course."

"To learn typing, or office skills?" Alex asked. Anders shot her another look, and she shrugged.

"Fieldwork," she whispered to him.

"Ha! Jobs? No. They teach us power stands, and power handshakes and power bathroom breaks. And the coffee, how can you make bad coffee in Norway?"

"Oh?" Alex replied.

"Come on," Peder said. "We need to leave now."

He led them down the escalators and out onto Operagata, past the Oslo Central Station and toward the Royal Palace.

"The original campus of the University of Oslo," he pointed out the Domus Media, a beautiful 19th century dome. "I can't socialize the way I used to. I don't have money for beers. My cell phone is last year's model. People are distant when they find out you are a Naver," Peder complained.

*Hard to imagine Norwegians being any more distant,* Alex thought, but did not say.

"Appalling and impressing people in equal measure?" Alex whispered to Anders, who laughed.

"You asked for it, I tried to warn you," Anders whispered.

"What's a Naver?" Alex asked.

"Unemployed," Anders answered before Peder could.

"Receiving unemployment benefits," Peder clarified.

"My notion of a non-materialistic, egalitarian Norway is exploding with his every complaint," Alex told Anders under her breath.

"It's not typical of a Norwegian to unload like this." Anders replied.

"Does anthropologist mean therapist in Norwegian?" Alex sighed.

"The worst part is all the noise," Peder continued, oblivious to Alex and Ander's side-whisperings. "I'm not fussy about noise. But at home without anywhere to go, all the noise is amplified, you know, children playing, people going to work. The high pitch start of the old trams is now discomforting, yeah."

"What is? The sound?" Alex asked.

"Noise is a constant reminder of being left out."

"FOMO?"

"A neighbor's loud party, yeah. When you're there it's cool and when you're next door alone, it's F-ing loud," Peder explained.

"A ruckus?" Alex asked.

"Yeah," Peder frowned.

"Silence can be comforting or unsettling," Alex dictated into a voice memo.

"Alex is making a sound project," Anders explained.

"Are you studying me?" Peder looked her in the face.

"No. I'm recording a voice note for my research."

"A voice note?" Peder asked.

"I dictate my notes. I have dyslexia, it's faster and easier," Alex explained. "Most of us use assistive technology now, we just don't call it that if we don't have to rely on it."

"Cool," Peder replied. Dyslexia gave her street cred with the navver.

They crossed in front of the National Theater T-Bane station and toward the Cultural History Museum.

"Wait," Anders took Alex's wrist, "There's a cool sound art installation in here for your project."

They entered the T-bane station and Anders pointed to the domed ceiling. All three looked up.

"It looks like an inverted seashell," Alex marveled.

"Crenelations move the sound waves," Anders said.

"I've never noticed it." Alex said.

"You did not look up. It's an inverted dome. It's sound art. Listen: Whoooooo," Anders's breath created a reverb. It echoed and joined Alex's, "Wow! Say more," Alex demanded and turned on her recording app.

"No one notices the dome," Peder said.

"Or the echo? Weird. Do we always need a visual cue to notice sound?" Alex asked.

"Let's see. There's a bench. We can sit and watch people pass by ... do they notice or not?" Anders suggested.

"Natural researcher," Alex said.

"Yeah, so I'm on the clock," Peder reminded them.


They followed Peder to the Europa Hotel.

"A hotel?"

"The other door," Peder pointed at a door hidden between the hotel and a shop.

"Convenient. Right by the tram stop for the University of Oslo Blindern campus," Alex noted.

"You knew him, yeah? At Uni?" Peder asked.

"I..."

"Yes, where she lent him a book," Anders saved her.

"Harry Hole, lives around the corner," Peder announced.

"Who?"

"She hasn't read Nesbo," Anders replied.

"Shameful," Peder said. "Jo Nesbo's famous detective."

"I thought he was fictional?" Alex asked.

"He is," Anders said. He approached the stairs.

"Not with my heavy bag," Peder said and directed them into the elevator.

"What's the point of elevator music?" Alex asked.

"It calmed people who feared heights?" Anders suggested.

"Was there music in cage elevators? A piano player in the lobby? No one fears elevators anymore," Alex said.

"Entertainment," Anders said and added, "Shameful the need to be entertained for a few short minutes." Anders glared at Peder, "It's bad enough wasting electricity when there are stairs, but adding music?" Anders shook his head.

Peder was uncharacteristically silent.

"Why do companies insist on playing music while people are on hold?" Alex asked.

"To signal a connection," Anders said, "Like dancing, we stay together in a common story, movement, rhythm, beat."

"Unless we're listening to different songs at the same time." Alex said, thinking of the silent disco. "Music insists on attention. It's hard to pay attention to anything else while you are on hold listening to bad music," Alex said.

"Block it out," Anders said.

"I can't," Alex answered, wondering why others could. And why music could help one person concentrate and hinder the next.

"Muzak is a genre created to increase worker production in factories," Peder said. Anders and Alex looked at each other. "Programmed in 15-minute blocks, gradually increasing the tempo and volume, making it brassier in instrumentation, to speed up the workers' pace," Peder said, speeding up his words as he went.

"You never cease to surprise me, old friend," Anders slapped Peder on the back.


The disloyal sun shone brightly into Roger's West facing apartment.

"Ten minutes, yeah? Not risking the job." Peder pulled up his sleeves revealing a straight line of scratches up and down his fore-arm. Drugs? Brambles? Bed bugs? Was he living in a hostel?

"Thanks, man," Anders said.

The apartment was a sparsely decorated one-bedroom flat with a living room, dining area and a bedroom with nothing but the requisite furnishings in each...a table, a sofa, a bed.

"It's as sterile as a hotel suite," Alex observed. "Must hand it to you, Peder, this place is immaculate. Not a speck of dust."

"I haven't touched it since last week."

"Before he was murdered?" Alex asked.

"Yes, and before the police searched."

"Did he always keep it this neat?" Alex drew her finger over a table, "No dust?"

"It's odd, yeah. He kept the windows open usually which produced mega dust. Bookshelf is over there," Peder pointed.

"Hey man, want to show you this funny video," Anders distracted Peder.

Alex slipped into Roger's bedroom. It was bright, empty and as sterile as the rest of the flat, save for a bright pink pair of earplugs on the bedside table. Even in sleep Roger desired silence.

"What did you find?" Anders walked in and asked.

"Poignant," Alex pointed to the earplugs. "Why the obsession with silence?"

"Could be the screechy, scratchy sound. Don't you hear it?" Anders asked.

"Yeah. An old pipe? Rats in the walls? Not unusual for New York City."

"For Oslo it is strange -- it sounds like an animal?" Anders listened.

"Think he entertained women in his big old bed?" Alex asked, jumping on the bed.

"Or men," Anders said, pulling her off the bed. She peeked under the bed and found an Apple watch charger. Was it Roger's charger? Had he worn an apple watch? She held it up to Anders, "The data could be interesting. How did the police miss this?"

"Who says they did? The watch could be with your lipstick in an evidence bag."

"You know about my lipstick?"

"All of Oslo knows about your lipstick," Anders said.

A painting of a man, side profile, brown hair, aquiline nose hung above the bed.

"It's Roger," Alex said and snapped a picture. She zoomed in on the artist's signature. "We could find the artist," she suggested. "Terje is a Norwegian name."

"OK, guys. Enough." Peder said, coming into the bedroom. "Thought you were looking for a book?"

"No books here. Quick peek at the bathroom?" Alex begged.

"Two minutes. He didn't keep books in the bathroom. You might find a magazine, not the kind you're looking for," Peder conceded. "Weird American habit."

"I need to use it," Alex insisted, when Peder tried following her into the bathroom, crossing her legs for emphasis. She closed the door behind her and went straight to the medicine cabinet.

"Where's all his stuff?" Alex asked Anders who peeked his head in.

"What did you expect?" Anders asked.

"A packet of condoms, anxiety medication, nail polish, make-up – any sign of a private life or a partner. Don't you find it suspicious?" Alex asked.

"What? The toothbrush? Or toothpaste, dental floss -- bottle of Benadryl?" Anders joked.

"American allergy medication. A recent trip home?" Alex

placed her hands on her hips and looked around, "Lacking junk is suspicious for an American. We are consummate consumers."

"My bathroom looks like this," Anders said.

*No surprise there*, thought Alex, given his minimalist uniform of black jeans, black t-shirt and occasional black or cream sweater.

"Well, he's a good citizen," Alex said.

"Huh?" Anders asked, coming closer to inspect.

"He rolled his toothpaste from the bottom and did not pinch from the top. I pinch from the top which drives everyone I share toothpaste with insanely crazy," she said. They watched each other in the mirror.

"You've shared toothpaste with many people?" Anders asked, looking her in the eyes via the mirror.

"My sample size is small, but still, I don't get what the big deal is? So you waste a bit of toothpaste. The convenience is a real payoff. You save time. Which is more valuable than toothpaste, in my book. Did he spend his nights elsewhere? This place does not feel lived in."

"No idea," Anders said and left.


"Find anything interesting?" Alex asked, joining him in the living room.

"This is more your area."

"What do you mean?"

"Sir James Fraser, *The Golden Bough.* Anthropology," Anders said.

"Look at you. Have you taken an Anthro course? These are indeed classics in my field," Alex said, coming next to him, "Now this is interesting." She pulled out a book about birds. "Was he a bird watcher?"

She opened *The Third Bird* which was not about birds.

"It's like five hundred pages," Alex said handing it to Anders who took a quick look and reported back: "About a secret society that came together to pay attention to things -- in silence."

"Aha, the origin of *Silent Singles*," Alex said, taking the book from him and placing it in her bag.

"No way. We are not taking anything," Anders took the book back and placed it on the shelf.

"Typical, rule-abiding Norwegian," Alex said, "Admirable as it is annoying. This is important. We are *borrowing* it."

"Write down the title. We will borrow it from a proper library," Anders told her.

"Lawful good," Alex concluded, impressed and annoyed. She took a snapshot of the cover and flipped through the book. "No bookmarks, dogeared corners, sticky notes or marginalia: nothing."

"Let's go," Anders said and headed to the door.

Alex shook the book, and a yellow sticky note flew out. It was dry, dusty and faded. It bore a single word scribbled in faint pencil: *RITMO*. She put it in her pocket and replaced the book onto the shelf.

# Fieldnotes: Attention!!!!!!!!

Email from Professor Whiner: *What is your theoretical foundation for making these claims Alexandra?*

Alex ~~For heaven's sake, I'm not making theoretical claims.~~ Attention is central to my theoretical approach. Attention catalyzes awareness into action. Attention is action and not the presupposition. Awareness is distinct from attention. Listening; awareness; and attention are all separate processes. ~~I'm hyper aware but not great at attention. My own response bores me to sleep.~~

Whiner: How's the literature review on sound coming?

It's not. I don't see the point of reading deeply in one area. I prefer connecting epistemologies -- diverse ways of thinking, schools of thought and theories. A literature review for me is not a random review of texts having to do with my fieldsite -- like Adorno on sound; it is a genealogy of ideas. Let's call it a kinship chart for theory. Hegel and Rumi, Corbin and Kojève; Ibn Arabi and Jung. None of them directly relevant to my current task at hand. I may appear to jump from topic to topic, but I'm making connections. I'd rather be writing an intellectual genealogy that shows Munch's influence on Ibsen's last play. Ibsen's play and Munch's painting are not a random connection. Roger's murder is informed by this connection; I'm sure of it, but not sure how.

Can't add two Norwegian greats to any of my pre-assigned "reading lists," unless I make a case for the sound painted into the scream or the sonorous depth of Ibsen's works. Grasping at straws, Alexandra, Whiner would say. Making connections in the field, I'd retort ... if I had the guts.

Lit Review so far:

"Cognitive Neuroscience of Attention."

Awareness facilitates rapid scanning of information, while attention leads to a higher probability of retaining the information. Awareness is a frequent precursor to attention.

~~ADHD: attention with noise. Get this, I found a "bird" book in Roger's apartment, turns out it's all about attention! I borrowed a digital copy from Butler Library.~~

*In Search of the Third Bird,* by Graham Burnett

~~Millions of pages of text. No audio version —uncool for a researcher writing about attention.~~

*The associates of the order of birds have across time and space engaged in collective practices of sustained attention often to works of art... At the heart of "birdish activity" is the magic matter of the* mind and senses working dynamically (and non-uniformly) within the total manifold of all – attention.

Whiner: Ah, so you've contacted RITMO, you are collaborating?

Alex Yes. I'm on it.

*What? OMG, he told me about RITMO before I left NYC.*

Whiner: Two books in two months? Step it up, Alexandra. I need not remind you of your deadline and the dire consequences of your lack of attention. Let's not have an autoethnography, Alexandra.


RITMO -- of course! I knew it looked familiar. I totally forgot Whiner's suggestion to reach out to Professor Stillstanding when I arrived. Had I done so, I'd be further along in solving this murder – not to mention in my academic research, for what it's worth.

*Silent Singles* was a secret society for paying attention. A secret only Roger knew. He was a stranger to us and we to him. And yet, we showed up in silence and did his bidding. Sheep without rhyme or reason. Did he talk to anyone? Doubt it. Did he intend for us to speak to each other? Doubt it. Were we unwitting subjects of a prank? Doubt it. Or was this a lonely attempt at connection? More likely. I wasn't exactly innocent, flirting with Roger at every turn.

"Paying attention in company."

Graham Burnett, author of *The Third Bird*, writes: Attention imploded the idea of human subjectivity in modern times. We are where our attention is. At the crux is human agency: we choose where we want to place our attention. This society, order of birds, (also called ESTAR, from the Spanish verb "to be"), were adherent to strict protocols to "be" in a state – especially temporary states of actions or conditions (to **be** happy, Norway **is** cold, the doors **are** locked). To be, or not to Estar. Is being a choice? If I'm in my head and not "in the classroom," it's my choice. If the teacher, or topic, cannot grab and hold my attention, my attention wanders. Estar is an irregular verb. I am an irregular verb. As was Roger, we have/had that in common -- but in what way? The personality of the victim will uncover the motive of their murder.

What's the point of coming together to pay attention? What's the point of being in a group if you are alone with your thoughts? What was Roger up to? Who *was* Roger?

Silent, but together. As a species, silence is dangerous if not discomfiting and yet, the minute we feel an awkward silence, we react with chatter. Silence is an evolutionary advancement of a species without the worry of lurking predators. A species who has the privilege to meditate, to be still, to go within and forgo vigilance. Silence is a privilege. In the animal world, silence signaled danger -- a warning Roger did not heed.

William James – the philosopher who taught us my favorite

hack, to "act as if," and the founder of modern religious studies, suggested that free will is defined in the moment we choose to give our attention "here versus there." Yes, there is involuntary giving, or stealing of attention, like being woken by the hotel PA system. William James would say I can choose to stop listening. But I can only stop hearing by blocking the noise with earplugs, headphones or other noise -- or by leaving the scene altogether -- which was the point of the announcement. Attention, and the attention economy, is at the crux of human agency and subjectivity in the Anthropocene (the current age where we humans inadvertently, and sometimes purposely, are destroying the world).

What wasn't I paying attention to the night Roger was killed?

The minute Anders appeared he stole 100% of my attention.

Sounds haunt me less than the noise – distraction at the disco. Distraction is less dangerous than the time it takes us to return from it. How long was I distracted for? The police assumed, with our headphones off, that Anders and I were sonic witnesses to Roger's demise. As if music was my only distraction. Like a dog sniffing out a treat -- my senses were engaged elsewhere. I close my eyes and see stairs: Anders ascending; me descending.

# Chapter 10

## *Silent Standing*

"Is this a ritual, or a special occasion?" Alex asked, following Professor Stillstanding, RITMO's director, from office to office, handing out Daemer toffee chocolates to each team member and wishing them a happy weekend.

"Every Friday," Professor Stillstanding answered. "We just concluded a big study on stillness. I call it *Still Standing*. We proved that we are always in motion."

"I can see that," Alex joked. He gave her a quizzical look.

"How ... how did you do it?" she asked.

"Easy. I wore electrodes all over my body while I stood still. We proved stillness is an impossibility." He threw a candy on the desk of an absent worker.

"I'd squirm with electrodes taped all over my body. I cut tags out of my clothing," Alex said.

"Yeah, anyway, we are always moving, even if it's a micro twitch," he said and took a handful of chocolates for the next delivery.

Standing still was the tyranny of school. Being still in school? Still in school...*Oh my God, I'm still in school!* Haunted by the demand: Alex, sit still, pay attention. Paying attention, listening and moving are distinct processes clumped together in school. She paid attention in school, just not to her teacher. Nor did she *listen* to her teacher.

"So?" Professor Stillstanding asked.

"I was thinking of all the punishments I've received for micro-twitching. Fidgeting, moving, helps me think. Walking is when I do my best thinking," Alex said.

"Yes, stillness does not equal attention."

*Is attention homeostasis? Even in stillness, there is movement, and in silence there is sound. Nothing is ever still; the world is always vibrating. Movement pushes dark clouds away. Movement causes accidents. Stillness makes me sad. Stillness invites predators.*

"Stillness for me, is unheimlich, it's the opposite of homeostasis," Alex thought aloud.

"Exactly. Everyone moves, yeah, but in differing degrees."

"I'm like a hummingbird."

"Even they rest. So, to your point about moving to think -- we studied classical music concerts. Norwegians, we move when we listen to music. We feel it, physically. My mentor Daniel Leviton says listeners are sensitive to the movements, and gestures musicians make. By watching a musical performance without hearing it listeners can detect expressive intentions of the musician. Like John Cage's 4'33'."

Alex made a note to look up John Cage.

Professor Stillstanding unlocked his office, and they entered what looked like the workshop of a mad scientist, at least a musical one. There were antique recording devices, including a theremin, a Ms. Pacman game console, and a myriad of instruments -- including a silent disco headset. Alex picked it up. Her heart raced.

"For our rhythm study."

"Oh?" Alex fingered the switches.

"We are studying rhythm in groups. Do people pick-up each other's rhythm by watching, or do they need to listen to the same music?" Professor Stillstanding asked.

"How? Observation?"

"I'll show you, come with me," he said and led her to the back of the building.

"We use headsets with different channels to see if people pick-up each other's rhythm. We watch body language to see if people sync, and if they do, whether it's because they're listening to the same song or because they are attuning to body language, or both. The headset lights indicate if dancers are on the same channel and song. We use professional dancers to coax people into new rhythms or different beats from their headset channel. Professional dancers can keep different beats and pay attention to what's happening around them. They have incredible peripheral vision."

"Like lizards," Alex said.

"It's imperative to see where to land on the dance floor, or where a partner is in space, or where the stage begins and ends. And to watch for headset light changes as you dance and detect a partner's rhythm change. They are super assets for our study."

Professor Stillstanding opened a door and led her into a sound studio outfitted like a faux disco -- headsets on hooks, a spin table, and a disco ball -- ready to party.

"We attached probes to dancers," Professor Stillstanding was saying.

"What did you find?" Alex asked.

"Unfortunately, our first night in public was interrupted by a murder."

"The silent disco at Kulturkirken Jakob," Alex muttered.

"We do know from studio work that if you increase the tempo, you eventually face a transition, like moving from walking to running. We go from one pace to another pace because we cannot both run and walk at the same time -- it's either or, it's very categorical. You can walk faster, faster, faster, faster and then...you will start running. It's like a horse going from a trot to a canter. It's not the same gait. Yeah. The first thing is the pace; the point of the pace transition may differ, based on whether you are increasing or decreasing the rhythm. And we see the same thing with dancing."

"How so?" Alex asked absently. She could not take her eyes off the photos pinned to the back wall.

"If you increase the tempo, you will get to these transitions quicker. And it's fascinating when testing this systematically at a silent disco -- you see people dancing to a steady beat on one set of headphones, while others are increasing slowly until they align."

"Right," Alex said, "Anders," she said, approaching a photo.

"You know him? He's one of our best dancers. He's wearing the same probes I used with the classical music concert goers. So there's obviously like a suspense thing happening where people kind of wait and kind of lean forwards and kind of wait."

"Suspense?" Alex asked. She couldn't take her eyes off the photo. "With the audience. And him?" Alex asked.

"Anders was a dancer we used to coax people at the Kulturkirken Jakob disco into a different rhythm. Dancers are the perfect medium: they embody music. Incredible hyper-focus and intense physical energy makes for a talented artist."

*Hyper-focus and intense physical energy --ADHD*, thought Alex.

"Look, he reaches to another dancer without looking at her. He senses where she is and uses his peripheral vision. You know him? I'm dying to see his solo show. It opens at Danse Haus this week. Are you OK?" Professor Stillstanding asked.

"I was there," Alex admitted.

"It hasn't opened?" Professor Stillstanding rubbed his chin. Norwegians were never wrong about dates; they had superb internal calendars owing to days of total dark and total light.

"No, I saw him at Kulturkirken Jakob, at the Silent Disco."

"It must have been, hmmm, yeah?" He studied her.

"I met Anders there." Alex said, *I was his research subject,* Alex thought. The shoe pinched on the other foot. "You recorded people at the silent disco?" she asked.

"We had observers on the ground."

"And they didn't witness anything?" Alex tried to sound casual.

"They were on the dance floor," Professor Stillstanding said.

*Anders wasn't*, thought Alex. *Surely a bathroom break was permissible.*

"We scrambled half the headsets. Our post-docs observed body movement to see whether people kept the proverbial beat with their group by listening to the same music or by dancing together on different stations. We did it here, in the lab, but it's artificial. People anticipate a change –they're aware of being watched."

Alex nodded her head. She was not aware of being watched. Who else had been watching her?

"I feel a bit queasy. Something I ate," she said grasping her stomach.

"Yeah, yeah, the air, it's a bit bad in here." Professor Stillstanding led her out, "I'll email you next time we go into the field. It would be great to have another set of eyes, an anthropologist's observations. We have psychologists, musicians, dancers, theorists. You'd be welcome, especially as you like to dance. Next time? Professor Whiner spoke highly of you."

"Really?" Alex was genuinely surprised, which did not faze a Norwegian. They were nothing if not humble.

Alex thanked him and left.

"My ear pods." She turned backed. Professor Stillstanding was gone, but the studio door was ajar.


It was dark and she had no clue where the lights were. Her stomach rumbled. She turned on her iPhone and shone the light around the studio and saw a small white ear pod case on the spin table. She went to retrieve it when the door slammed shut. She ran to the door. It was locked.

Alex pounded on the door to no avail. Her heart raced. She spun around and shone her light in every direction.

"Who's there?" she asked. "HELP!!!!" she screamed into the soundproof room.

She stood still, silent, in place, listening. She was alone. She

slinked down cross-legged on the floor and unlocked her phone --
no signal. She felt along the wall to the door.

She couldn't help thinking of the sauna. She would start
carrying a door wedge with her everywhere she went. Norway was
an open society, but with too many doors.

*Breathe, Alex. Breathe.* Had she heard Roger's last exhale?
Would her next exhale be her last?

*I can't breathe. Anders can help. Anders knows how to breathe.
What else does Anders know?*

Alex stood and shone her flashlight app at a cabinet in the far
corner. A little peek wouldn't hurt.

She opened the door and saw a row of disco headsets. They
looked just like the ones at Kulturkirken Jakob, only thicker. Bigger
heads? Different brand? She took one out and examined it. One
eyed troll, thought Alex, spotting the red eye of an infrared GoPro
type camera. They had been recording that night. Where were the
recordings, and why had Professor Stillstanding lied to her?

Adorno warns us to pay heed as even the music of integrity and
essence of a genuine consciousness can degenerate into ideology
and a socially necessary illusion. Was all this an illusion? Was
sound a distraction? Was silence the distraction?

She dictated a note:

*Headphones make music personal...* She thought she heard
something and stopped recording.

"Hello?" Alex called out to the empty room. "So this is the
sound of silence?" There was no answer. She made a mental note
to ask Professor Stillstanding if this studio was a true echo
chamber.

She thought she heard a bang. Did Roger's ghost linger? She
wondered. And if so, could she hear it? Only a believer in ghosts
would hear one.

She continued her survey of the lab and found a small mole-
skin notebook. The writing was in both Norwegian and English.
Not unusual for the University of Oslo.

*Fairchild 660: magic happens in the sidechain -- monitors the input level and produces a corresponding voltage when the signal exceeds the threshold. This voltage is applied to the control grid of the amplification valves to decrease the amount of gain added to the signal. The more the input signal exceeds the threshold, the greater the control voltage, and the more gain is reduced, resulting in compression.*

Compression, pressure, air. The release and compression of organs controlling air make sound. Singing, breathing... frowning. The human voice is the greatest organ,

*A frown painted with a blush of Perfect Plum Pout lipstick -- which cost a fortune and my freedom*, Alex scribbled in the mole-skin notebook. She immediately regretted it and tore the page out. She crumpled it and slipped it into her pocket.

The Hammond organ's electric motor sends sound in a circle; listeners ears rapidly fluctuate frequencies. Like Janet Cardiff's sound loop. Was Roger's grunt a before or after?

Professor Stillstanding was researching ambient sound.

Alex continued reading: Integrated Listening System: music in special frequencies combined with motion. Low gain hearing aids programmed to filter out background noises. Silence only exists in echo chambers, otherwise the world is loud.


Alex shouted: HELP!!!!!!


She dictated into her Notes app:

Laboratory techniques are not devoid of scientific value. 2, 3,4 and then more...

*And yet, they fit their victims like a glove. Sound is not about what is there, but what isn't there. For example, if a train is supposed to be there and you don't hear it ....*

. . .

The door swung open, and Alex dropped the notebook. The light went on before she could shut the cabinet. A tall woman wearing a ballerina bun swiftly entered the room.

"Why are you standing in the dark?" she asked Alex.

"I left my earbuds behind and came back for them and got locked in," Alex said, shutting the cabinet.

"And?"

"Yes, I found them. But I couldn't get out, the door was locked."

"You need a swipe card," the woman said, glancing at the moleskin notebook on the floor.

Alex bid her farewell and slipped out the door.

# Fieldnotes: Tacet Love

Dear Will,

Remember telling me I'm like tinnitus -- *in a good way?* There's no good way to have tinnitus. The agony of repeated sound drives people to suicide. Are my letters less tinnitus, and more earworm? Your replies are auditory hallucinations. Voices in my head. In other words: they don't exist. I remember voices so well that I can have an entire conversation with you in my head. Crazy, right? You're my earworm, a memory out of whack and on repeat. Oliver Sacks calls them a special form of involuntary musical imagery – out of control, unpleasant and intrusive. ~~Was I special? Out of control, unpleasant and intrusive. A happy song or a sad song?~~ There's a cure – silence. ~~Are you cured?~~

Composer John Cage inadvertently cured people's tinnitus and earworms with his silent opus. He called it "Tacet" -- a musical notation for musicians not to play. Only in Cage's *Tacet,* (or 4'33) he instructed musicians to pantomime playing – moving bows and arms and fingers and breath, in silence. Imagine composing silence ~~(you're quite good at it)~~. No two performances sound the same because the ambient sounds of the space differ. Versions on the violin, guitar, full orchestra, string quartet and piano all cured people's earworms. Cage believed silence only existed in echo chambers. The music *is* the creaky chair, a musician's sigh, an audience member's sneeze, a cough, a crinkle, a shuffle; as people sit silently, but not still. Sound is molecules in motion. We hear what we pay attention to. Attention is a gift we give to what holds our interest. ~~Your silence has my full attention; I am writing to an echo chamber.~~ Faces elude me, but I can recall a person's voice as if I'm listening to a recording. I can make them say things in my head I wish they would say in real life. Silence contains acoustics – ~~yours is active and loud. Your silence is a sad song on repeat. The record scratches, I replace it with a brighter tune, and I hear Anders say... A-lex? And you say good-bye.~~

# Chapter 11

## *Singing in the Rain*

An exquisite smell of sautéed garlic came from the Eilert Sundts Building as she walked by Moltke Moes Vei. Alex was on her way to the tram after a useless meeting with a colleague of Roger's – a real dead end-- and was too hungry to pass up the university cafeteria.

She was exiting the cafeteria with her falafel ball and Baba ghanoush bowl when she ran headlong into Professor Thorvald Storesund.

"Alex," Thorvald exclaimed.

"Hi," Alex said, startled. "Professor, I mean, Thorvald."

"Where are you planning to eat that?" he pointed to her take-away container.

"By the fountain."

"It's too chilly to eat outside. And we can't have a visitor eating alone. Come to the department, we do the quiz on Fridays at lunch."

"Quiz?" Alex said.

"Yes, like your Jeopardy show. Come."

"OK," she said reluctantly.

"Goody!"

Was he conjuring the sarcastic American "goody," as in *I was hoping you'd say no but now you said yes, oh goody,* or a Norwegian English goody which could mean *wonderful to have you at the quiz.* Translating a Norwegian word to English would have been easier than trying to figure out how a Norwegian was using English. Either way, he was leading her away from the elevator bank and toward the stairs.

"Is the quiz in the department? On the ninth floor?" Alex asked.

"Yes! The stairs are better for us and for the environment," Thorvald said opening the door to the stairwell. No wonder he kept so fit for a retiree.

Alex huffed, puffed and sweated her way up the spiral staircase to the ninth-floor lunchroom where Thorvald retrieved his lunch from the fridge and the *Guardian Newspaper* from the counter.

"Quiz time," he called the lunchroom to attention. She wondered if his wife forced him out the door every day with a lunchbox. According to the department website, he had been emeritus for at least five years.

Alongside teaching an occasional lecture, writing a penultimate study of a drowning island, watering the plants of the faculty in the field, he was also the quizmaster.

"Twenty-four centimeters, by..." Thorvald tapped his fingers on the table before coming up with the correct answer for allowable circumference of carry-on baggage measurements on Norwegian Air.

"The topic of Princess Beatrice's advocacy work?" Thorvald asked, reading from *The Guardian.*

"Dyslexia!" Alex shouted the answer, correctly.

"The name of the new Labor Party secretary's dog?" Thorvald laughed and guessed, "Fido," incorrectly.

The quiz concluded with a seventy-five percent accuracy, according to Thorvald's scorekeeping.

"Wait," Guro, the department manager, jumped up, "Final question time. We add a local question at the end of the game. My job," Guro explained to Alex, before asking, "On which bridge did the Vålerenga Men's Choir perform the Vålerenga football team's theme in this year's candle lit night?"

Like ghosts gathered in the fog, Alex remembered the ethereal image of men in white plastic ponchos, their blue and white flags waving in the wind from the Anker bridge as she passed them on her way to the silent disco.

"Only Norwegians would show up in the pouring rain to hear a men's choir sing a soccer anthem," Alex said.

"Thorvald?" Guro asked him. Thorvald's neck and cheeks reddened.

"Quiz is over, tally up." Thorvald licked his fingers, scribbled on the scrap of paper he kept score on, and announced, "Five points higher than last week. Alex has brought us good luck." He flashed his winning grin, snapped shut his lunch container and stood to leave.

"Wait," Guro stopped him, "The bonus question answer is the Anker Bridge. Our generous colleague knew this as he was there singing his heart out in the pouring rain but left the points for someone else to claim. Hurra Thorvald," Guro announced.

Thorvald took a brief bow and scurried down the hall.

"Come again!" Guro called after Alex who was in pursuit of Thorvald with a quiz question of her own.

"Yes, thank you, this was lovely," Alex called back.

Thorvald's head was bowed down over a stack of papers. His purposeful posture said: busy.

Alex backed away, afraid of interrupting him, when he looked up.

"Hei," Thorvald greeted her warmly. Years attuned to listening for signs of witchcraft in the rainforests of Melanesia lent him the hearing of a bat. Either that, or he had spectacular peripheral vision. Was he a dancer as well as a singer?

"Singing in the rain? You're in a choir?" Alex boldly entered his office. At Columbia, the line between the hallway and a professor's office was like the third rail of the Subway: hot and activated and not to be crossed.

"Norwegians like to sing. Good material for your sound project." He moved deftly into mentor role.

"You never mentioned it."

"Why would I?" he lifted the *I* -- to either indicate a question, or as a Norwegian inflection.

"When I first came to see you about Roger's murder - well, you didn't mention being nearby. I mean, it is quite a coincidence." Alex's cheeks flushed; her heart raced; she hated any kind of confrontation, especially with authority.

"Coincidence?"

"You were singing right outside of the disco when Roger was killed," Alex explained.

"Ahh. Which is why we all have alibis."

*That was quick. I wasn't asking for your alibi,* thought Alex. She tried a quick calculation in her head: alibis or opportunity? Her dyscalculia did not help in moments like this. Surely the police did their own calculations.

"We sing in an annual candlelight river fest. No pre-meditation here," Thorvald insisted.

"Unless there was. It's annual, well-planned and known by all?"

"It's a major city of Oslo event," he said.

"Not many people were watching you," Alex tried not to offend.

"It was pouring rain."

"Why not cancel?"

"It's Norway. If we canceled for inclement weather, we wouldn't do anything."

*Inclement? Try torrential. So this event would happen come rain or shine -- great cover,* thought Alex.

"Yet people skipped the event. Why sing without an audience?"

"We sing for enjoyment, not for show. If others enjoy it, all the better, but it's not a requisite." Thorvald pointed out. "And besides, by the time he died, the choir was long gone."

*So was the murderer.* She remembered the receding ambulance screeching off with Roger's dead body in the rain as she and Anders watched from the door. The crunch of gravel. Steam rising from open mouths of the ghostly figures on the bridge -- their song silenced by the distance and the rain.

"Are you sure?" *Breathe*, she reminded herself.

"Hmm," he muttered. He leaned back in his chair, tussled his hair and squinted at the ceiling. A pair of glasses sat next to his keyboard suggesting his bat powered hearing was less from listening for magic in the jungle, but an attentional filter evolved to sound due to poor sight.

Alex bit her lip and tasted blood. Finally, he swung upright.

"The men would not have seen anything," he concluded. *If I could see you singing from the door, you could see the murderer leaving from the door*, Alex thought.

"Were you wearing your glasses?" Alex asked.

"Perceptive," Thorvald said and instinctively swept them into the desk drawer. "No, I was not, it was raining," he explained.

"Why not wear them now?"

"It's a crutch, I'm strengthening my eyes by resisting."

This same logic assumed assistive technology was cheating, leading students who need it, to refuse it, and the added time for tests and assignments, because they want to be like everyone else, and not cheaters. *But we are not like everyone else. We don't any of us have the same brains. And those of us with dyslexia and dyscalculia and ADHD are time blind and word blind and assistive technology equalizes our stasis if not status. It's no different than wearing glasses or a hearing aid,* thought Alex.

"You all may have seen the murderer leave the building," Alex blinked.

"I can see how upset you are by all this. Witness to a murder and being so far from home. It's super upsetting, but you must let the police do the investigating," Thorvald told her. His voice was gentle.

"Why, when we first met, didn't you mention being right there at the scene?"

Was he being Norwegian and divulging only what was strictly necessary? Or was there more to his omission?

"Why would I? You're not investigating this – or are you?" he raised his voice.

"No, it's... I don't know," Alex answered weakly. "I am a witness and may be a suspect. And I wasn't paying attention, which the police find hard to believe. My whole life I'm accused of not paying attention and the one time..." Alex choked back tears, "I was the last person to see him alive. My lipstick was used to make a primitive sign. My fieldsite is the Botanical Gardens, I have a swipe card," Alex divulged it all despite herself.

"I'm sure you didn't murder Roger." Thorvald gave her a sympathetic look.

"Well, so am I. Wait, *Roger*? You knew him?" Alex wiped her tears.

"I knew of him. He gave a talk at the Travelers Club."

"Like the Automobile club? AAA? Not the anthropology association."

"It's an intellectual dinner club. Retirement project."

"A gentleman's club?" Alex asked.

"More like the Rotary club. We opened it up to women. I mean, we have women speakers. We highlight adventurers."

*Armchair anthropology?* None of this was the point, Alex forced herself to stay on topic.

"But you *knew* him and you never said," Alex repeated.

"I *knew of* him. He had not been identified to me when you and I first met." He held her gaze.

"What was his talk about?" Alex asked.

"Ahh, good question. He gave a talk on climate change."

"He was a climate activist?"

"Scientist. A seismologist." Thorvald clarified.

"Do you have earthquakes?" Alex asked. She would look this one up. She was not going to rely on Professor Storesund's expertise anymore. She would double check everything from now on.

"We do, little ones," Thorvald answered.

"Little what?" Alex asked, her thoughts returning to the room.

"Earthquakes. The last and only recorded big one was in Oslo in 1904, a 5.4. Small by US standards, but was felt in Sweden, Finland, Poland."

"Small places by US standards. Would it capture the attention of a US seismologist?"

"Seismology is a study of the earth's vibrations. Glaciers, as well as earthquakes. And glaciers we have in spades. Or we did have before they started melting," Thorvald said.

"Earth songs?" Alex asked. "The vibrating or humming or singing of the earth –seismology."

"Yes, the earth hums. Hmm." Thorvald hummed.

"So, he was speaking about glaciers?" Alex asked.

"His talk was on oil." Thorvald added, "We have oil."

*Typical Norwegian understatement.*

"So I heard. Drilling for oil can cause earthquakes," Alex said.

Alex saw protesters outside of the palace with *Stop Drilling* banners.

"He ruffled a few feathers."

"Do you remember whose feathers in particular?" Alex asked.

"If I did, would the names mean anything to you? Besides, it's not a murderous crowd. We *do* host the Nobel Peace Prize. We are a peace-loving people," Thorvald said.

"What if his work became policy? A Rachel Carson type. *Silent Spring*. Could be worth killing for."

"It's already policy. Norway has the most successful EV rates in the world – close to 100% electric vehicles."

"And yet you mine fossil fuels. Did Roger call the EV project hypocritical? Surely the police have followed this line of inquiry?" Alex asked.

"Roger worked on sound and noise pollution."

"Noise pollution?" Alex asked.

"Yes, noise: sound out of place," Thorvald bit his nail.

"Who decides what's out of place, what's in place, who and what belongs and where? *Is* noise sound out of place? City sounds are hardly out of place. We expect jackhammers, yelling and sirens in a city. And yet, who wouldn't call it noise? Do we call it sound since it belongs in the city? I'm from New York City and find the sounds of suburbia: leaf blowers, mowers, and trimmers going at a hapless hedge akin to dental tools."

"Ah, worse than blaring New York City rush-hour horns and sirens?" Thorvald asked.

"It's noise, plain and simple. We New Yorkers would welcome the grass, leaves, hedges and weeds. Does decibel matter?"

"Decibel is a matter of class and culture. Loud is inappropriate in polite society. Norwegians are quiet."

"Are you suggesting America is not polite society?" Alex asked.

"Noise is a cultural construct. Noise is an opinion. One person's noise is another person's melody. Noise is sound we don't like. What I consider deafening and harsh, others find joyous," Thorvald elaborated.

Alex did not admit the blasted Munch playscape was the sound of pure ruckus. She pulled out her phone and wrote a note:

Is noise a ~~nuance~~ nuisance?

"Did Roger's research on noise threaten anyone?" Alex asked.

"Not really. He called out the cruise ship industry, of which Norwegians are at the forefront."

"Why the cruise ships?"

"When we humans returned to our caves during the pandemic lockdown, the animal kingdom flourished mostly due to the subsequent silence. Finally, animals could send uninterrupted contact calls," Thorvald began.

"Cheetahs could hear their babies crying to them," Alex agreed.

"Cheetahs don't swim," Thorvald pointed out. "But yes, all those inarticulate sounds, like a chicken cluck, signaling foraging locations, safety or danger could finally be heard. Dolphins who were aborting due to sonic stress from cruise ship and cargo liner clamor were giving birth. Whale song wasn't being drowned out by motors. The pandemic illustrated the difference between sound and noise and how detrimental human noise is to nature."

"This explains Roger's interest in RITMO. They study ambient sounds like cooling systems and fans. Bothersome noises for some soothe others. Fan noise is a top choice in sound machines."

"Sound machines?"

"Some people block noise to sleep; others need noise to sleep."

"Look," Thorvald glanced at his watch, "Oslo's not a bad place to be stuck. Let the police do their job. They will figure this out. Nobody from the Travelers Club, or RITMO killed him."

"And the choir? Was he friends with someone from the choir? What time did you stop singing?" Alex asked.

"Are you cross examining me?" Thorvald laughed and studied his nails.

"As you pointed out, I'm trying to clear my name and go home."

He looked at Alex without expression. She wondered if he played poker – more likely chess.

"We stopped singing at around 8 o'clock," he said and bit a cuticle.

*Around the time Roger was killed.* She thought. Her heart thumped wildly.

"My choir mates are not murderers."

*Famous last words*, thought Alex.

# Fieldnotes: Sound Waves

*When we think of noise, we picture loudspeakers radios and sound like Frontline armament, subways, thundering, and rattling. What is noise? Is it simply random, pain-level sound? Technically noise is a sound that contains all frequencies.* Diane Akerman *History of the Senses*

Is noise a ~~nuance~~ nuisance? Nuisance -- worst word for a dyslexic to spell, back to dictating (Siri is a better speller). Is noise deviant, a deviation from the norm? Sound is ever present whereas noise is not. It *sounds* like a cultural construct, or a neuro-difference – such as an intolerance for certain noises: slurping, chewing, licking -- misophonia. And the choir -- being in or out of tune is a cultural opinion. (I'll spare you my very deep rabbit hole on disability as a cultural opinion in which I use the metaphor of a tuning fork).

In drumming, being 'off' – if done consistently - is a feature, rather than a flaw. Micro imperfections, deviations from playing musical notation exactly alike, gifts music its emotional resonance. Imperceivable microscopic rhythmic imperfections are responsible for our emotional response. Humans are micro rhythms: purposeful deviations from notation.

If sound contributes to deep sea anxiety and the disturbed

mental state of dolphins, then it surely messes with human sanity. And yet, and this is where I am stumped: we humans are so unique in our sonic preferences that what bothers one person may soothe another. Roger craved dead silence (bad pun), while Liv surrounds herself in sound like a warm blanket.

Why silence Roger? Why did Roger prefer silence? Silence doesn't always soothe. Silence signals danger. Like crickets going still and silent upon hearing a predator. Because silence denotes danger, animals, especially humans, use gentle humming to relax us when we feel fear. Evolutionary musicologist (cool career choice) Joseph Jordania suggests early humans, or hominids, used humming as a form of contact calls. Does humming have a fingerprint, a signature? Who is Liv trying to contact? For whom is Roger listening?

Roger authored an article on ships' interference with animal airwaves and sound waves, and the harm they cause marine animals. Ocean liners make too many waves, sound and otherwise. Is our murderer a wellspring of sonic noise? A cruise ship magnate, oil tanker captain, cargo ship owner? Roger footnotes a naval document from 1979 on underwater sound based on the doppler effect. Get this: submarines have their own contact calls: echoes and radar signaling back and forth and sometimes interrupted by floating debris like kelp. Kelp is ocean noise – it blocks signals and sends false echoes back. "Noise" gets in the way of recognition: ocean ADHD!

In 1842 physicist Christian Doppler observed a change in frequency of a wave in relation to an observer moving relative to the source of the wave. Think of a car horn's change of pitch as it approaches and recedes. The frequency is higher during the approach and lower during the recession. No shit Sherlock. Stand on the corner of Operatgata on any given afternoon and see for yourself. It's common sense to anyone living in this century -- there was less noise in 1848. This part is cool, though, Lord Raley (science was for the wealthy, back in the day) noticed that if an observer were moving from the stationary source at twice the speed of sound, a musical piece previously played by the source would be heard at the correct tempo and pitch but played backwards?! Craziness! Musical dyslexia! Roald Dahl's vicar's sermons in song. Stereotype alert: we don't see everything backwards, just B, D and C.

At the end of the day, everything comes back to the human receptor. As Graham Burnett says, no matter how good your radar is, if the person looking at the radar screen isn't paying attention, you're totally screwed. With the invention of radar came the problem of paying attention to screens. It's called the vigilance decrement, the drop-off in vigilance to a statistically low frequency phenomenon. Will's my dolphin dopamine and I am a statistically low frequency phenomenon that has dropped off his radar. We may not need sound to communicate, but we do need motion. The molecules are still, the contact calls have ceased, the ocean is placid.

# Chapter 12

## *Silent Watching*

Oslo blinked its eyes open from hibernation and went straight back to sleep. Spring stirred from slumber in spasms of wind, rain, sun and clouds in various degrees. One minute sunny, the next rain.

"I need windshield wipers," Alex yelled at the dripping trees. She balanced a take-out pizza in one hand, and her umbrella in the other, resisting the urge to wipe her glasses. The icy rain slickened the river path from the Mathallen food hall to the Oslo school of Architecture and Design where Liv was subletting an apartment. The pizza would be cold and soggy by the time she arrived. Alex stopped at a bench, set down the pizza and wiped her back-up glasses. Were they magical lenses? She squinted into the distant fog, hardly believing her eyes.

"Only in Oslo," Alex muttered. Dancers, ankle deep in the frigid river, were posing for a photo shoot wearing nothing but misty blue tutus and fuzzy halter tops.

Alex shook her head. *What lengths artists will go to for their art.*

. . .

"Come in," Liv's forced enthusiasm was not lost on Alex. She hugged Liv and tried handing her the pizza.

"You weren't at work; I was worried," Alex explained her surprise visit.

"Dangerously dehydrated from the sauna. I am resting," Liv said.

"Hence this offering of pizza," Alex said and handed Liv the box.

"It's not Saturday," Liv said, reluctantly accepting the offering and ushering Alex into the kitchen.

She set two plates on the breakfast bar and retrieved the single stool.

"I can stand," Alex said.

"Nonsense. I'm not ill," Liv snapped.

"It's OK to be out of sorts. You have reason to be." Alex studied her.

"Mm, pineapple and ham, thanks, it's good," Liv avoided eye contact and took a bite.

"I'd be freaked out too, if I'd been locked in a sauna," Alex said.

"Alex, I'm fine. How are *you* doing?" Liv asked, recovering herself.

"I don't know. I thought this professor would help and advocate for me, but..."

"Why would he?"

"He's a friend of one of my professors. She at least trusts me."

"Right," Liv said, and stabbed at her pizza.

"You are sure you're, OK?" Alex asked.

"Great," Liv said.

"Great, come out with me tonight. I am going to a dance performance." She was dying to gush Anders girl talk, but Liv was off men, especially Norwegian men. Alex probed no further.

"Dance?" Liv's face soured.

"Yeah, you've heard of it, people twirling about."

"No thanks, I hate dance," Liv said.

"How can you not like dance? Don't you like sculptures?"

"Sculptures?" Liv took another bite of pizza.

"You keep extolling the virtues of Oslo's unique sculpture parks."

"Who doesn't like sculptures?" Liv dabbed her mouth with a napkin.

"Dance is sculptural," Alex explained.

"A sculpture is not supposed to move. It's supposed to stay still so I may gaze upon it," Liv said.

"But you like paintings? And you like film, no? And a film is a moving painting," Alex explained.

"Ever the visual anthropologist. Film is different. It has a story," Liv said.

"Dance has a narrative, language and alphabet," Alex retorted.

"Not one I care to learn," Liv insisted.

"I thought you weren't into theater?" Alex commented on Ibsen's collected works in English on Liv's mantel.

"It's called an education. We Norwegians are readers."

"Ouch," Alex said.

"Sorry, I meant, it's like Nordic design, everyone has an Ibsen boxset on their mantle."

"Next to Nesbo?" Alex quipped.

"Yeah," Liv said, unamused. "He's on my bedside table. We have 22 libraries in Oslo. Including a *Future Library* – just in case."

"Like the seed vault? Seeds and books. Good priorities."

Alex ran her finger over the box set. She missed touching books. She saved luggage space by going digital.


The mighty Akerselva River, engorged and overly satiated by the recent rain, rushed at full force as Alex stepped onto the bank. She was north of Kulturkirken Jakob, where, days ago, Roger's life ended in eternal silence. She threw a stick in the river; in minutes it would pass under the Anker Bridge along the riverbank by Kulturkirken Jakob. The thought saddened her. Her foot slipped slightly. Any further and she'd be as powerless as the stick, broken to bits with each crash into river rock. The river was relentless. There would be no time to catch her breath if she fell in. She backed away. Alex planned to record each of the twenty waterfalls that powered industry from mills to waterwheels to turbines. Flour mills gave way to floating sawmills, which turned to textile factories. Timber turned to paper, and paper to plays -- which explained Oslo's writerly success and many libraries.

Waterfalls powered electricity along wires, allowing industry to move away from the river and to other parts of the city, abandoning buildings. Salmon, trout, and mussels gave way to sewage. The riverbank hosted weeds and brambles, and a dangerous dereliction deterred visitors until the 1920s when the riverbank was converted to a green space. The salmon returned to spawn and run through the twists and turns of the long river. People returned to fish the salmon and enjoy an afternoon walking, playing and picnicking. Today the School of Architecture and Design, the Film Institute, Dansens Hus, and the Mathallen food court hugged the shores of the river in former red brick factories, at the edge of Grünerløkka and Vulkan, Oslo's hippest hoods.

Alex's phone beeped a fifteen-minute warning. Running was her best option. She backed away from the bank carefully and took off as fast as she could without slipping.

She arrived at Dansens Hus out of breath and sweating. She procured a ticket and slipped into the darkening auditorium as a spotlight hit the stage and illuminated a silhouette she knew intimately from his strong jawline, long arms and firm legs.

Anders was a moving sculpture, dancing with the light in a perfect *pas de deux* between sound and silence. Breath danced with body. Toes tapped a metronome. A landing thump, a grunt of effort, a runaway sigh articulated cause and effect. Did he hum in his head to keep the beat? She made a note to ask him later. Alex closed her eyes and listened to the sound of pleasure tap along the wooden floor like a code. Desire in the dark. The dark. His hands on her hips. Anders coming up the stairs as she was going down. A lie by omission. She was jealous of every other woman in the audience. Were any here at Anders's invitation? She did not want to know. He had not invited her to his show, and she had not told him she was coming. He was visible to her; she was invisible to him.

The dance ended and Alex quickly left before Anders saw her. Thankfully, a talk-back would give her enough time to disappear before he appeared in the lobby. Oslo cultivated a casual art scene, and Anders would be expected to mingle among his fans in the beautiful café bar.

The air was still moist and fresh from the rain. Alex navigated the sleek slope down to the river path and was approaching the bank when she heard footsteps behind her.

"Alex?"

She startled at his touch.

"Hyper-focused?" he laughed and turned her toward him for a hug. He was wearing black tights and a puff jacket. "Running away?" he asked.

"I could ask you the same question. Don't you have a talk-back?" Alex asked.

"Choreographer is taking it. I spotted you leaving. Thanks for coming," Anders said.

"You ran out here to thank me?"

"How did you hear about the show?" Anders asked.

"Not from you," Alex said.

"You never asked," Anders replied and sucked in a deep breath.

He disarmed her, once again.

"Where did you learn to breathe?"

"The womb," Anders joked, "Pilates. Dancers practice Pilates. You need to use breath to build a strong core."

"Oh," Alex said, she was shivering.

"I'll walk you home," Anders offered, "I need a second to say goodbye to my producer."

"No, I need--"

"Headspace," he said, "I have it too."

"Headspace?"

"ADHD. The theme of the performance was attention and the ..."

"The inability to sit still." Alex concluded.

"The desire for movement," Anders corrected her.

"Akram Khan choreographed a dance of a young boy who squirms through school with a chair and piece of chalk as his only props. It's brilliant. A brilliant commentary on the school's demand to keep children immobile. Still in school. It's a bit of a paradox because dancers with ADHD can also hyper-focus," Alex said.

"Hmm, yeah, otherwise, we'd get injured. Paying attention with your body is different from paying attention with your mind. It's a physical meditation. Swimmers with ADHD find the movement quiets their million racing thoughts," Anders said.

"The quiet of the water would drive me crazy."

"But it's not quiet, is it? You hear swishes and splashes and rhythm – it's what regulates us, our bodies, our minds...our thoughts," Anders said.

"The sound? Or the swimming? Sounds amazing, pun intended," Alex said, "I'll start swimming."

"Or dancing," Anders said and pulled her out of the path of an oncoming cyclist.

"*Faen ta deg!*" the cyclist yelled at them.

Alex took hold of Anders.

"What did he say?"

"*Let the devil take you*...a teen blowing off steam."

"He nearly killed me."

Peripheral vision. What else had Anders seen and Alex missed?

"RITMO," Alex ventured.

"What about it?" Anders asked.

"Was I part of your research ... is that why you danced with me?" Alex asked.

"Am I your research subject?" Anders answered.

"Professor Stillstanding told me about your performance."

"You met him?" Ander's phone beeped. "I need to go," Anders said. Norwegians were never late. Nor did they skip or miss appointments. He leaned in close, and Alex closed her eyes, anticipating the touch of his lips, when instead, he hugged her. She kissed his chest and pulled away.

"Later," Alex said and turned toward home. She could feel his eyes on her back. *Protector or predator?*

"I'll call you later. We can meet," he called after her. Her heart fluttered at the sound of *meet* the last emphasis on "Te" in a Norwegian accented choreography of question and finality – the promise of a future embrace. "*Sees senere,*" Anders blew her an air kiss.

Alex's knees went weak. *Be careful Alex*, she told herself. *It's a crush, a tiny crush.*

She wound her way down the river path, gingerly sidestepping where the river spilled over onto the sidewalk. A gentle nudge, a tiny push is all it would take to be swept in and away. She took a deep breath of fresh Norwegian air. *Jasmine and piss -- Protector or Predator?*

# Fieldnotes: Swan Song

Procrastinating is an art best done in libraries. Though this is not procrastination. This is fear and avoidance -- eventually I will need to go home. For now, I'm on the road less taken, off to the labyrinth of shelved song, in search of inspiration. I find the letters of Robert Frost.

1914, Frost to John Bartlett:

*It is so [by listening to sentence-sounds] and not otherwise that we get the variety that makes it fun to write and read. The ear does it. The ear is the only true writer and the only true reader.*

*I have known people who could read without hearing the sentence sounds and they were the fastest readers. Eye readers we call them. They can get the meaning by glances. But they are bad readers because they miss the best part of what a good writer puts into his work.*

1914 -- before anyone knew of auditory processing deficits, and before the invention of audiobooks (I wonder if Anna Gillingham read his letters?) Robert Frost championed ear readers. Frost understood the way I "read." No one needs to read every single word when meaning can easily be gathered from context. Beautifully written prose or poetry where every word counts is the only reason to read every word. We should all be writing poetry.

Poorly written texts are like laboring through a field of weeds in search of single flower – the gist of the piece. Gleaning meaning from a glance is my super-power. Grad school was a game of guessing meaning from abysmally written assigned readings and then in seminar discussions, offering a morsel "no one else had thought of," (because they read every word). My peers stumbled when decoding the meaning of theory, despite their superior reading skills. Critical thinking is done in the gaps between intention and guessing. Decoding and comprehension are utterly different skills. Teachers assumed an inability to decode letters meant an inability to comprehend meaning. I am an avid reader – just not with my eyes. With my eyes, I read, if not letters, then faces and places: trees, footprints, snowflakes and expressions; especially the escaped expressions caught back too late.

4 July 1913, Frost to John Bartlett,

*I am possibly the only person going who works on ... versification. You see the great successes in recent poetry have been made on the assumption that the music of words was a matter of harmonized vowels and consonants.*

*I alone of English writers have consciously set myself to make music out of what I may call the sound of sense...The best place to get the abstract sound of sense is from voices behind a door ...*

It reminds me of Adorno, who says the aura of disguise and miming attracts children to theater, not because they want to experience art, but because they want to confirm their own pleasure in dissimulation. The closer opera gets to a parody of itself, the closer it is to its true self. Like fictional ethnography? "Cloak-and-dagger," is a "scene in which two lovers sing to each other while murderers lurk left and right behind pillars." Adorno.

Voices behind the door.

I should go to the opera.

I should check my email. My heart races at the thought of it.

I've been putting it off. As if not reading it will mean it was never sent.

Frost to Bartlett:

*If I didn't drop into poetry every time I sat down to write, I should be tempted to do a book on what it means for education. It may take some time to make people see—they are so accustomed to look at the sentence as a grammatical cluster of words. The question is where to begin the assault on their prejudice. ...*

*Just so many sentence sounds belong to man as just so many vocal runs belong to one kind of bird. We come into the world with them and create none of them. What we feel as creation is only selection and grouping. We summon them from Heaven knows where under excitement with the audile [audial] imagination. And unless we are in an imaginative mood it is no use trying to make them, they will not rise. We can only write the dreary kind of grammatical prose known as professorial.*

God save us from the prose known as professorial! God love Robert Frost.

Time to face the music and read the prose known as professorial.

Email from Professor Whiner:

Is this a collaborative project, Alexandra? Explain.


Seriously?? Explain what exactly? Anthropology is by nature a collaboration. And by implying otherwise Whiner discounts my interlocutors' agency. We don't plan for collaboration. We do it inherently from the moment we leave our desks for the field. In graduate seminars, we collaborate in discussions. In the library, we collaborate with books. We read theories of long dead anthropologists and collaborate with their ideas. We are always collaborating. The universe tends toward collaboration. It is out of joint when competition precludes collaboration. Theater, opera, dance is collaboration. Anders in a solo show collaborated with the light, with the stage, with the director, the stagehands and the tech folks – the dressers.

In the spirit of publicly permitted voyeurism and education, the windows of the costume design studio on the first floor of the Oslo Opera House are open exposing, the workroom to the public. Detritus of a long day: empty coffee mugs, scraps of chiffon fallen to the floors, sticky notes on desktops, and pins in overstuffed pincushions form a backdrop parade of mini maquette dancers lined along the windows in lace and silk. This week's exhibition features Swan Lake's black swan. Her plume of silky black feathers and perfect posture reminds me of Liv. I stared so long, a tailor scowled at me and dropped the needle from her pursed lips. Shears in hand, mid-work, she looked ready to take a stab at me lest I move on. Who else is poised to stab?

# Chapter 13

---

## *Silent Snow*

Alex had her finger over the call button on FaceTime, dreading the moment she would have to disappoint Hugo, a glaciologist she had met at a talk at UiO and who had invited her to record sound in the Arctic. She took a deep breath and answered the FaceTime call:

"Alex! Hi!" Hugo said. "It's ..." he took a short breath, laughed and said, "Cold!" He clung to railing of the rattling airplane stairs so as not to blow away with the arctic wind. A figure covered in a large red winter parka stepped forward to greet him.

"No one is ever prepared for this weather," he said. "Minus 20 Celsius today, I'm told."

"What's behind you?" Alex peered into the screen.

"Fire engine should the plane catch fire as it lands. I only have a few minutes to chat while we drive into town. The whole town will be out to greet us at base camp. Planes are infrequent and bring mail, food, news."

"How long is the drive?"

"2-kilometers. But it takes a bit of time in this weather," Hugo said as he entered the SUV.

"What's the big antennae for? TV?"

"Ah, it calculates the position of earth and the universe. And there's the dog yard. We use dogs to sled out to camp sometimes."

"And other times?"

"Snowmobile. Route safety is an issue – the crevices. It's a 20-kilometer ride out to the glacier. It will take us 2-5 hours. We have a tent in case there's a blizzard. But there will be light all the time. The weather changes quickly ... like suddenly it's warm and everything melts and it's hard to drive and then it freezes at -20."

"How far is the research camp from Svalbard?" she asked Hugo.

"Svalbard?" Hugo asked.

"I'd love to see the seed vault."

Behind Hugo a large sign with a picture of a polar bear read: *Visste du at det er strengt forbudt å skyte isbjørn annet enn i nødverge?*

"What does it mean?"

"No shooting polar bears except in self-defense," Hugo said.

"Do you have a gun?"

"A spear. We carry a weapon, but ideally, we avoid disturbing them and when we do, we move away. When there are Polar bear cubs, mamas can get a bit defensive. And we only fight back in self-defense," Hugo said.

"Too bad this rule doesn't extend to humans. We've taken this idea of self-defense to a dangerous place. We've made it about defense of national lines and resources and it's no longer about life and death; it's about capitalism and ownership."

"Yeah," Hugo replied. He was distracted by a message on his satellite receiver.

"So, when we get to the fieldsite, I lower you into the glacier, you set-up sound probes, and I pull you back out," Hugo said.

"Right," Alex nodded bravely. She had imagined herself 'watching and wondering' (Dutch ornithologist Nikolas Tinbergen's maxim). But she would not disappoint a spear-carrying climate scientist.

"So, do you have an arrival date?" Hugo asked.

"Not yet, but soon," Alex said, leaving out the fact that she had asked the police about the trip and they informed her she was not to travel outside of Oslo, and especially not to the arctic where planes were as frequent as earthquakes. It was a hard no.

"What do we do when we aren't freezing to death?" Alex changed the subject.

"Research, gym, sauna, kayaking and a mean game of Scrabble," Hugo grinned. Scrabble was a dyslexia nightmare, even worse than the polar bears and freezing cold temperatures.

"The trip to the glacier is a 24-hour excursion, right?" Alex asked.

"That's right. Lots can happen in 24 hours," Hugo said and abruptly signed off.

It was the last thing Alex wanted to hear.

# Fieldnotes: Gud Vibrations

Was it 18 aftershocks? Me and numbers -- oil and water. Roger and Statoil: a seismic fault? In 1936 Danish seismologist and geophysicist Inge Lehmann discovered the earth's inner core. She recorded all sorts of seismic waves resulting in the Lehmann discontinuity. Imagine having a seismic discontinuity named after you? Danish women rock! I love puns!

Seismology: anything that makes a vibration, including a melting glacier.

A melting glacier screaming in agony... insert Munch meme...

The song of a glacier's demise.

The glacier was scrying crying ~~Scrying~~.

Hugo. All climate scientists should be screaming. My opportunity to help Hugo record a glacier's last breath has been upended by my witnessing a man's last breath.

Geologist Ugo Nanni lowered a recording probe deep into a glacier to catch the sound of its demise -- the crackling, whistling, sonorous grunt of a massive glacial death. Glacial humming – a mourning I relate to.

What is the tempo of mourning? Emotion comes through a break in rhythm.

Brakes, breaks, slowing down.

Tired has no walls.

Tacit knowledge is body memory. Does a glacier remember?

Humming: a human's seismological vibration. A vibration imprinted with a voice.

Is a hum unique to an individual like a fingerprint? Is a hum as familiar as an individual's voice? Is it a code? Is it encoded with individuality? Is it true that you cannot think and hum at the same time?

What sound will we make

What sound will we hear

as we depart the world?

We wonder how death will *feel* physically, emotionally, spiritually but how will it sound?

ALEX

It's getting lighter later. My eyes are heavy and yet reluctant to close until I see the seed vault in Svalbard, the northern lights, the reindeer in Tromsø, the cathedral in the snow, the Bergen railway, the Geirangerfjord, Stavanger, Bodø, Volda, the arctic. I am desperate for voyage.

KIT

What's stopping you?

*The police.*

Girl, you need to get over your fear of flying if you're going to be an anthropologist. Armchair anthropology is no longer a thing.

ALEX

Trust me, I trust the Norwegians. And trust is the inverse to fear. No fear of flying here. I'd die to careen through a crevice in Norway's mountains. They go through a survivalist boot camp to get their driver's license. No Norwegian would get behind a wheel drunk. I appreciate their commitment to keeping people alive.

KIT

Are you on task? You asked me to keep you on task; I'm never sure what the task is?

ALEX

Seismology, sound and spontaneity – (the key to good fieldwork, being in the mix of things, following leads and allowing the project to morph and evolve with each new encounter). Speaking of encounters …I kissed him.

KIT

What?

ALEX

He backed away. My lips landed on his chest.

KIT

No!

ALEX

You told me to make the first move.

KIT

I did?

ALEX

You and Conan O'Brien's Norwegian sex therapist.

KIT

Oh no.

ALEX

Oh yes. Is it possible to fall in love so quickly? Is it possible to love two people at once? Love is the least of my worries.

KIT

I knew it. What's going on?

ALEX

Nothing. Turn of phrase.

KIT

I'd come visit you if you promised not to put me
on skis again.

ALEX

Norwegians learn to ski before they can walk.

KIT

You promised to pick a warm fieldsite. What's up,
Alex? If you don't tell me what's going on, I'm
getting on a plane.

ALEX

I'm a bit homesick, and I miss you. Nothing I can't
manage.

KIT

How about I fly in for a long weekend?

ALEX

Not good for the environment or for your new job.
Is it possible to love two men at once?

KIT

Of course. You have a big heart. Big enough
for two.

ALEX

It never worked for Munch. He was always the
bonus guy. Love was madness, obsession. He
only knew how to love by losing himself.

KIT

Sounds like he didn't lose himself. Losing yourself
in love is not going mad but setting aside
your ego.

ALEX

Who me?

KIT

No, silly, Munch.

ALEX

Right. He preferred unavailable women.

KIT

Thrill of the chase. Try not to get caught.

# Chapter 14

## *Sugar and Snuff*

The siren broke into Alex's sleep before she was cognizant enough to ascertain whether she was dreaming. A man's voice was so crisp and clear that it sounded like he might be standing outside her bedroom door with a megaphone. She reached for her glasses and slipped out of bed. She listened at the bedroom door. The sound was coming from outside. She went to the living room, slid open the balcony door and slipped outside in her thin pajamas. Crowds of people in pajamas and sweats covered in puffy jackets, hugging themselves to stay warm, were gathered in the square below. Across the way, blue lights blinked from the hotel where the gruff male voice announced via a speaker in both Norwegian and English: *A fire has been reported, please leave the building!!!!!*

Alex looked at the clock. It was five am. She felt sorry for the weary travelers who had been plucked from their sleep by a hotel fire alarm. She went back inside and fell on the couch, hugged her knees to her chest and announced to the room: "An assault of sound. Powerful as any army, it commands: *Wake up, pay attention* and I obeyed. And the fire threat isn't even in my building."

Alex scooped espresso into the Italian coffee maker. She was told to "pay attention," so often she grew adept at tuning things out. But this one proved difficult. There was no use trying to go back to sleep. She sat down with her cup of coffee and wrote:

The mind is a powerful force and yet, despite our attempts to mentally block it, sounds, ideas, cruel words, wiggle their way in and penetrate our mental fortresses despite our best efforts. Loudspeakers assault and kidnap our attention.

Can a repeated phrase become an earworm if it's not music? Norwegian is musical. Even English spoken by a Norwegian sounds musical, which may explain why I am still hearing: *A fire has been reported* on repeat in my head, even though it finally stopped. No need for translation. The loudspeaker was clear, close, urgent -- eerie. Emotion and volume were enough to relay the untranslated message. I would have run the moment the man cleared his throat – had I been fully awake.

Adolf Hitler conquered Germany with a loudspeaker. Ayatollah Khomeini hijacked the Iranian Revolution with audio-cassette tapes and a megaphone. The French philosopher Michel Foucault regretted his own use of a megaphone in Iran. The megaphone is a powerful tool and should be treated and used with care. Once released, a word bounces out, echoes, reverbs and cannot be retrieved. Foucault of all people should have known this. He professed the power of a well wielded word. Once in circulation, we cannot control the power of a word, as power moves to each new user of the word. Like spilled mercury, it morphs and is impossible to recapture. It can only be soaked up and tossed out. Foucault was desperate to retrieve his writings on the Iranian Revolution, but they were already out there, bouncing about. Once transformed to sound, words --in the head or in the air or in print -- can reverberate for centuries. Bang.

But then there are other sounds like, the call to prayer, or church bells, that become part of the landscape, and as such easily integrated and – ignored.

Alex rubbed her eyes, closed her notebook and took her second cup of coffee out to the balcony where morning rush hour was in full swing. Office workers crossed the cobble-stoned square to the tram in one direction and toward bars and cafés in the other. Children climbed the playscape --a last-ditch denial that school loomed right around the corner.

It was unseasonably warm and Osloites were sipping coffee on the pier and the wharf, legs dangling over the docks and on benches -- anywhere with a patch of sun.

Alex joined the crowds for her morning walk along the edge of the Fjord. As she passed beneath her own balcony, she observed a solitary man on a bench at the edge of the Munch playground jotting notes on a clipboard. *Suspicious,* thought Alex. She glanced over his shoulder and saw a mishmash of little marks. *Fake writing?* She waited for him to turn and when he did not, she passed in front of him to see if he would follow her.

People noticed her in Oslo because she was an outsider. She was different. People familiar with the landscape, and who saw the same people day in and day out, noticed a stranger who, like a weed, was out of place. For Alex, everything and everyone was new. Everything felt weedy and beautiful and overgrown in all the right and wrong places. She couldn't differentiate one person from the next. Had he followed her?

He was doing surveillance. For whom? Of What? In truth, he never once looked up at her balcony or turned in her direction.

*Paranoia will destroya.*

Her phone buzzed and she jumped.

"Hey, are you coming in today?" Liv asked.

"Eventually. I'm out recording," Alex lied.

She deftly switched her phone from one hand to the other as she passed a harmless gang of teens. Simple street smarts.

"What's today's sound?" Liv asked.

"Sound?" Alex asked.

"Your recordings?" Liv asked.

"Oh, right." Alex crossed the street toward the Akershus Fortress.

"Ghosts. Haunting. The Fortress."

"The Fortress?" Liv asked.

"Ghosts can't speak, but they can make sounds," Alex said. "They don't have lungs and vocal cords, so they bang into walls and pots and pans. 20,000 Hz...Phantom power," Alex said.

"Huh? Ghosts don't have mass. They're ethereal, and without form. They have nothing to bump with."

"The wind is invisible, and it makes sound and moves objects," Alex said, "It has force. It's made up of molecules and materializes through action. Like ghosts."

Alex thinks of Åsgårdstrand where sound molecules of Munch's shot fired over a century ago still rings in sonic purgatory. Or Kulturkirken Jakob where Roger's last exhale knocks about organ keys and on closed doors.

"Ghosts are sound molecules looking for release -- too angry to deflate," Alex suggested.

"Do you believe in this stuff?" Liv asked.

"Keeping an open mind. Our fascination with ghosts is one instance where sound is the heightened sense."

"Are you chasing the ghost dog?" Liv laughed.

"What?"

"Legend has it when the fortress was built, a dog was walled in to guard it for eternity."

"And?" Alex asked.

"Well, it died of malnourishment and loneliness -- what else?"

"Some guard dog."

"His ghost howls at the waves lapping at the edge of the world," Liv said solemnly.

"The five thick cannons at the edge of the fortress are far better protection than a dead dog," Alex said as she entered the grounds and came upon the cannons.

"Norwegian dogs don't bark. They're extremely well behaved," Liv said. "So, imagine how unusual a barking ghost dog is. Ahh," Liv yelped.

"What is it?" Alex asked.

"Another stroller parked at the door. My hands are full. Now I must put everything down to move the darn thing."

"Yeah, people see our lovely Lily House and assume it's an abandoned building."

"We should spread a rumor that it's haunted," Liv suggested.

"We'd get *more* foot traffic," Alex said. "It reminds me of my professor at Columbia, Marilyn Ivy, she taught a course on ghost narratives. She says one cannot tell a real ghost story because ghosts resist representation and transgress expectation. You never expect to encounter one as they are a split between a phenomenon and its origin—"

"Oh my God Alex, please tell me this is not what you study?"

"Ghosts are relevant to sound studies. Think of a voiceless body or a voice without body. Ivy says they are the rift between an auditory phenomenon and its visual source."

"Shouldn't anthropologists study the real world?" Liv asked.

"For one thing we are discussing the real world if we are talking about a cultural phenomenon and for another --the real world is overrated. Ghosts seem to know this. At least the well-behaved dead do. According to Ivy, ghosts are the dead behaving badly, or the dead pointing to the living behaving badly. It all comes down to how we memorialize the dead. Ghosts are unsettled dead. They inhabit the uncertain territory between the seen and heard; the differential gap between the fissure and rupture... a rift between an auditory phenomenon and it's a visual source -- ghosts."

"Must make for some interesting field conversations. Speaking of which...I need to jump," Liv tries to say over Alex who continues...

"Tell me if this doesn't sound almost Ibsen-esque: Ivy writes about a mountainous area in Japan, where the dead were thought to go, and the bereaved went to find them. There's a story of a woman who was so distraught about the loss of her child that she wandered into the mountains behind the temple site, following echoes of her own voice, repeating the name of her dead child. She thought she could call her child back from death. Can you imagine? An attempt to rebind spirit and body."

"Why are you telling me this?" Liv snapped.

"Sorry, it's just anthropology. Stories, folklore, conversation... you're the one who brought up the ghost dog."

"I wasn't asking for an anthropology lecture."

"I haven't even started...Ivy's obsessed with the idea of the uncanny, a ghost is uncanny because they shouldn't be present, but they are..."

"Later. I really have to get back to work," Liv said and hung up.

"Liv?" *She's stressed,* thought Alex, and continued along the path.

A sign in English above a stick figure sculpture asked: *Please show consideration as the sculpture is a work of art.* A man's dog showed consideration by taking a piss on it.

"What necessitated such a sign, do you think?" Alex asked the dog's owner.

"To a dog it's a metal pole. Makes you wonder about the value of art. If it were a flagpole or a light post, would they ask us to show it consideration?"

"Your dog doesn't seem to know the difference."

"Hmm." The man replied as his dog came between Alex's legs and sniffed.

"Hey," she cried and backed away. The man unwound the retractable leash allowing his dog to get closer. Alex retreated and the dog whined.

"He likes you," the man called after her.

Alex ignored him.

"His name is George," the man said as he and George caught up to her.

"George?" Alex sidestepped the dog.

"Yes," the man said. George licked Alex's ankles.

"Well, George, I must be going," Alex said and sped-away.

"He doesn't like many people," the man called after her.

Alex took out her phone and made a note:

A dog with a human name. A metal stick figure with personal rights. What can a stick figure say about personality? Ethnicity, race and gender are all erased. And the autonomy of art? The value of objects? The perfect commodity fetish like a stick figure drawn in Perfect Plum Pout.

The unkept man with the clipboard remained on the bench in front of Alex's apartment building when she returned.

"Enough," Alex said under her breath and started toward him when Kit texted. She paused to silence her phone notifications, as if Kit would pop out of her phone and catch her out in a lie -- by omission. *She knows me too well. She power-pops into my head more than one should.* Alex felt for her phone and stopped herself. *No, it's too risky – she reads me too well.*

"Hei," Alex called out a word that worked in both English and Norwegian. The man looked.

"What are you doing here?" Alex asked Peder, incredulous.

"Counting people. And you?" he asked gazing past her.

"I live here."

"Rich American," he set down his board.

As a poor American graduate student, Alex was tired of oil-rich Norwegians crying poverty.

"So... you and Anders?"

"Is everyone in everyone else's business in this claustrophobic fishbowl?" Alex asked.

"No, we are not close. I assumed. He's OK. Yeah. The type who crosses to the other side of the street on a dark night to make a woman feel less threatened."

"Yeah, he's a good guy," Alex agreed.

"It's excessive. When we were in high school, he dropped a dance partner, and he still feels guilty."

"Was she hurt?"

"No. She got up, brushed herself off and moved on. But not him, he felt bad for weeks. She dropped out, which was a total coincidence, and he blamed himself. Inflated sense of responsibility if you ask me. He said it was 'a feeling.' Norwegian men have taken feelings and feminism to an excess. It won't get him laid." He looked Alex up and down.

"On the contrary, he has more chance of getting laid," Alex said. "Women prefer feelings."

"And he's made a move?" Peder asked. He wiped his sweaty brow with the back of his hand.

"Are you OK?" Alex asked, wondering not for the first time, if he was on drugs.

"I'm doing a sugar and heavy metal detox." He produced a round disk shape container. It looked like others Alex saw outlined in tight jean pockets around the city. He opened it, pinched a wad of sticky brown moss and stuffed it in his cheek.

"What's that?" Alex asked.

"Snuff. So, Bjørvika?" Peder mumbled. He sounded calmer after his hit of non-heavy metal, sugar-free tobacco.

Detoxing from sugar and pesticides while stuffing snuff inside his cheek -- the Norwegians were full of these kinds of contradictions. Activists who protested the drilling for oil while living off the government's larder. A peace prize funded by a dynamite empire. Exporting bullets while embargoing guns (she needed to verify this).

"Why are you counting people?"

"Nav office got me this job. Investors are opening a restaurant and need data on foot traffic." Peder said. "It's the first job I've been offered since Roger fired me."

*Fired?* If Roger fired him, why did he have his key? Did the police know he'd been fired?

She eyed his backpack and asked if he wanted a coffee.

"Yeah, sure. Triple cap, oat milk. *Tak.*"

Alex tallied the cost of her distraction and decided it was worth it.

She crossed to God Brød, missing a near collision with a cyclist who sped by her.

"They're worse than cars," Alex muttered.

Peder finished his coffee and Alex leaned over and spilled the remainder of her drip coffee all over his lap.

"What the...?"

"Sorry. I'm so clumsy," Alex said, wiping his thigh with a soiled napkin.

"Yeah," Peder agreed.

"My apartment is nearby. I can offer you a bathroom."

"OK, sure. There's the same number of people every hour anyway," he said setting down his board and standing up.

Alex showed Peder to the bathroom and waited to hear running water before unzipping his backpack. She rifled, blindly at the bottom where heavy objects eventually sink and unearthed a tin of cat food, but no keys. His taste in coffee was expensive given his penchant for cat food.

The water stopped. Alex froze. She was zipping his bag when Peder re-emerged from the bathroom.

"What are you doing?" he asked, snatching back his bag.

"Wiping the coffee. Sorry, what a mess."

"I need to hightail it back to the bench."

"See you around," Alex said, closing the door on his back and hoping she'd never see him again.

# Fieldnotes: Sucking Air

I'm so tired. I would nap on my balcony lounger if I didn't feel so exposed. I close the curtains at night now and deprive myself of the view I love…of the Munch Museum lit up against the dark water, lights twinkling in a U-shape along the Fjord and out to sea. Why doubt the safety of my cozy apartment? I feel outwitted by an unseen adversary. I sense the murderer knows me. And while I have no idea who they are, I know they are exceptional. And if Norwegian, they will hide their exceptionalism. Norwegian society does not encourage tall poppies. The law of Jante ensures a field of flowers blooming at the same height. Norwegians are adept weed-whackers. No one should stand out, not for their deficits, nor for their strengths. Jante makes recognizing an outlier difficult, assuming the murderer is Norwegian. Newcomers to Norway assimilate well to Norwegian culture if pictures of the May 17th celebrations of veiled Muslim women waving Norwegian flags and leading their students in the parades is anything to go by. The murderer could easily be a recent immigrant or an ex-pat. There is a desire to belong and to be a part of this gangly group of former Vikings. And more important is the imperative to bottle hot tempers in this cold landscape. Viking anger management training inadvertently over-corrected.

I close my eyes and imagine Anders's ice blue eyes against the gray night; Roger slumped along the corridor; a stick-figure outlined in Perfect Plum Pout.


Professor Bach: Dear Alex, Norway! How exciting. I understand your defense is delayed. Send me your new dates when you have them.

Alex Dear Professor Bach, Apologies, change in topic --I'm working on sound. I understand if you can no longer serve on my committee due to the delay and topic change.

Professor Bach: Ah, yes, sound, the world is quite loud these days.

Alex Silent too. Too silent.

Professor Bach: *Halt die Ohren steif...* hang in there, Alex. Hang in there in German is literally: *hold your ears stiff*. I know Columbia's stellar at proverbial weed-whacking. Bloom where you are, and when you come back, I'll be here in New York, New York. Enjoy this moment. You'll never have time in life again just for research and reading, trust me, embrace it, inhale it.

~~Dear Will~~

~~Fieldnotes~~

~~Literature Review~~

Random Notes

Life in Norway is a painful inhale of sharp freezing air. We suck air in through our mouths, to our lungs, larynx and voice box, which siphons it out and through an opening between our vocal cords and boom: vibration. We speak; we sing. The quicker the cords, the higher the pitch. Like an organ. Air comes in, music comes out.

Sound waves hit our eardrums setting off a chain of mechanical neurochemical offense or a mental image we call *pitch*. Pitch is both a purely psychological construct, and a note's frequency relative to its position on the musical scale. If a tree falls in a forest and no one hears it, does it make a sound? No. Because sound is a mental image created by the brain in response to vibrating molecules. Get this: pitch cannot exist unless a human, animal is present. A suitable measuring device can register the frequency made by the tree falling, but not the pitch. Pitch only exists when it is heard. Basically, color, sound, and taste only exist as an interaction with a physical sense organ. It is a purely psychological phenomenon related to the frequency of vibrating air molecules. It is entirely in our heads. Do we need to pay attention to register pitch, or is it enough to "be there?" As a person with ADHD, I can safely say it is never enough to simply "be there." Being "there" does not preclude attention. One must be there and present.

What happens when sound escapes the material and becomes ethereal? What happens when it inhabits our minds? We enter the attentional realm -- my favorite, or least favorite place, depending on the context. When we lose control of our attention and allow sound and noise to occupy our mental space, we lose control of our agency and power to loud neighbors, a dripping, beeping, banging -- earworms, tinnitus, or worse -- auditory hallucinations. The sound of rain again and again. The ultimate protest is to block sound/noise. To take back our soundscape. But how? Earplugs, headphones, humming -- seeds.

Silence exists as form. It creates space; it has power. Think of protestors who occupy space and take power with sound or are made powerless through silencing. Silence can be usurped by sound. It can also be a form of protest. The world is divided between silencing and sounding off.

# Chapter 15

## *The Last Hum*

When Alex told Liv about her diorama project in Bozeman, (leaving out the murder and blood), Liv suggested Alex would love the old Oslo mansions in Frogner -- a dreamscape of life-sized Victorian dollhouses. Alex was admiring a particularly plucky mansion with a turret above every window when she heard singing -- not the drunk party kind, or the choir rehearsal slipping out the church door kind, but something in between.

*Sound!* Alex exclaimed to the wind and set about finding the source of the singing. It could be the perfect opportunity to capture singing on the streets of Oslo. Alex peeked through a particularly thorny bush and saw a sliver of people gathered in the garden of one of the mansions. She retreated from the bush, scratched and bleeding, but not before noticing a splintered wood gate with an easy to unhook latch. Beyond the gate was a door, which meant that she was not technically trespassing.

She knocked tentatively at the door. When no one came, she followed the sound of singing around the wrap-around porch to the back garden where the singers were seated at tables covered in pink tablecloths. They drank champagne and plucked strawberries from glass bowls and dipped them in cream. Alex stood as still as she could behind a bushy pine, just short of crashing their party, and listened to the joyous singing. She waited, thinking of a way to introduce herself and to ask for permission to record the singing without looking like a complete fool, when suddenly everyone stood, pushed their chairs back, placed their hands under the table in front of them, lifted it, place-settings, and all, and walked the tables from the back garden to the front garden.

Norwegians moved with the sun. Which meant Alex had just lost her opportunity to approach them without full-on trespassing.

She returned to the gate, only to find the latch was stuck. She pulled it and pounded it, to no avail. She was stuck until someone came by, which meant missing her walk with Anders, whom she could not call as her phone battery was dead. She was just about to give-up and announce herself to the party when it occurred to her to climb over the fence.

Alex landed lightly on the other side of the fence, where she winked at the cat in the window as she slipped by and out to the street.

She ran past the Frogner tram stop, through the gates of Vigeland sculpture park to the monolith looking for Anders. She rested at the base of the monolith. Naked bronze, granite, and cast-iron bodies embracing, twisting and contorting under rare blue skies, looked like a midsummer celebration gone wild and then stilled for eternity. Was it Medusa, or Narnia's Snow Queen who froze the party mid-action?

"It's like the people reaching out to the heavens in the judgment card," a British tourist remarked to her boyfriend. The tower of embracing people was like a reverse tornado spinning endlessly toward the sky.

"Tarot? Again? It's like a religion with you," the man said.

"Vigeland called this monolith his religion," Alex told them. "A whirling embrace."

The boyfriend took his girlfriend's hand and led her away.

A cloud slipped by and chilled the air. A minute later, the sun re-appeared like a tantrummy child returning from an unjust time-out to mercilessly remind anyone and everyone that the elements were in charge. Norwegians agreed. Nature in Norway was regarded with religious respect. The Norwegians comprehended the sublime; they respected nature's danger as well as her gifts. They wore sunblock.

It was hard to believe this was a popular cross-country ski spot in winter. She wiped the sweat from her forehead and looked around for a shady bench. All the benches were exposed to the sun, as three quarters of the year Osloites sought sun and not shade.

She squinted in the distance and caught Anders waving at her. Heimlich, Hegge – Anders smiling at her in the distance was all things home and hot.

"Was giving up on you." Anders patted the small space on the blanket next to him as she approached.

"Sidetracked," Alex admitted. "Sorry. There was the most amazing scene," Alex told Anders the story of the moving garden party. Anders laughed.

"Yeah, it's typical."

"You Norwegians are extremely comfortable moving furniture around. A professor moved a seminar table from the ninth floor to the eighth floor – by way of the stairs. Either to save energy or because it didn't fit in the elevator. And the guy's retired."

"What would you do at your university?" Anders asked.

"Buy more tables."

Did Norwegians move the furniture around inside their homes as well? She had not been invited inside a Norwegian home.

Anders moved the picnic basket to make room and Alex squeezed in, pushing his boxy knee out of the way.

"Occupational hazard," he said of his loose hips, and folded his legs into a tent to make room.

"Be comfortable," she insisted and knocked her knee with his.

"My legs splay out naturally," he said, nudging her back.

"You're lucky, you'll go into old age strong as an ox."

"On the contrary," Anders started to say.

"Say that again," Alex begged, "I love the way your voice goes up and down."

He nudged her playfully.

"I was saying on the...," he stopped, self-conscious, and continued, "Twenty-five is retirement age in ballet."

Ballet? She thought he was a modern dancer but refrained from commenting.

"I'm an old man." Anders said. His searing look made her squiggles squaggle.

"You Norwegians will eat on the side of the road if there's a sliver of sun," Alex said admiring all the people out picnicking.

"Yesterday was the unofficial, official first beer. We take our first beer of spring outside the minute it warms up – around Easter."

"When you all read murder mysteries?" Alex looked around. She thought of her rowing coach, "Eyes inside the boat Alex." She was always looking around instead of ahead at her coxswain.

"How's it going with the *Silent Singles*? Any solutions? And how did you come upon the group anyway?" Anders asked.

"I had a friend whom I lost to Tinder... she no longer has time for me."

"Why didn't you join her on Tinder?" Anders asked playfully, but she could tell he was fishing.

"Because I have, or, had a—"

"A boyfriend. Which is it?" He asked and stroked her knee.

"Huh?" Alex asked.

"Have or had? Tense is important in this situation."

"In this tense situation," she said.

He stroked her arm.

"Honestly, I don't know," Alex admitted.

"Right. But now, you are in the present tense?" Anders either stated or asked.

"Yes. Here I am. Few people are reading." Alex commented on the couples strewn about the park in amorous embraces.

"Yeah, you chose to meet at *the* Oslo snog spot," Anders squeezed her shoulder.

"Snog?" Alex laughed so hard she snorted. "I haven't heard that word since Oxford." Alex seldom mentioned Oxford. And when she first mentioned it to Anders he said, "Oh, a smart one," and she explained Oxford's tutorial system was ideal for people with dyslexia.

"So, is this full-on picnic basket in hopes of a snog? I thought we were meeting for a walk," Alex said.

"We can do both," Anders answered. "What do Americans call it?"

"Making out. Though I like the term my mentor Lilian used. She was born in the 50s and called it canoodling."

"Your mentor?"

"My mother died when I was in high school, and my drama mentor, Lilian, became my guardian. She was a professor at Columbia. She sponsored me at Oxford. She was wonderful. Without her I would never have gone to college or grad school. With dyslexia they say one mentor or good teacher in your court makes all the difference. What's in the picnic basket?" Alex asked, deflecting any further discussion of her past. Anders opened the basket and Alex found her favorite Freia chocolate with the air bubbles.

"You remembered."

"You said they remind you of Flake bars from England," Anders said.

Anders would be hard to get over.

"I thought you might be hungry. I am," he took her hand and nibbled at her knuckles.

"Hey, I'm inedible."

"I disagree," He put his lips to her ear and whispered, "What else is on the menu?"

She turned away and looked at the lake. "Snog and swim?"

"Water's cold." He turned her face back to his.

"I see you brought the brown cheese," Alex rummaged through the spread.

"It's not the ideal way to seduce an American, but fresh waffles are difficult to pack," Anders said, watching her with delight.

"Is that what this is? A seduction? In which case brown cheese is the way to go with this American, I love it!" Alex said and took a slice.

"You really are unusual -- brown cheese is an acquired taste," Anders made a face.

"I've been told *I'm* an acquired taste," Alex joked.

"Yummier than brown cheese." Anders laughed, sat back and readjusted his legs.

"And your Norwegian?" she asked. She plucked a strawberry and took a bite. Her mouth began to tingle. Her mother had always said, *Pretending not to be allergic won't make the allergy go away.*

"Wait," Anders took her hand, and she thought for a minute that he noticed her allergic reaction. Instead, he began to sing.

"What are you doing?"

"We sing before meals," Anders said, scrunching his freckled nose.

"Wait," Alex pulled out her phone to record him.

"Do you record everything?"

"Yes, I'm an anthropologist," she said.

"Is this allowed?"

"Yes, we are in public."

Anders sang a beautiful bar of Norwegian and took a bite of strawberry.

"Ah, I forgot my battery is dead," she threw down her phone and took a swig from her water bottle.

"The sun stings," she said.

He touched her cheek with the back of his hand, "You're getting burned, shall we move to the shade?" Anders asked. "Want to see the ducklings?" He stood and pulled her up. "It's shadier over by the lake." He packed the picnic basket.

"I could listen to you speak for hours," Alex said, following him to the lake. "When you retire from dance, you should become an audiobook narrator. I mostly listen to audiobooks. For me, a person's voice is their most attractive feature."

Clouds passed dotting the lake with moving shadows.

"In Hollywood a good voice is more important than looks. Careers were destroyed when the silent film era ended, and people heard the actors' terrible voices for the first time. I never forget a person's voice," Alex continued.

"Is that so?" Anders asked and set down the picnic basket.

"I love your voice," Alex said.

"I love your intelligence, it's super-hot," Anders said.

"My intelligence?"

"And your kindness," Anders squeezed her hand.

"We're well hidden here, are you worried people might see us snog?" Alex said, looking up at his eyes, "You said it's a strong possibility."

"It's not," Anders said, and Alex found herself surprised to be on the verge of tears.

"It's not a possibility or even an eventuality: it's happening," Anders took her hand and kissed it.

Alex's relief surprised her.

"Look," she pointed at the baby ducks following their mother in line from reed patch to reed patch. She missed her mother. Dusk was especially lonely in Oslo, but not tonight.

"If there were a fire and you could run out with only one object, what would it be?" Anders asked.

"My phone... I rely so heavily on assistive technology. What about you?"

"My phone, because it's what connects me to you when you're not around."

Alex thought of Will, who tried and failed to make a connection. And then she felt Anders behind her, lift her hair and kiss the back of her neck – connection. She heard humming in the distance, and for a moment her loneliness gave way to happiness. She turned to Anders and the world went dark.

# Chapter 16

## *Black Metal/Black Gold*

Alex opened and closed her eyes. Was her head cracked? It felt cracked in half right down the middle of her forehead and burned where light seeped. Can you dream pain? Alex wondered.

"Alex?" asked a familiar singsong, Norwegian voice. Her knees went weak and felt something akin to dreaming. She fluttered her eyes and an unfamiliar chandelier -- bulbs hanging like grapes from a vine-- came into focus. Above her was an ornate ceiling molding: leaves, flowers – green wallpaper; an older building? The walls in her decade-old Bjørvika apartment were smooth and white and the lamps antique. Where was she?

*Hush now...* she often thought in songs. Silent lucidity? A constant soundtrack played in her head. She made a mental note to lookup whether this was normal. Not that she believed in normal. As Jonathan Mooney put it, *Normal Sucks.*

"A-lex?" the inflection on the A and X. *Norwegian. Desire.*

"Anders?" She focused on his face. Was she drugged? She attempted to sit up. "Ouch!" she cried. "What happened to me?"

"You were hit on the back of your head."

"What?" Alex whispered.

"Vigeland park, we were having a picnic." Anders adjusted the pillow behind her head.

"In the park?"

"Yes," Anders frowned. "You don't remember?"

Alex felt a large bump covered by a band-aid on the back of her head.

"I need a doctor," she said.

"We went to the clinic. The doctor checked you. You don't remember?"

She shook her head. "Ouch."

"Don't shake -- you might have a concussion."

She could only hope it was not the same clinic where Liv was treated after the sauna. They would recognize Alex. Anders knew nothing of the sauna incident. What if Liv wasn't the target in the sauna? What if Alex was the intended victim?

"Anders?"

"Yes?" Anders answered.

"Did you report this to the police?"

"Yes."

"I'm scared," Alex said and turned to face the wall. She didn't want him to see her cry.

"You're safe here. You'll be OK." Anders sat on the edge of the sofa and rubbed her back. "I'm going to gently maneuver you to your side and then back –okay?"

"Oh, no," Alex said as he rolled her over, "I'm so dizzy. What if I am seriously injured?"

"We need to get your ear crystals back in place. Without them we'd have bouncy vision when we run. Our vestibular system and ocular reflexes keep our gaze level."

"How do you know about this stuff?"

"I'm a dancer -- we rely on this more than anyone! Think of the inner ear as this fascinating labyrinth -- like your soundwalk. It's dotted with pip organs sensing head movements and relaying signals to the brain, which then integrates them with sensory information from eyes, muscles and joints to keep us in balance. When we get an inner ear infection the inflammation in the ear disrupts the vestibular system and we lose our balance. It's an occupational hazard," Anders said while gently maneuvering her head to the side and pulling her back up to sitting.

"Wow, you're strong," Alex said, wondering if an ear infection had caused strong, talented and coordinated Anders to drop a fellow dancer at school.

"Why am I here? I should be resting at home," Alex said.

"You couldn't remember your door code."

*Dyscalculia sucks* thought Alex. Her teacher was right; she would not always be able to rely on assistive technology. Without her phone the numerical part of her life: phone numbers, door codes, passwords, money, was lost to her. Norway was close to cashless.

"I need my phone. My door code is in it."

"You wrote it in your phone?" Anders asked.

"It doesn't say, *door code*, but yes -- how else would I remember it? It doesn't take a bump on my head for me to forget a code. I don't remember sequences. I have dyscalculia. I remember a detail about myself!" Alex exclaimed.

"Dys-what?" Anders asked.

"Dyscalculia is a math disability. There's no superpower component, unless you count (pun intended) time spent writing poetry in my math exam books instead of equations. So much wasted time pretending to solve problems that I didn't understand. Like now," Alex said.

"We all have characteristics that do and do not work," Anders commented.

"By "don't work" you mean by societal standards. We're all off-beat. Our synapses are composed of micro-rhythms assuring we are all a smidge unalike. I take comfort in this idea. Before we consider race, gender, culture, ethnicity, class, education, our synaptic core creates difference. We are all on and off the same groove at any given moment, dancing distinctive styles to the same song. Stop looking at me like I am a marvel of science," Alex insisted.

"You're marvelous," Anders stroked her forehead.

"Did you know that memorizing groups of numbers by chunking, like an area code – 2 1 2 for New York City, helps us remember phone numbers? If we already know the area code, we need only memorize 7 numbers instead of ten."

"No, I didn't," Anders commented patiently, "Music is a highly effective trigger for memory."

"I wonder why?" Alex scrunched her forehead.

"Because of emotion," Anders said, stroking the frown lines on her face.

"I thought it was the rhyming, the alphabet song is still the only way I remember the order of the alphabet," Alex admitted.

Anders stroked her hair.

"You didn't remember your landlady's number or her married name. Have you ever met her?" Anders asked.

"No? No, I haven't." Alex said, "It's not unusual? I mean if it were an Airbnb."

"Yes, but isn't she also your benefactor?"

"Yeah...funder," She rubbed her forehead. Thinking hurt.

Anders took her hand and rubbed it. "You feel cold. How about a coffee?"

Alex's mother boasted that her daughter's dyslexic superpower was reading people. Alex hoped her mother was right. In Anders she read goodness and boyish innocence. Attraction could fog the best detectors.

"No," Alex scrunched her face.

"No cocoa?"

"No, I don't remember her name. It's. What's going on? My memory isn't *this* bad," Alex panicked. "I'm good at diffused attention."

"Hmmm?"

"Paying attention to many areas at once."

"Which has to do with what exactly?" Anders asked.

"Retaining numerical knowledge, like a door code is not my strong suit. I wonder. We memorize a door code the same way we memorize spelling but spelling we can lookup; there is a correct way. A code..."

"They said you may experience temporary memory loss, but..." Anders scrunched his face into a frown and studied her.

"They?" Alex asked.

"Doctors. Temporary," Anders eased her back into a reclining position. "Do you remember if you have a pet?" he asked.

"A pet?"

"You are desperate to be home. Is there a fish, cat, dog you need to feed?" Anders asked.

"A cat!" Alex exclaimed.

"What?"

"Something is speaking to me," she said.

"A cat?" Anders asked, "Is speaking to you?"

"It's an interesting turn of phrase – speaking. Speaking a silent thought. An unspoken thought vying for our attention. To speak is to request attention. We think in language. Did we think before language, as babies? I'll look it up. Chances are we discussed this in a grad seminar, and I totally zoned out. Speaking is simply to communicate and ... attention is ... I've lost the thread."

"You need to relax," Anders said.

"I need my phone."

"Your phone was stolen," Anders caressed her arm.

"I was robbed?"

"You couldn't remember if you had it with you at the park. It wasn't with you at the clinic, and I couldn't find it when I went back to look for it at the lake. I texted you when you were late but got no reply."

"I need to erase my phone! What if the thief has my door code?" Alex said. "How long have I been asleep?"

"A few hours," Anders said and rose. "I'm making you tea," he insisted. He wrapped the blanket around her tighter, hygge.


Anders brought her a steaming mug of tea.

"You were humming in the kitchen, and it made me wonder if each number on my door's keypad has a different sound. Can a code be discerned by listening? It could be in the back of my mind -- if I hum it..."

"Alex, what is it?" Anders asked as he propped her up against a pillow, so she could drink.

"The lake..." Alex said, she remembered hearing humming -- Ane Brun, *Take Hold of Me*-- as she was whacked over the head. And it was playing on her headset when Roger was murdered. Alex did not believe in coincidences.

"Frogner?" Anders asked.

"A frog lake?"

Anders laughed. "You asked the name of the lake. It's the least important detail of yesterday." He caressed her hand. "What do you remember?"

"I don't know...nothing. I felt pleasure on the back of my neck and then..." Alex closed her eyes and laid back. Anders laid down alongside her on the couch. She turned toward him and remembered how the sun caught the stubble on his chin.

"I've been dying to touch your cheek," she said.

Anders placed her hand on his cheek -- Velcro and Satin. He leaned in and kissed her nose, the edge of her ear and neck. She pulled his shirt off.

"Whoa," Alex breathed. A beautiful rusted red tattoo -- a mermaid -- was branded across his back. She traced it lightly, admiringly with her finger.

"Huldra," Anders said.

"Who?" Alex asked.

"A siren who lures men to their death. There's a sculpture of her in Ekeberg park."

Alex continued to trace Huldra's beautiful long limbs with her finger.

"It's like a petroglyph," she said, quickly withdrawing her hand. Her head hurt. "She has a tail?" Alex noted.

"Like a fox," Anders confirmed. "What is it? Are you OK?"

Anders asked. She never told him about the drawing on the mirror at Kulturkirken Jakob on the night of Roger's murder.

"My head..." she said vaguely. She closed her eyes and rested her head on his shoulder to avoid talking and giving anything away. Only her thoughts escaped her as she fell asleep.

Alex and Anders dozed off and woke to a thumping noise.

"My neighbors," he said. "They're in a Norwegian black metal band. Distorted guitars, fast drums, vocals we thankfully can't hear."

"It's so loud."

"More treble and less distortion means it seeps right through walls and noise cancelling headphones."

"Weird -- is it on purpose?"

"Black metal, salmon and oil are our three biggest exports."

"So I'm told."

"People meditate to it."

"Crazy." Alex rubbed her eyes. She was thinking of Edgar Varese's idea: Music is organized sound. Anders was right -- Norwegian black metal was meditative. The minimal and repetitive drumming patterns felt like falling -- off a train, off a bike, off a cliff...to sleep.

"I can't believe this." Alex jerked awake.

"Sorry, want me to go up there and tell them to cool it?"

"No, it's not them. I finally memorized my door code after weeks of keeping a piece of paper ... my jacket." She tried to sit up. "Ouch," she slumped back down.

"Where do you think you're going in this condition?" Anders sat up and placed a pillow behind her.

"Inside my jacket pocket. I have a slip of paper with my door code written on it. In case my phone battery died!"

Anders slid off the couch and went to fetch her coat.

He handed it to her, and she hugged it like an old friend. She slipped her hand into the right pocket.

"I'm so messy." She said and released a fistful of papers onto the couch: receipts, gum wrappers, and a sticky note. "It's here!"

she exclaimed, "Detritus saves the day." She tried to stand but failed.

"You are not going anywhere." Anders insisted. He gently pressed her down.

"I need to wipe my phone. I need my iPad. I need *Find-my-iPhone.*"

"*You're* in no shape to go anywhere. *I* will go."

Anders reached out his hand and she handed him the sticky note with her door code.

# Chapter 17

## *Silent Spirit*

"Of all my clothes, you bring me this?" Alex pulled and tugged at the tight, short mini dress she bought on a whim at an Oslo second-hand store.

"It was hanging in your closet." Anders sipped his coffee and watched her struggle.

"Yeah, because I never wear it," Alex answered.

"It was the *only* clothing in your closet," Anders chuckled and handed her a cup of coffee. He poured the waffle batter into the pan.

"I hang the clothes I never wear in the closet," Alex explained.

"And the ones you do wear?"

"It's what chairs and dresser tops are for."

Anders shook his head. The few clothes he owned hung neatly in his closet. Unlike Americans, Norwegians were not gluttonous consumers. Anders limited his clothes to one of everything, which was unheard of in the United States where the *what if* mentality reigned supreme: *What if ... they stop manufacturing it, what if ... it's never on sale again, what if ... I break it, tear it, stain it?* Which explained the toilet paper hoarding during the pandemic.

Alex took a sip of her coffee and scalded her lip. She set down her mug.

"Hot," Alex said.

"Yeah," Anders said, studying her.

"Will you zip me up please?" Alex asked.

"I'd prefer to unzip you," Anders made a play for her dress.

"Later. What goes up must come down," Alex batted his hands away from her thighs.

A siren went off and Alex held her ears, "Is it a danger alarm?"

"Maybe my neighbor burned her toast?" Anders said or asked.

"It sounds really close by," Alex scrunched her nose as if this would help her hear. She disliked any noise signaling danger these days.

Anders opened the window, and the incessant beeping became louder and more insistent.

"Is your neighbor's house on fire? This is more than burnt-toast alarm."

"It's not us," the neighbor said, coming around the corner. "We just re-installed all the fire alarms. I assure you it's not us. It sounds like it's coming from your house," she said and tried sticking her head out of the window.

"I'll check," Anders said and closed the window.

"I'm coming with you," Alex insisted, scared of being trapped inside.

Outside, the noise was deafening.

"The cloud coverage doesn't help," Alex said, holding her ears.

"It's coming from the back alley."

"It sounds like a fire alarm."

"Nice place," Alex admired Anders' picturesque cottage – a former worker's cottage worth a small fortune. They circled the house in search of the source of the urgent beeping. Kampen was quiet, residential and occupied by Oslo intellectual elites who enjoyed the neighborhood's former working-class creds, where they could play out their socialist philosophies without living anywhere near the present-day working class.

"The beeping is surely connected to the recently reinstalled fire alarm system. It can't be a coincidence," Alex commented as they peered over the neighbor's fence where the beeping originated.

"I can hear you; you're on the wrong track. We don't hear anything inside the house," the neighbor informed Alex, huffed and slammed her window shut.

"She hates my parents for putting a fence around the house."

"The fence is cute, what's her problem?" Alex asked.

"It reduces the community space in the name of ownership. Norwegians don't outwardly demarcate ownership of land. In the city, yes, but in the countryside, we own land but allow others to traverse it. Oh, man...we've never had this problem before," Anders covered his ears.

"I've been hearing that a lot lately," Alex said under her breath.

"Do your parents have a security alarm?" The incessant beeping disturbed Alex's sense of safety. Had a wire been tripped by an intruder?

"This is Kampen," Anders said.

"Your point being?"

"It's safe."

"Shouldn't we call the fire department? A professional. Or your parents. You guys have firefighters?" Alex rarely saw fire engines in Oslo.

"My parents live abroad," Anders said without elaborating.

"Do you smell rubber? Something electrical is burning, from your place," the neighbor came outside.

"Someone may have set a fire ..." Alex started.

"Why? To what end?" Anders asked.

"The trash cans," Alex marched over to the row of multi-colored bins and lifted the lid of the neighbor's purple bin. She would get to the bottom of the bin, and the sound before fear and noise drove her insane.

The sound assaulted them as Alex opened the lid. Beep, beep, beep, beep...it shrilled. She peered inside and found a pile of old fire alarms beeping away. She motioned for Anders to look.

"Katrin, you forgot to remove the batteries. And... batteries are disposed of in a special place," Anders yelled at his neighbor and Alex could feel years of his pent-up hostility release.

Alex laughed both in relief and at watching Anders yell. She had never seen a Norwegian lose it, which was odd considering their famed meme. The whole escapade reminded her of her favorite children's book and amateur detective --*Nate the Great.* Her mother read *Nate the Great* and *Harriet the Spy* to her daily before dinner. It explained her penchant for solving mysteries.

Anders took a deep breath and motioned for Alex to follow him.

"I need a little walk," he said. Alex understood.

As they came around the corner, Alex spotted a tall familiar figure pushing a wheelbarrow.

"Thorvald?" she muttered.

"You know him?" Anders asked.

"He's an anthropology professor. How do you know him?"

"We play soccer together. He's competitive." Anders did not elaborate.

"Isn't competition the point?"

"Yeah, but..." Anders started.

"He's a public figure -- an anthropologist, not a murderer," Alex sounded unconvincing.

"He can be an anthropologist *and* a murderer."

"Give me one example," Alex said.

"Sure, give me a minute," Anders pulled out his phone.

"You're being ridiculous. This is because he beat you in a soccer match?" Alex said and ducked, "Did he see me?"

"Now who's being ridiculous?" Anders asked.

"Why the wheelbarrow?" Alex asked.

"Dead body?" Anders joked, and then frowned, "Oh, no. I forgot -- today is the Dugnad."

"Huh?" Alex asked.

"The Dugnad is a communal workday. A neighborhood or a block or a building come together to work on our communal living area. Today it's the playground planting flowers and building a trampoline. We all do it together," Anders said and set out toward Thorvald.

"I'm overdressed," Alex said and grabbed his arm, "Wait."

"Yep, black is more funeral, than Dugnad."

"Will Roger have a funeral in Oslo?" Alex asked.

"They cannot release the body yet."

"You're full of useful facts." Alex said.

"TV. I'm Norwegian. We like this shit." Anders said.

"I need to leave," Alex said, pulling at her dress hem.

"But the Dugnad! We'll have beer and hotdogs. Besides, I need to keep an eye on your concussion," Anders took her arm. "You have time," Anders drew in a sharp inhale as if to settle the matter.

*Someone wants me dead; I'd say I'm pressed for time,* thought Alex.

"As enticing as beer and hotdogs wrapped in tortillas sound, I have a headache," Alex said.

"I'll take you..." Anders started.

"Anders!" a neighbor called. She held-up a sharp rusted object. Anders turned and Alex slipped away. She looked back and saw the woman approach Anders and hand him a trowel.

"They waste no time," thought Alex, thankfully.

"Wait!" Anders called back as he saw Alex leave.

"Bye," she waved back at him, as the neighbor handed him a pair of gardening gloves.


Children and their minders swarmed the Natural History Museum and Botanical Garden Grounds. The Water Lily House was isolated and off-limits to the public, which is why *the door should not be ajar*, especially on a Saturday, thought Alex. Norwegians kept strict boundaries around work and leisure – especially Liv. No one worked weekends if they could help it.

"Hello?" Alex called as she entered the greenhouse. Strong beams of light saturated the dirty windows but provided little visibility in the steam.

"Liv?" Alex wiped her fogged glasses.

Liv would not forget to lock the door.

"Liv?" Alex rattled the plastic sheet demarcating Liv's office. Norwegians trusted their co-workers to respect their space – a trust Alex was about to break. Her Find my Phone app had indicated Alex's phone was in this building, the only explanation being that Liv found it and placed it in her office for safekeeping. It was worth a peek. Alex pulled back the heavy plastic barrier and entered Liv's office. Her heart beat rapidly.

"Nice dress," Liv laughed.

Alex turned around, startled.

"I didn't see ... hear you," Alex said, wondering why Liv was not playing music. "Clearly," Liv said, studying Alex, "Late night?"

"I may have left my phone here," Alex explained.

"Yes, you did. Obviously," Liv looked her up and down, "I couldn't reach you by phone, so I tried to drop it off. But you weren't home. This explains why you are dressed for a Saturday night on a Sunday morning," Liv commented.

"I stayed with a friend."

"I thought I was your only friend," Liv's smile was cold.

"I had an accident," the lie slipped out.

"An accident?" Liv asked, concerned.

"I hit my head. I'm a bit out of it. I can't remember anything from yesterday."

"Nothing? Weird. Yeah, your phone was found in the gardens and returned to the office." She went to her desk and retrieved Alex's phone and handed it to her.

"Thank you," Alex rubbed her phone. She was dying to turn it on. "I was being held for observation at the clinic," she lied. "I have a bit of a headache."

"May I help you home?"

"No. You are busy. I'm OK. Are you working over the weekend?" Alex asked.

"Yes," Liv did not elaborate.

"OK," Alex said and turned to leave.

"Temperatures are rising. Need to get seeds in the ground," Liv explained.

Alex exited the gardens and crossed the street while her phone powered on. It beeped with a new text.

UNKNOWN

Don't trust him.

She looked behind her. The street was empty save for a lone mother with a stroller. Alex changed her course home. Habits could prove deadly.

# Fieldnotes Glorious Fieldnotes Notes

*A bird does not sing because it has an answer. It sings because it has a song.* Chinese proverb

*The assumption hidden in the etymological nest of spiders is that the world will still make sense to someone who is blind or armless or minus a nose.* Diane Akerman, a History of the Senses

"Verse without words." A person's tone. Urgent. Fearful. Ecstatic. Can you "hear" tone in a text? Angry. Unhinged. Unforgiving.

What sounds the mind does create for our own pleasure. And yet, how do we differentiate the "sound" voices in our heads from the psychotic? What does it mean to be of *sound* mind; or for a theory to be *sound*. Why has the word sound come to stand for sane or plausible? Why don't we say a "seen mind" or a "seen theory." What of folks who hear voices in their heads? Auditory hallucinations are different from thinking or silent reading.

I imagine silence ending with the arrival of a letter. I open it and decode the squiggles and squaggles and release of voices – it's like magic. Words rise from the page, slip through the silence to speak inside my head. An echo chamber of code, an amphitheater of dialogue, a drama of description, all happening in the silence of my mind. As a child I wondered if anyone else spoke to people in their heads. When and how do thoughts become sound? *Hearing* voices is a psychiatric break, mysticism or magic – depending on the culture. Voices in the head were a heresy in Augustine's time. When Saint Augustine introduced silent reading, people feared the devil was putting words in people's heads as they sat silently, staring at a text. People read not aloud, but to themselves. Was it magic, sorcery, witchcraft? As a kid with dyslexia, reading was a magic spell cast on everyone but me. The words refused to speak to me. Letters were a junkpile of disappointment. And then, one day, I began decoding, and it was like magic. Send some magic, Will. Something I can hold. Reading is somatic (felt in the body) and referential (signs and codes). When we read to ourselves, our ears *hear* nothing (physiological) – but we listen (psychological).

*I'm listening, Will. Your silence speaks volumes. But I refuse to continue to write inside an echo chamber.*

In the Persian fable, *Leili and Majnun*, Majnun goes crazy for Leili and loses his "senses" and the ability to construct language. The further he moves from sanity, the closer he moves to metaphor. There's a connection between language and sanity. Majnun, means crazy or possessed. Snippets of poetry come to me in the silences of my mind. People with dyslexia can rhyme. Neither rhyme nor reason are available to me now...lost in a sea of rationality, it is the last place I will find clues to Roger's murder.

Fragments from my fieldwork. How might they fit together in a narrative?

A painting of baby Jesus, of Mary, of a man in pain

A stick figure in red

An object sharp enough to plunge into the heart

A wall pierced by bullet holes

A baby's cries blocked by seeds from a faraway Pacific Island

A painting, separated from its cohort.

A museum like a mausoleum.

A scream, seen but not heard.

A scream heard but not recognized.

The sound of silence.

Write to me, Will.

# Chapter 18

## *Silent Sitting*

A lex awoke abruptly from her unplanned nap. It hurt to sit up and so she rolled carefully off the couch. She pulled on her sneakers and her jacket and snatched her phone from the charger as she headed out the door.

*Estimated time of arrival: 558.* If she walked fast. *No running with a concussion*, she reminded herself. Securing an appointment with Terje was no easy task. She would power through.

She hit the river stretch between Grünerløkka and little Tøyen like a cross between a marathon walker and a duck waddling at high speed, careful to keep her concussed head steady. Her adrenaline was pumping and, she hoped, priming her brain for focus.

She was making OK time when a fence appeared.

"No! It's not on the map," Alex complained to the foreman. The construction blocked every imaginable path across the street.

"There must be a way through. Over there," Alex pointed to a gap in the makeshift fence, "Can't you please let me slip by, please?" Alex begged, cringing at the ring of entitled Americana.

The foreman shook his head without removing his noise-canceling headphones.

"Please?" Alex forgot or never learned the Norwegian word. Was it *takk?* Please and thank you?

The foreman signaled a circle, indicating she would have to circumvent the construction. She put her hand to her pounding forehead and yelled over the jackhammer.

"Please?!"

*Always double check*, Kit would say. Who had time to double check? Not Alex. Time was never on her side. And now, faced with a stickler for rules foreman, she must backtrack.

She arrived at the bottom of Kampen Park panting and with a pounding headache. She popped a Tylenol and took a swig of water. How many was too many Tylenols for one day? Did 24 hours start with the first pill or at the beginning of the day?

Her destination, the majestic castle *cum* Bavarian hunting lodge "artist building," taunted her from atop the hill. The pedestrian path wound through a small, charming park and ended at her destination 15 minutes later than she was due there. Terje was waiting. Shortcuts, in Alex's experience, often ended up taking longer, and yet the less appealing, if not dangerous makeshift dirt path straight up the hill was obviously the faster route. Dark clouds, impending rain, and glass shards made the path ripe for a creepy Nordic noir. She squeezed through the opening in the rusted fence and began the ascent.

Midway up the path she heard humming. She looked around. In the distance were after-work runners: air pods in ears, tan tights, expensive running shoes – the Oslo uniform assuring no one stood out. She removed her heavy, hot, puffer jacket and wound it around her waist. She wiped the sweat from her brow and scampered up the hill, where she emerged from the bushes like a prophet from the desert: tired, thirsty and a hot mess.

"Are you here to visit Terje?" an artsy looking twenty-something called out to Alex.

"Am I so obvious?" Alex wiped her sweaty brow and approached the building.

"Yeah," they laughed.

"Terje asked me to let you in," she explained. "Top floor." She swiped her card and opened the door.

"Right." Alex wound her hair into a bun, wiped her fogged-up glasses and marched-up the seven flights of cold cement stairs, where Terje waited for her at the end of the corridor.

"Yeah, no worries about being late. I'm organizing." Terje said and led her inside his large attic studio. His soft gray hair, warm expressive grey eyes and wisp of a smile lent the appearance of a living portrait -- still and silent against a gallery of blue.

"Come in, look around."

Alex eyed a large filing cabinet.

"Go ahead," Terje observed her.

She opened the first drawer. He studied her with interest, curious to see which ones she chose to examine. She gingerly pinched the corner of a drawing.

"Don't be so precious with it," he insisted.

"They remind me of Japanese watercolors," she said.

"Have you been?" Terje looked at her.

"No. Have you?" Alex asked.

"I studied blue dying processes in Kyoto one summer long ago."

"Cool," Alex said. Terje's blue oxford shirt was the same color as the one Roger wore the night he died. The sad pages in a comic were called the blue pages, thought Alex. "So, Roger..." Alex said tentatively.

"My friend Stine runs the Travelers Club and—" Terje began.

"Traveler's Club?"

"Yes."

"Does he know Thorvald Storesund?" Alex asked casually.

"You heard about the fight?"

"Does everyone know everyone's business in Oslo?" Alex mused.

"Pretty much."

"What happened?"

"Roger and Thorvald went to blows -- verbally. Roger put down Norwegian climate politics and it got heated. You're an anthropologist? Go ask Professor Thorvald. Don't academics have open office hours? Being public servants and all."

"Right. And how did you meet Roger?" Alex asked.

"Roger asked club members to recommend an artist to paint a portrait of his girlfriend for her birthday. And they suggested me."

"It's a brilliant portrait," Alex said.

"You've seen it?" Terje stuffed his cheek with snuff.

Alex nodded and blushed under his watchful gaze.

"Impossible, no one has seen it -- not even Siri," Terje went to a stack of paintings leaning against the back wall, pulled one out, and placed it against the wall.

Alex caught her breath, "The light, her eyes. Like Munch's vampire, but without the ferocity," Alex said, thinking, this woman was fragile. Her paper-thin white skin looked like it might easily tear.

"Siri -- strong and soft," Terje agreed. "Roger visited me in my studio with a terrible photograph of Siri. I prefer not to paint from photographs. He wanted to surprise her. We sat, drank a coffee -- coffee?" Terje went to his small kitchen counter and scooped coffee grounds into a French Press. "Why are you claiming to have seen a portrait that never left my studio?" Terje did not turn to look at her.

"I saw the one of Roger," Alex admitted.

"Right," Terje sighed, "Roger and I drank a coffee together that day and I asked to paint him. He was handsome, but it's not why I wanted to paint him. Often, I don't know what I am seeing until I paint it."

"And did you find it? What was it?" Alex asked.

"No, he was as visible as the faded photo of his soon-to-be ex-girlfriend."

"The one he gave you to paint from?" Alex asked.

Terje nodded.

"Roger -- you captured --I couldn't put my finger on it either, but it's there," Alex said.

"You knew him?" Terje asked.

"Why sell it?" Alex deflected the question.

"Paintings are to be sold. He wanted it, and pleasure is in the process."

"And was it? Pleasurable?" Alex asked.

"Hmm, portraiture is like anthropology. We get to know people. We talk," Terje said, "Mind if I smoke?" He asked, lighting a cigarette.

"And did you?"

"Did I what?"

"Get to know him?"

"No, he barely spoke."

"People thought he was rude," Alex said.

"Because he was silent? I enjoyed it," Terje pursed his lips. "Talking isn't the only path to intimacy, to knowing someone."

"Snubbing small talk is considered arrogant in the US," Alex said.

"Not in Norway. Siri I would have enjoyed speaking to, but he didn't agree to my idea of gifting her a sitting."

"Jealousy? Was he possessive?" Alex asked, hoping for a hook.

"He wanted to surprise her with a finished portrait. You Americans like tangible, material things. He offered a good sum."

"He had money?" Alex surmised.

"Old money. You can tell, no? He grew up with it, was accustomed to having it. Not the type to clean his own messes."

"Family money. Do you have any idea what they did?" Alex asked as she sipped her coffee. "Wow, this is good."

"His grandfather came to Norway to capitalize on salmon farming in the 1960s."

"I thought Norway was wild and organic?"

Terje laughed. "Sivert and Ove Grøndvendt began raising juvenile salmon in nets in a fjord west of Trondheim in the 1960s. Along with oil and death metal it's our biggest export."

"You disapprove?"

"I don't love death metal."

"And salmon?"

"My grandfather was a fisherman. The Norwegian govern-

ment killed the traditional fishing industry by forcing the fish-
ermen on the West coast to move inward toward the center of the
country. It destroyed the coastal communities. It's like his family
colonized mine?"

"Hmm," Alex took notes.

*Fishing industry -- Americans? Government -- inter-genera-
tional grudge?*

"Yeah. He brought me photographs of Siri -- none of them
good." Terje shook his head at the memory. "I painted her. And,
when the painting was ready, they were broken up. He paid for it
but never retrieved it." He looked back at Alex.

"They broke up before her birthday?" Alex made a note.

"Must have. He gave me a deadline of her birthday. He would
need time to wrap it, or whatever," Terje stood and shoved his
hands in his pockets.

"When was her birthday?"

"December. Sagittarius."

"Is everyone in Norway a Sagittarius?"

"Spring is mating season," Terje laughed.

"I can see why you kept it. She's mesmerizing."

"Does it look like I throw anything away?" Terje stuffed a pinch
of snuff in his cheek.

"Why would you? What will you do with Siri's portrait?" Alex
asked.

"I'm waiting. We'll see. I must decide -- should I take this to her
or not. One day they will find her in my collection. So, it's a
dilemma. Roger paid for the painting. It's his and, as such, belongs
with his estate."

"You want her to have it."

"You're perceptive. *Siri* means beauty," Terje said, examining
his own painting.

"She is beautiful."

"Tell me, besides the color, what is it you find interesting
here?"

"You're a storyteller. I'm dyslexic and I spent most of my life listening to audio books and reading graphic novels -- I read images."

"Dyslexia? I have dyslexia. Is it why I paint this way?" Terje asked or suggested.

"Yes, most likely," Alex answered. "We are visual thinkers and as such, visual storytellers."

"Oh. I didn't know. You should see my handwriting. I may be able to draw, but I can barely write."

"Dysgraphia – or doctor's handwriting. The result of thinking faster than we can write," Alex explained.

"You speak fast too," Terje noted, "It's difficult for non-native speakers of English."

"Sorry," Alex apologized, "I'm verbose and speak quickly, even for an American."

"How do we know which ones of us dyslexics are fast?" Terje asked.

"Fast?" Alex asked.

"Are we all fast processors with slow uptake?" Terje asked.

"No. Educational testing, old school IQ tests – unfortunately – are what they rely on. You can have a high IQ, with low processing speed ..." Alex started.

Terje retrieved a stack of notebooks and set them down on the coffee table.

"My tower of Babel," he said, opening the first book and handing it to Alex. "Now look at this one." He then took one from the bottom of the pile and handed it to her.

"Totally different handwriting?" Alex noted, trying to look without looking.

"Look closely -- it's in Norwegian, so you won't understand my private thoughts." He insisted, "You're not prying. Aren't anthropologists naturally nosy?"

"I'm too self-conscious to be a good one, but I do ask lots of questions," Alex said. She pulled a notebook from the middle of the pile and examined it. She took another one and compared them.

"Totally transformed, took two decades," Terje said.

"And you documented it?" asked Alex.

"No, better: I did it deliberately. Is that the right word? It's an art project."

"How so?"

"I made an effort to change my handwriting." Terje felt for his reading glasses.

"They're on your head," Alex said.

"Thanks," he put them on and joined her on the couch.

"Wow," Alex exclaimed. "It's ..." Alex thumbed through Terje's notebooks. "Each book presents a slight shift in handwriting, as if slowly revealing a face from behind a mask. Or masking a face from exposure. Year to year, it's such a subtle transformation. But take a book from one decade and compare it to the next decade and, wow, it's like reading a new person. Going by visual symbols alone, since I don't understand Norwegian, the change in personality is evident. Nice job. I went through five years of occupational therapy in elementary school for my dysgraphia and guess what?" Alex asked.

"Nothing changed."

"Exactly."

"Because it was not your project," Terje suggested.

"You nailed it. Never thought of it that way. A lack of student agency explains truancy rates."

"*Dexter*, left in Latin, like the devil. And also dexterous. At one time, left-handed people were forced to become right-handed. A psychological shock therapy based on mythology." Terje sipped his second espresso.

"It's eugenics. Perfectionism is abuse. My professor at Oxford signed so many essays in one week, her signature changed, and her bank rejected her signature on a check." Alex took a sip of coffee.

"Signatures, handwriting in general is a large part of our identity," Terje was thoughtful.

"Do you feel different?" Alex asked.

"An anthropology question? Sure, it's been ten years. We are always changing. My body can attest," he chuckled and set down his espresso. "Why the interest in Roger's portrait?" He stood to give her a moment.

"You've heard," she said.

"Heard?"

"About my lipstick? I assure you; I cannot draw – not even a stick figure."

"No one mentioned lipstick," Terje said, and added, "You at the disco, I know about. My brother-in-law is friends with one of your professors at Columbia. He used to teach in New York."

"Oh..."

"Don't worry, they're a bunch of academics. We are artists. Come, look," Terje led her to the window. "From here Oslo looks like a medieval village. It's all perspective. We see rolling hills, steeples and a sliver of water where the Fjord begins."

"It's beautiful - construction cranes and all," Alex said, spotting Bjørvika in the distance.

"Your eye went to the construction cranes: it's all to do with perspective," Terje said. It sounded like an omen.

# Fieldnotes: Collective freeze

*There are no coincidences, just encounters.* Paul Eluard

Something is niggling at me. Fernette Eide says people with dyslexia often get to an answer before we can prove it. Through reflection and using episodic memory and patterns we discover the solution. I feel it. The puzzle pieces are falling into place. Concentrate, Alex.

This is where missing information comes not from data but from imagination, an educated guess (Jack Horner, the paleontologist taught me how this works with bones). My bones are sound. Am I using sound because it is conveniently tied to my research, or because Roger's "Silent" theme is at the heart of this?

The murderer has been one step ahead of me. Not anymore. I know when I'm being played. This has become about me. But why try to kill me? If I'm the murderer's next target, it must be about *Silent Singles* – it was my only tie to Roger.

Or is it a coincidence – our interest in sound? Are there three coincidences? More than three = connection.

Roger did not like sound. Roger was an advocate of quiet oceans.

Roger was killed at *Silent Singles*.

Roger's girlfriend happens to be a musician.

Three's a charm – is a crowd the answer?

I'm so dizzy. The doctors said it's not a concussion but vertigo from an out of place inner ear crystal. Anders did an Epley movement on me – moving my head around to bring the ear crystals back into alignment. It stopped the positional vertigo but not the dizziness. When I stand, I no longer feel like a motionless spoke on a fast-moving wheel. But as Hemingway said: Never mistaken motion for action. Action triggers sound, and action makes me dizzy. Like taking off the disco headphones off and feeling the world go from rhythm and movement and noise to sudden stillness and silence. It's like falling from a fast-moving train slammed to a sudden stop. Walking to a running phase transition -- trot to canter. Clave: a beat of a drum. A drummer speaks to a dancer through the beat. Tapping: the unseeing map the world. Contact calls: a cluck is a code for "come." Clave: the word for code in Spanish. Everything comes down to codebreaking, decoding, re-coding. Reading signs and symbols.

Lost door codes. Not speaking -- and response between drummer and dancer. Dancer. Peripheral vision, space to articulate -- choreography ... composing language through movement vs text. Slave to a score. Samba...beating to your own drum. Sheet music – Emotion. Lover's mouth a dot in Sufi poetry, silenced, Majnun. A dot, an island sinking, drowning. Puncture wounds in walls. Puncture wounds in hearts. Tacit knowledge... body memory. What *does* the body remember? Who died and left behind a crying infant? Breaks in rhythm, in waves, brakes ... slowing down.

# Chapter 19

---

## *The Last Gasp*

Whwhen Terje closed his studio door, Alex quietly retraced her way back down the corridor to the last studio. She knocked lightly. The woman who answered was dressed in black silk overalls, her long black hair wound up in a bun, and was far more beautiful in person than in her portrait.

"I'm a friend of Terje's, his studio is down the hall. I'm making a sound project, and he suggested I pop in and introduce myself," Alex said.

"Hi," Siri said, "Yeah, the man who made a portrait of me. I must go meet him. Velkommen, it's a bit messy. I moved in this week and I'm already late to set up my new show."

"What's the show?" Alex asked.

Siri pointed to a large sculptural object. It looked like a giant Chinese hand fan attached to a balloon.

"My organ."

"Organ?"

"A musical lung -- it sings by losing air. Like a sigh," Siri explained. "Radar, echocardiograms, ultrasounds, measuring the flow of blood, satellite communication, and the Hammond Organ owe their existence to the doppler effect. An organ operates on air pressure. Imagine?"

"Doppler gave astronomers the ability to measure electromagnetic waves and detect the speed at which galaxies and stars recede from or approach us. Useful for dodging asteroids," Alex added.

Siri laughed and pumped her instrument. "Listen," she said.

"It's more like a screech, or a scream," Alex said holding her ears.

"All sound is music."

"Really?" Alex laughed.

"Ah, it changes when you do this," Siri pulled a pipe out of a socket, deflating the balloon.

"Now, it sounds like a silent pause," Alex noted, bending over to look at the open socket.

"Here, while you're down there, I could use a hand," Siri handed Alex a long thin brass pipe. "Hold this? I'm going to add a ..." Siri struggled to jam a plastic tube into a joint. "It's an accordion."

"It's so cool."

"If you understand the concept of air and time, you can create an organ," Siri explained.

"Just like that." Alex wondered if Siri knew the RITMO crowd but did not ask. "Sound travels slower than the speed of light," Alex added.

Siri gazed out the window. "Thor's roar always follows a bolt of lightning."

"Quivering molecules of air. Rushing, crusting and withdrawing waves of air molecules activated by the movement of an object rippling out in all directions. I read it somewhere," Alex said.

"Yes, like when a cricket shakes her wings thereby shaking air molecules, which shake neighboring molecules, and soon you have a song," Siri said as she plunged the last pipe into the organ and pumped it with air. She then released the air creating a different sound: the sound of a final and last exhale. A sound that made Alex's heart race. She swayed.

"Are you OK?" Siri caught Alex.

"Sorry, lost my breath." Alex steadied and sucked in a deep breath of musty air.

*Sound in reverse causes a bang, a puncture, or a spike through the heart,* thought Alex.

"It belongs in a church," Alex breathed. She heard it at a church, at *the* church, Kulturkirken Jakob, the night Roger died. "It grunts," Alex stated.

"Exactly," Siri agreed, "It's not the sound we expect, right? The organ creates sound not by pumping air in, but by losing it."

"A music of lost air. Breathing out," Alex said, "A sigh."

"A spiritual experience," Siri agreed, assuming Alex was having one.

"Like a last exhale. The poetry of a lost breath," Alex continued. *The sound of Roger's last exhale was an organ. Why and by whom was the organ pumped that night?* Alex wondered.

"Breathing is personal. We all breathe differently. How we breathe and sound as we breathe is unique, cultural," Siri explained.

"Like Norwegians sucking in air when making a point – the high point you reach in pitch at the end of a sentence. We communicate through air. Through a language of breath. Sound is breath," Alex said, composing herself.

"The sound of a lover's ecstasy, or their snores," Siri smiled sadly.

Alex was reminded of the pink foam earplugs on Roger's nightstand. They were Siri's. Roger snored, thought Alex. *The victim's character determines his fate.* Siri hardly seemed the type to kill a man for snoring.

"Other sounds are an exclamation point, or a period," Siri continued.

"Writers misuse exclamation points to make a point when their actual function is to denote screaming. Sincerity is bred in our mistakes rather than in our perfection. Did you know Duke Ellington believed a piano tuned to a perfect pitch was less genuine?" Alex asked.

"No, I didn't."

"Harry Hole quoted Ellington in a Jo Nesbo novel, or the other way around, Nesbo quoting Ellington...anyway," Alex said.

"You like Nesbo?" Siri's eyes widened.

"I listened to my first Nesbo and, oddly, I do. Wasn't he a musician?"

"Yes, we have many artists and writers," Siri said politely.

"You're lucky the Norwegian government is so supportive of artists. When building or renovating a public structure a percentage of the budget goes to art, no?"

"It's true." Siri replied.

"Churches too?"

"Well... they get renovated and these artifacts of process ..." Siri went on a tangent, sounding like a grad student on steroids, using lots of words to say nothing.

"Does Kulturkirken Jakob have an organ?" Alex asked.

"They do," Siri said.

"Does it make a grunting sound?" Alex asked, assuming Siri knew Kulturkirken Jakob intimately if she played the organ there.

"Grunting? Have you been there for a performance?" Siri asked.

"I was at the silent disco," Alex admitted.

Siri slumped against the wall.

"Sorry, I ..." Alex said kneeling beside her.

"My ex-lover was killed there."

"Lover?" Alex feigned surprise.

"It was sex with a sell-by date. Roger knew my long-term boyfriend was out of town for six months -- in New York City for a show. Roger was here for six months doing research, and so it worked out. We met each other's needs."

"Sounds more French than Norwegian."

"Sounds human to me -- aren't you an anthropologist?" Siri asked.

*Ouch*, thought Alex, given Siri was being the cultural relativist and generalizing.

"When did your boyfriend return?"

"In time to kill Roger," Siri paused, "Sorry."

"No, I'm sorry, I was being nosy. It's ... Roger's cat ... I wasn't sure if you--"

"Cat?" Siri looked at Alex.

"I was his cat sitter, and I fear the poor creature is trapped in his apartment."

"Must be a post break-up cat -- I am allergic. Figures that I was replaced by a feline," Siri said, "Why don't you take it? You have my blessing."

"I don't have his keys, and I don't know any of his friends."

"Neither did I. And the police?"

"They did not find the cat. She's shy."

"I have a spare set of keys." Siri went and retrieved the keys and handed them to Alex. Norwegians were too trusting, thought Alex. "Please take the cat," she insisted.

A cat was the last thing Alex needed.

"Thank you, Tak," Alex said as she opened the door to leave. "Good luck with your show."

"You know what Miles Davis and Picasso had in common? They were less interested in the objects they created and more interested in the space between the objects. For Miles Davis, empty space was the air he placed between one note and the next – leaving the listener time to anticipate the next note. It was his genius," Siri said as she closed the door.

The space between her studio and Terje's was close like a painter and his model, and narrow, like that between a question and an answer. How did Siri know about her portrait and how is it Terje did not know that she knew? Which one of them was lying?

She arrived at the last step and saw a crack of light from under the door. It reminded her of a Leonard Cohen line: the crack where the light gets in, but was it light?

# Fieldnotes: Killer Beat

Was the murder choreographed -- killer rhythm? Did the murderer kill on a particular beat? And if so, how did they time it? Were they privy to the playlist? Where was Roger's headset?

ALEX

Thoughts on rhythm? Do we all have it?

KIT

It's a constant. If you eat, sleep, walk -- then you have rhythm. Prosody is spoken rhythm.

ALEX

Anders seduced me with his voice; it dances as beautifully as his body. Norwegians excel at prosody.

KIT

Rhythm isn't always syncopated, think of jazz's deviations.

ALEX

We all know jazz is deviant lol. Pulse quickening.

Rhythm is visual -- watch any moving body. You don't need sound to discern it. A beat can be picked up without hearing a sound. RITMO is testing to see if people catch on to another person's rhythm by watching or if they need to listen to the same song. I fell for their decoy dancer.

KIT

At the silent disco? Improvisation demands trust.

ALEX

I'm always improvising, yet I rarely trust myself.

KIT

You trust yourself despite yourself.

ALEX

Everything in dance is about trust: trusting the music, trusting a dance partner not to drop me, for example. And what happens when trust is broken?

KIT

The beat goes on. I'm sure dancers fall and are dropped all the time. Rhythm is perception and time. Time is born when tapping a steady pace and steady beat. Timing is cultural. Western dance does not value repetition as an aesthetic impulse the way African dance does.

ALEX

Mind wandering ... exploring new idea, divided attention.

KIT

Instead of mind bifurcation; think collaboration. Distinct parts of your brain in conversation. Who is defining function?

ALEX

Attraction vs distraction. Will is ghosting me.

KIT

Attention as selection for action. Call him.

ALEX

Overload. I'm off.

Notes....

Rhythm: a duration of a series of notes grouped together into units.

Meter: created by our brains by extracting information from rhythm and volume.

Key: a hierarchy of importance between tones in a musical piece. Clues.

Melody: main theme of a musical piece -- the part you sing along with. The murderer.

Harmony: relationship between pitches of different tones. Something is out of joint.

Tempo: speed or pace of a piece. I'm running out of time.

Contour: the shape of melody -- up and down. Norwegian goes up and down; up and down. Anders leaping through the air, up and down.

Timber: distinguishes one instrument from another. Like an organ and a human voice? And when both play the same note?

Volume: a purely psychological phenomenon related to the energy that an instrument creates and the volume of air that it displaces -- Siri's organ and Roger's grunt.

Reverberation: the perception of how far the sound is and how large the room is often mistaken for an echo.

Reverberating thoughts: a warning is echoed.

## Chapter 20

---

### *One Dog Day*

The Sørenga foot bridge shook with every step. Water lapped at the edges, soaking her tennis shoes. Alex clutched at the metal railing, freezing her fingers. Still, she was grateful to hold onto something stable and secure. She felt queasy, wet and afraid. She needed distance, perspective and solitude, which was not hard to find in Oslo in April.

Midway across, the bridge swayed in the wake of a passing ferry, throwing Alex to the railing where she leaned over, face to face with the frosty Fjord's rippling tides. As the water calmed, she spotted a tiny pink woolen mitten floating solemnly along the surface of the murky water, softly carried by the water's now gentle undulations. Alex prayed that its owner was warm and dry.

She set foot on the Sørenga side of the bridge and walked along the dock, passing the gelato stores and pizzeria's, their terraces closed for the season but still blasting music from speakers. *Taylor Swift* met squawking seagulls and construction noise as Alex made her way to the end of the dock where she paused beside the diving board to catch her breath. She folded forward to stretch and felt something soft and wet touch her back thigh. She shot up and swung around to find George sniffing her.

Alex backed away, realizing too late that she was right on the edge of the dock. Another step and she'd be taking a fully clothed frosty dip in the Fjord.

"Hello," said George's owner, coming closer than any Norwegian ever had. Norwegians liked their personal space, and even this was too close for an American. Alex pulled her neck and head back without moving her feet. Her balance was precarious. He took a step closer, a feat Alex had not thought possible. His breath was rancid and heavy on her face. George was panting at her side.

Alex glanced down at the sliver of dock, then took her chances and ran. The man released George who ran after her faster than she thought possible for an overweight bulldog. He panted and sniffed and gained on her. Running away from a dog was never a good move. She stopped short and felt in her pocket for a sacrificial offering. All she found was a Freia chocolate bar, doggie poison (a lost opportunity in Roald Dahl's opus). She only planned for the heavy cream, dense sugar and cocoa to propel far enough through the frigid morning air to give her a lead on George. She unwrapped her precious Freia bubble bar and passed it in front of George's nose to sniff; he approved. And knowing dogs, like humans, craved what was bad for them, she threw the chocolate bar as far as she could. If, as she suspected, George was his owner's entire world, then he too would run after the chocolate to save his dog. The Freia bubble bar did not disappoint. George and his owner were soon occupied in the age-old battle of disciplinarian versus sugar addict, while Alex ran.

George, against all odds, turned away from the chocolate bar, and his owner, and pursued Alex. *Why me?* Whimpered Alex, thinking of how Daniel Leviton likened attention to walking a dog: it can be unpredictable and out of our control.

"Sorry, George," Alex apologized and ran across the bridge and straight into a tall Norwegian man dressed in a fluffy pink robe.

"Alex?" came the avuncular greeting she was coming to know so well.

"Thorvald? What are you doing here?"

"What do you think?" he asked and smiled. "What does your

anthropologist spidey-sense suggest I'm doing here?" Thorvald asked.

"Spying on me?" Alex replied.

Thorvald laughed heartily.

"Not in my bathrobe, though that would be a good disguise."

"Not really -- I recognized you right away. Pink becomes you, especially with your flushed cheeks. Were you running?" Alex chortled. She'd try harder to maintain decorum.

"I'm going native, taking a sauna," Thorvald laughed.

"What are you doing up so early?" he asked Alex.

"Is it? It's so light out," Alex said. She did not bother to check the time as she left her apartment.

"Six AM. I hit the gym at five, sauna at 6, work by 8," Thorvald explained.

"Aren't you retired?" Alex asked.

"And who's your friend?" Thorvald pointed to George, panting at Alex's side.

"George is a little fixated."

"He's not fixed; hence the problem," Thorvald pointed out. "Smell is a dog's highest attentional sense. When a dog sniffs something interesting on a walk, he will ignore everything else."

Thorvald patted George's head and told the dog: "She appears interesting but is a bit of a troublemaker -- between us." He eyed Geroge's owner who was watching them from a safe distance on the other side of the bridge. Was he intimidated by Thorvald's fluffy pink robe? Alex wondered.

"Here's a good fact for your sound research..." Thorvald was saying.

She tuned back in to hear Thorvald say, "Protohuman ancestors threw themselves in the path of new predators when they left trees to explore food sources on the ground. Recognizing threatening sounds was a vital part of survival and why sound took priority in the flow of information through the attentional filter," Thorvald was saying.

"Right," Alex said grateful for the professorial ability to lecture at will, anywhere. George's owner was no match for an academic lecturing in a pink bathrobe in the freezing cold dawn.

"Neurologists haven't worked out all the hierarchies in the human attention filter; only that we filter distraction by irrelevance," Thorvald went on.

"Irrelevance is subjective. Like me in school," Alex said, hoping Thorvald would get the hint.

"Hmm," he said in what Alex was coming to know as Norwegian neutral.

George barked.

"If his attentional filter is primed for sniffing and he chose me over chocolate, it proves George's individuality. We met recently at the fortress. He wants my attention. He is taken with me," Alex said.

"Then why is he standing all the way over there?" Thorvald asked, disrobing.

"No, not him. George, the dog."

"He sounds deranged," Thorvald said and pulled a sweatshirt and sweatpants from his pack.

"George is a little obsessive," Alex explained as she watched Thorvald dress.

"I meant his owner. George is crying for help. He needs saving if you ask me," Thorvald waved at George's owner. "I'm late, Alex," he said by way of good-bye and strode off toward his bike.

"Wait," Alex ran after him. "What if he's the murderer?" Alex yelled after Thorvald, who was on his bike and already halfway to Operagata.

# Chapter 21

*The Silent Yarn*

Liv stood alone on the Anker Bridge with her headphones on, singing along to *Men at Work.*

"Do you come from the land of Allah?" Liv belted out. Alex wondered, not for the first time, whether Liv had auditory processing differences. Liv couldn't live with silence, and Roger, couldn't live with sound. It meant something -- but what?

Alex tapped Liv on the shoulder.

*"Do you come from a land down under,"* Alex corrected her. "You of all people should know an Australian accent."

"I was in England," Liv slipped off her headphones.

"Australia's still part of the Commonwealth," Alex said.

"You're late," Liv stated. "I said bull sculpture, Acker Bridge, 6pm."

"It's 6:10." The rain dripped in Alex's eyes and fogged up her glasses.

"Why the sudden interest in knitting? Besides, I thought you were on a date?" Liv asked.

"My plans changed."

"How is it that you have never knitted?" Liv asked as they crossed the bridge to Kulturkirken Jakob.

"How is it that you do?"

"I'm Norwegian."

"Too many directions, too much left and right. I don't know. I couldn't figure it out. Never thought of you as a knitter," Alex eyed Liv who was more comfortable shoveling a ton of dirt for recreation.

"This is how Norwegians socialize. It's either book clubs, choir or knitting."

"And you chose knitting?" Liv knitting was less surprising than Liv hanging out with other Norwegians.

"Choir would have offered more endorphins – but, alas, no alcohol. This is a sip and sew."

"You've been here before?"

"Once or twice. I'm not a regular. It's an effective way to quiet the squirrels."

"Squirrels?" Alex asked.

"The crazies in your head. You've never heard the expression? The incessant inner dialogue we carry with us. Voices always talking, talking," Liv said. "After all, they're not paying rent, are they?" Liv laughed.

"Rent?"

"Rent in your head. They inhabit it and drive you crazy for free!"

"The squirrels?"

"Yes, Alex, the thoughts. They are like squirrels in our head, talking to each other – and we can't let them drive us crazy."

"And knitting helps?" Alex did not want to evict the squirrels in her head. She enjoyed her inner dialogue. At times it was her only company. Norway was lonely. And her ADHD brain was a big jumble drawer -- it never ceased to entertain her.

Liv led the way down a spiral staircase to the basement.

Alex stopped cold.

"What is it?"

"Over there," Alex pointed to the bathrooms.

"What?" Liv looked around, worried.

"Roger--"

"Oh, I totally forgot. I mean...I don't associate this place with --. Forgive me Alex," Liv said and put her hand on Alex's arm.

"It's OK." Alex patted Liv's hand. "Where are we going? Where is everyone?" Alex asked.

She was here in hopes of finding and playing the organ. Though she was not sure how she would play it, or hear it, or what good it would do. Getting into Kulturkirken Jakob was half the battle.

"We go through the basement and up the clock tower stairs. People rarely notice the stairs in the exit alcove. They end in a landing below the clock tower. It's wonderful. They've created a poetry space. You'll love it. It is the definition of hygge."

"Can hygge be spooky?" Alex asked as they felt their way up the stairs.

"The lights are off. I don't know what's going on here. I mean we're not super late. I'm never late."

"Sorry, it's my fault," Alex apologized.

"You would not have found this place without me," Liv said. She pushed open a door and they entered a warm room dominated by a large clock and an exquisite Persian rug.

"Welcome to Oslo strikk og drikk!" a woman at the center of the knitting circle called to them.

Alex found an open seat next to a vivacious Asian woman speed-knitting a striped cap.

"I don't think I've ever seen fingers move so quickly," Alex told her.

She laughed and said, "Liv tells me you are an anthropology graduate student."

"Really?" The woman next to the Asian woman reached out and shook Alex's hand. "Astrid. I'm also an anthropologist visiting from Denmark."

"Astrid is my roommate for the next few months. Where are you from? I'm Nora."

They returned to their knitting without dropping a stitch.

"New York City." It was one thing to be American, and another to be a New Yorker.

"New York," they said in unison.

"Like this," Nora showed Alex how to cast on her yarn. "I was once in New York, but I don't remember much," Nora said.

"Too much beer on the plane?" someone joked.

"No, it was when I was first adopted, and they flew us all from China to Oslo through New York City. I only remember that I made a wee on my seat."

"Nothing's changed Nora?" A woman across the room laughed, "Remember the Hytte trip last year?"

"You're an actress?" Liv looked skeptical.

"Yes, why?" Nora replied.

"You're lucky, you've never had to deal with being type-cast as a Viking maiden."

"Hadn't thought of that," Nora replied tersely.

"Have you?" Astrid asked Liv who pretended not to hear the question.

"Lovely rug," Alex changed the subject to the large Persian rug that adorned the room. Its warm blue and red floral pattern created a seriously hygge vibe.

"It's on loan from the Persian singer Mahsa Vahdat. She left it here for safekeeping with Erik Hillestad, her music producer, and Kulturkirken founder and longtime director. She says it is assurance that she will always return to Oslo," Nora smiled.

"What a cool idea this is. How often do you meet?" Alex yanked at the end of her ball of yarn.

"We meet once a month," a man with a round head and even rounder belly told Alex.

"Oh, I must've missed the last meeting," Alex feigned confusion, which was easy, as dates were not her strong suit.

"Don't worry, it's not sequential. You have not missed anything. With knitting you pick up wherever you left off," Nora said.

"Speaking of projects, what are you doing in Oslo?" Astrid

asked. Count on the academic to go straight to the project, thought Alex.

Alex explained her project to Astrid who politely nodded in interest.

"Astrid studies Caribou hunters in Greenland," said Nora.

Liv wedged herself in between Astrid and Alex. "Hei," she said.

"Watch out with her, I've seen her Facebook page," Liv whispered to Alex.

"What about it?"

"You learn a lot about a person from social media."

"You mean Fakebook?"

"Yes, anthropologist. For example, the woman across from you, the one with the magenta yarn is a total snob. Posh hotel check-ins and couture dresses – desperate for attention attained through ownership of objects. She's all *look at me --look at what I've done-- look at how cool I am.*"

"It's sad, needing validation from cyberspace," Alex agreed.

"Oh, and the hypocrisy! The head of our climate initiative posts from a long-haul destination every month. The food bank outreach person posts photos of her zillion dollar meals," Liv complained.

"Did Roger anger someone on social media?" Alex whispered, thinking Liv was quite attentive to social media for one who hated it.

"Was he on there? Didn't he prefer to socialize in silence? Facebook is loud."

Alex looked at Roger's still active profile. Either no next of kin had been given access, or they chose to keep it open. Was it necessary to keep it active for the investigation? Or was it a memorial?

"He's quite chatty on Facebook. It's like a different persona," Alex noted.

"Maybe extraverted online, introverted in real life?" Liv suggested.

"Would a true introvert be so prominent on Facebook?" Alex scrolled through pages of comments ... mostly philosophical tidbits.

"Lonely is more like it -- unable to communicate with people in person," said Liv.

"Hmmm. Did he piss people off?"

"One in particular, I'd say." Liv responded. "This is why I stick with plants. Humans are way too complicated – and, frankly, not so interesting."

"Hei Hei," The leader called to Thorvald who appeared in the doorway with a large grin and an even larger bag of yarn. He pulled up a chair next to Alex.

"You knit?" Alex asked.

"Astrid invited me. Yes, we knit at home, in the department, on the T-bane. I'm retired," he said and took out his in-progress scarf.

*So you keep reminding me*, thought Alex.

"Seriously, does *everyone* sing and knit in Norway?" Alex asked.

"Astrid is Danish," he clarified.

*And is everyone always so literal?*

"Yes, don't forget it," Astrid chimed in. Alex liked her; she was petite but powerful. And her muscular arms were testament to the hours of tennis she said she played to abate the stress at work.

"We all know who the real Vikings were. You Danes were only in it for the helmets and the horns," Thorvald said. Alex would never understand the humorous but vicious competition between the Danes and the Norwegians. When an amateur skier arrived on the ski slopes, Norwegians would cry: *Dane on the slopes.*

"And we know who the mother of Norway is -- Denmark. *Kjarringa pa hadeland*," Astrid said, settling the matter.

Nora, Astrid's roommate, asked Alex whether she'd been to the theater.

"Everything's in Norwegian," Alex said, "I mean, it's Norway, but it makes it hard for me."

"We're going to an English Ibsen production you may enjoy," she suggested.

"Which one?" Alex asked.

Alex was half listening to Nora's description of the Ibsen production -- she was more interested in the exchange between Thorvald and Liv. This was the gift of diffused attention. The ability to move uninteresting sounds to the rear of her attentional force and drag others right up to the front was a gift of her dyslexia -- Thorvald and Liv were oblivious to her listening in.

"Nice to see you again," Thorvald nodded to Liv.

Liv pretended not to hear.

"The mystery at the Botanical Gardens," he reminded her.

"I don't recall. You must have me mistaken for someone else," Liv said, head bent, concentrating on her knitting.

"That's one tiny hat," Alex pointed at Liv's knitting.

"It's not finished."

"It could be if it were for an infant." Alex observed.

"Alex, I'm buying tickets. Astrid's driving -- want to join us?" Nora asked.

"Sure," Alex agreed absently.

"You don't remember? The organs?" Thorvald asked.

Liv was saved by the leader's gong. "Commence!" she called, and the knit-a-thon began.

*Organs? Plural?* Alex tried to imagine the sound of more than one organ.

Thorvald did a deft cross-stitch without taking his eyes off Liv.

The second gong sounded and Alex startled, dropping her ball of yarn.

"What's with the gongs?" She asked, crawling along the floor after her ball of yarn as it rolled and unraveled past baskets and feet, "I'm so sorry. I'm so clumsy," Alex said.

She followed the ball of yarn down the hall and out the door to the top of the stairs where she swooped to retrieve what was left of it, only to notice a small speck of glistening dust. It looked like a piece of gravel from the driveway. She pressed her finger on it and examined it: a seed. A Casuarina seed? She stood and bumped right into Thorvald.

"Need help?" he asked.

"What was this Botanical Garden to-do that Liv forgot about?" Alex asked, pocketing the seed.

"I'm a bit of a detective," Thorvald grinned, "When they discovered animal organs -- liver and kidneys -- left in ritual-like form in the Botanical Gardens, they called me in to advise them on whether removing the organs would be sacrilegious."

"No kidding? You guys bring in anthropologists to explain the cultural significance of litter?" Alex was impressed.

"What would you do in the United States?"

"Throw it out," Alex said without thinking.

"Surely not? How culturally insensitive!" Thorvald exclaimed.

"Cultural sensitivity is not our strong point."

"But US academics drone on and on about it."

"Doesn't mean we practice it," Alex sighed. "Why are you really here?" she asked.

"Helping you chase your yarn," he replied.

She held up her ball of yarn.

"Ah. The threshold is a place to pause – Goethe," Thorvald said.

"Why are you here now, knitting? You don't strike me as the type."

"No?" Thorvald chuckled.

"No."

"We anthropologists don't subscribe to type," he smiled broadly.

He was right, this was not a good look for an anthropology PhD student to subscribe to type.

"Isn't your fieldsite sinking?" Alex blurted, her nervous system was starting to misfire.

"Technically not. It's being swallowed by the sea," Thorvald said gently.

"It's kind of a metaphor."

"Not everything is a metaphor," he replied.

"Why have you waylaid me at the threshold?" Alex asked.

"Between us," he whispered, looked around, and said, "The police have determined the murder weapon is a long sharp object. Like a chopstick."

"A chopstick?" Alex asked.

"Exactly," he confirmed and held up a knitting needle.

"You think the murderer is a member of this club? Someone in there? Now? Roger did not schedule a silent sip and knit. How did you learn of the knitting group? And why are you investigating? I thought Norwegians trusted the police to do their job?"

"My wife's friend in Bergen met husband number two in a knitting group and we were joking about knitting needles," Thorvald was saying, "And—"

"Knitting needles are funny?" Alex asked. She did not get Norwegian humor.

"Inside joke. But it got me thinking they could also be deadly."

"Which is why you are here?" Alex surmised.

"Well, the object used to killed Roger ..." Thorvald stopped speaking and stood extremely still.

"What is it?"

"I thought I heard humming, out of tune." He made a face.

"I wouldn't know, I can't carry a tune to save my life."

"Then how do you know you're out of tune?" Thorvald asked.

"I've been told," Alex admitted.

"We better get back," Thorvald said and held his finger up for Alex to pause. He counted to five with his fingers and motioned for her to follow him back to the room where they found Liv waiting by the door.

"Alex, there you are!" Liv exclaimed, "Are you blowing this off?" she glared at Thorvald.

"Shop talk," Thorvald flashed a sheepish grin. "We academics can't help it." He patted Alex on the back, and they took their seats.


At the end of the evening, Liv and Thorvald had started hats and gloves, while Alex could boast a tangled mess of yarn.

"Multi-modal?" Thorvald raised an eyebrow and turned to leave.

Alex stopped him, "How did you know to listen for the humming? Until you paused, I hadn't heard anything. You sopped speaking right before we heard anything."

"You're observant," Thorvald said. "Listening is tantamount to survival in the jungle where visibility is obscured by heavy overgrowth. One is attuned to everything -- including witchcraft." Thorvald said as Astrid approached. "So long," Thorvald bid them farewell.

"He's too friendly to be an academic," Liv said, as they watched him leave.

"I'm an academic. Besides, don't let him fool you, he's clever," Alex added, "I'll meet you outside," she told Liv.

Alex waited by the door while Liv, who was more meticulous when it came to putting away her projects, collected her things.

"Will you be joining us again?" Astrid asked Alex as she stepped outside.

"Are you joking?" Alex asked, holding up her ball of tangled yarn.

"I couldn't help overhearing Roger's name. It's terrible what happened to him. I can hardly get my mind around it. He was the nicest guy."

"You knew him?" Alex asked.

"Vaguely. When he first arrived, we worked on similar data sets. He was interested in my project in Greenland. He sounded a bit paranoid honestly. He kept reminding me to keep my research under wraps," Astrid said as she unlocked her bike.

"Why? Would someone kill for your data?" Alex asked.

"I don't think so," Astrid answered. "I've been doing this for over a decade and nobody's attempted to murder me," she said. "Though his dating skills could be a motive for murder."

"What do you mean?"

"We went on one date," Astrid admitted, "He cooked me a six-course meal while I waited and watched. Then he dumped me right after dessert."

"Right after dessert?" Alex didn't mean to laugh, she liked Astrid.

"He was punctual. Honestly, I was done with him by the time we sat for the first course. Before he even spritzed his pan with olive oil to begin his 'process,' we were done. He poured me a glass of wine, told me to relax and put on music of my choice. Then he freaked out over the jazz station I chose."

"Controlling?"

"In the extreme," Astrid agreed.

"Aren't all good chefs?" Nora said, coming outside.

"How are you getting on in Oslo, aside from a murder?" Astrid changed the topic.

"It's difficult making friends," Alex admitted.

"Yes, I can understand," Astrid commiserated.

"Especially if they're being offed," Nora laughed.

"Sorry, ignore the Norwegian noir," Astrid gently touched Alex's arm, "It can't be easy."

"Thanks, you're unusual for a Norwegian," Alex ventured.

"Because I'm Danish," Astrid reminded her. "The weather is warming; time for my season opening spring dip. No better spot than a spa on the Nord Fjord."

"The fjord is warmer than it's ever been," Nora noted.

"Not a good sign," said Astrid.

"The bus!!" Nora exclaimed and ran. "See you at the play!" Nora called back.

"Are you coming with us?" Astrid asked.

"It sounds amazing," Alex answered eagerly.

"Great. Bring your bathing suit," Astrid said. "And Alex," she whispered, "Norway is a safe place, but not everyone in Norway is safe. OK?" Astrid gave her a gentle hug, mounted her bicycle and rode off toward the palace grounds.

# Fieldnotes: Silent Thinking

*I was all ear and took in strains that might create a soul. Under the ribs of death.* John Milton

Oh my God, I need sleep. How did it get so late? Thoughts... thoughts and more thoughts ...all leading nowhere.

Liv calls them squirrels – the unwanted, uninvited thoughts. Are thoughts loud? Are they neuro noise? Are they out of place? Where do all the squirrels go? When do they sleep? Anders swims to drown the squirrels; Liv uses music.

*Music is made not of notes of sound but of atoms of time.* Maria Popova

Music opens a path into the realm of ~~science~~ silence. Music reveals the human soul in stark "nakedness," as it were, *without* the customary linguistic ~~grapes drapes tapping's~~ trappings.

Language is a system of taps. I'm too tired to tap. Is it already midnight? It's too light out to tell anymore.

Music and contemplation.

Why is contemplation relegated to religion? The Catholic Church banned polyphony, the playing of more than one musical part at a time, fearing it led to doubting the unity of God.

Dozed off. Dreamt of Kulturkirken Jakob. In my dream I'm walking through the church alone at night followed by a pantheon of gods singing in different languages. A polyphony of voices in my head turn to squirrels running into the dark corners of the church and my mind.

A squirrel chews on a seed -- evidence is eaten. A knitting needle -- a seed and a set of headphones sitting on the pew by the bathroom door.

What did I hear, but not pay attention to?

We all hear things twice. Sound enters our outer ears in turns. What doesn't make it in our ears is held back, reflected and then allowed in, seconds later. This delay is how the brain locates sound. Think of people without sight relying on sound to map the world by tapping a cane and listening for echoes. There's a geographical quality to listening. A geography the police want my map of. Drowned in sweat, sound, silence and sorrow.

*Why didn't you hear anything if your headphones were off?* They demanded.

Roger's headphones!

ALEX

Kit?

KIT

You still up?"

ALEX

Yup.

KIT

Why?

ALEX

Nightmare.

KIT

What did it feel like? Pay attention to the feeling of a dream.

ALEX

It was sad, mad, loud, and rhythmic -- I can't explain.

KIT

Your sound research is stressing you out. When's
the spa trip?

ALEX

Tomorrow. Maybe they'll have a sound bath.

KIT

Turn off the work for a minute woman. Très brave
to run off to a spa with two Scandi women you
just met. They can outrun you in the wild. Try not
to get overheated this time. Terrible things happen
when you leave women alone in saunas.

ALEX

Norwegians don't suggest, they propose. And
upon accepting an invitation there is no confirming
or double checking -- and certainly no backing
out.

KIT

Can you trust them?

ALEX

I don't feel like I can trust... Yes, why wouldn't I?
Thorvald promised a search party if I get lost in the
mountains.

KIT

Cool of him. Though, if it comes to a search, it will
be too late. Think frozen body found months
later...

ALEX

Thanks for the lovely image.

*Statistically the chances of finding a murderer are less with each
passing day. I'll freeze to death in Norway if this becomes a cold
case.*

KIT

Want me to come?

*Does Kit read minds?*

ALEX

~~Yes.~~

We leave in three hours; you couldn't make it on a leer jet. And I doubt they fly to random mountains in the middle of nowhere for Ibsen plays. Signing off…need to pack.

KIT

Pack warm.

*Pack heat is more like it.*

## Chapter 22

---

### *The Silent Return*

Fog, dense and heavy, hung over the dark waters of the Geirangerfjord. The scene was set for Henrik Ibsen's *When We Dead Awaken*: a wood platform; two chairs awaiting actors; a patch of folding chairs nesting a snug audience.

Alex hugged herself and rocked back and forth to stay warm. All around them craggy, ominous peaks stood sentinel like warning signs of an avalanche.

"It's true," Astrid confirmed Alex's anxiety. "An avalanche could cause a tsunami in the lake. A sign in the lobby commemorates lives lost in a nearby village wiped out by a tsunami caused by an avalanche."

The Norwegian unrivaled respect for nature's danger and reverent appreciation of her gifts, put Alex at ease.

"Here, this will help," Nora uncapped a flask and poured a clear liquid into Alex's cocoa. She took a sip and spat it out.

Astrid propped her glasses on her nose and looked at the program.

"You wear glasses?"

"Occasionally." Astrid squinted.

"May I see your glasses for a minute?" Alex asked and reached out for them.

Astrid handed them to Alex.

"Your lenses are crazed," Alex informed her.

"What?"

"It's the squiggly lines; it's from too much heat."

"Probably the sauna," Astrid said absently, placing the glasses on her nose and peering back at the program.

"You read in the sauna?"

"No?" Astrid frowned and snapped her glasses off her face and slipped them back in her backpack.

The proverbial curtain was minutes from rising on the three actors and the al fresco performance on sanatorium grounds.

"It's how I imagined a sanatorium in the mountains when I first read this play," Nora said. She opened a thermos and handed around paper cups. "Cider not spiked. I once played Maia," Nora whispered.

"Who is she?" Alex asked.

"The lead: a young woman married to the older professor," Nora answered.

"Typical," Astrid snorted.

"And they're taking the cure at a spa in the mountains – like us! Cool, no?" Nora sucked in air, making a Norwegian statement.

"I'd prefer taking a cure in the sauna," Astrid quipped. "And what's up with the guy at the front desk asking if I want a tour of the dead house?"

"The ground here freezes solid. In the old days, they stored the dead in death houses until spring when the ground was soft enough to dig and bury bodies in," Nora explained.

"Does it smell like dead bodies?" Alex asked.

"Does the Fjord freeze? Why not throw the bodies in the Fjord? A stake would be heavy enough to anchor the body," Astrid suggested.

"The Vikings would not waste a good spike," said Nora. She taught Norwegian culture to foreign students and was a wealth of information.

"I don't get it?" Alex asked.

"Need to pull the spike out," Nora motioned pulling, elbowing Astrid.

"Enough Viking history, you two," Astrid insisted.

"Theater it is. The play -- *When We Dead Awaken* will be in English. They--," Nora stopped and nudged Alex who looked up to see the actress playing Maia appear on the platform.

"Finally," said Astrid and yawned.

The actress was joined by a man wearing spectacles and wearing a tweed jacket.

"The professor, I presume," Alex joked.

"I was once sold shoes for an academic job interview by an out of work actor/salesman who insisted he knew what I needed as he had once played a professor," Astrid told her.

"Really? What did he choose for you?" asked Alex.

"High heeled Mary Janes." The women laughed. The older woman beside them shushed them.

The actor cleared his throat and nodded his head to the woman playing Maia, as if she needed his permission to begin.

MAIA. Just listen how silent it is here.

PROFESSOR RUBEK. And you can hear that?

MAIA. What?

PROFESSOR RUBEK. The silence?

MAIA. Yes, indeed I can.

PROFESSOR RUBEK. Well, perhaps you are right, mein Kind. One can really hear the silence.

MAIA. Heaven knows you can—when it's so absolutely over-powering as it is here—

PROFESSOR RUBEK. Here at the Baths, you mean?

MAIA. Wherever you go -- at home, here-- it seems to me. Of

course, there was noise and bustle enough in the town. But I don't know how it is—even the noise and bustle felt dead.


The actors froze, cueing the audience for a transition.

"Up," Nora commanded.

"What?" Astrid was waking from a cat nap.

"What's happening?" Alex asked.

"The play ends at the top of a mountain. We will now follow the actors and watch the rest of the play at the summit."

"The summit?" Alex asked.

"Cool, yeah?" Nora wrapped her shawl around her and retrieved her empty cup. "Let's go," She gestured forward movement.

Astrid rubbed her eyes and moaned.

"Were you asleep?" Nora accused her.

"My grant was due this morning. I was up all night," Astrid said, "I thought we were sitting and watching a play. No one mentioned hiking."

"It's hardly a hike," Nora said. Nothing short of scaling a mountainside was ever a hike for a Norwegian.

"I'll go to the inn and refresh. You guys can tell me all about it over dinner," Astrid apologized. She was gone before Nora could protest.

"You're missing out," Nora called after her anyway. She took Alex's arm, and they followed the small crowd along the trail.

"Our folk school was in the mountains. We lazed around all day reading plays and doing monologues, making costumes and learning make-up tricks. Brilliant times," Nora told Alex as they climbed to the next stage.

"Why didn't Ibsen like the title *Ghosts*?" Alex asked.

"That's another play," Nora says.

"I just read it."

"Ah. His English translator, William Archer chose ghosts. The characters are not ghosts, they're entirely otherly. But the Danish or Norwegian *Gengangere* would be more accurately translated as *Revenants* which means "The Ones Who Return."

"Right," Alex said. *The one who returned*, she tapped into her Notes app.

Nora pointed to an older woman with bright red cheeks. Dark blue eyeshadow bruised her slim lids.

"She was once a famous stage actress," Nora said.

She looked like a porcelain doll, and Alex wondered if she was here to play the ghost. She swiped her chin with the practiced ease of one habitually fixing bleeding lipstick from thinning lips. She caught Alex staring and grinned, revealing wine-stained teeth, more black than red from chain smoking and a recent swig of red wine from the mini-bar.

They climbed up a path better suited for goats and sheep. Across the valley, small wood farmhouses painted red clung to the side of the mountain like mushrooms emerging after a rain.

"How did they manage to build there?" asked Alex.

"Norwegians, unlike Swedes, do not need instruction manuals to build a home," Nora said.

At the plateau the woman joined the actor playing Arnold, or Professor Rubek. Maia held back, behind the audience from where she began to sing. The audience turned to look when Arnold spoke.

"This part is in Norwegian," Nora whispered, "Arnold is now alone with this mysterious woman." She translated.

"I see," Alex said. Why did people explain action when they were translating? Being linguistically impaired did not make her unaware of what was playing out in front of her.

"He recognizes Irene, his former model. He's touching her face, remembering sculpting her, but also determining whether she is alive or spectral."

"Why would he question her existence?" Alex asked.

"She's referring to herself as dead."

"Dead?" Alex asked.

"Yes, she tells Arnold -- she calls Professor Rubek by his first name -- she says posing for him was suicide."

"Intense."

"She claims he captured her soul and imprisoned it in his sculpture which is called *Resurrection,* by the way," Nora translated rapidly. She knew the play by heart. In the distance Maia's song tickled and vibrated crystals and bones in her outer ears which then pressed fluid in the inner ear and against a membrane that slid past the tiny hairs, triggering nerves to send a telegraph to Alex's brain: listen. Maia had been singing or humming all along. Working alongside Liv, Alex was accustomed to blocking background music. Liv was always listening to music.

"Brilliant -- using the actress as a soundtrack," Alex whispered.

"That's not all," Nora replied. "They have shortened this version, given we are in the mountains *in situ* and all, but the gist is while Arnold found fame and fortune through his work, and especially due to the sculpture of Irene, he hasn't stopped loving her. If you ask me, he's a bit obsessed. She, on the other hand, hasn't stopped thinking about killing him.

"Also obsessed," Alex surmised.

"Did you notice the actor off stage with a knife in her hand poised to stab him?"

An image came to Alex of a woman standing in the shadows at Kulturkirken Jakob with a knitting needle, poised to stab Roger.

"Arnold tells Irene he has felt dead since they parted."

"I'm guessing it's a bad move, admitting this to a psychopath?" Alex whispered.

"You're getting it," Nora laughed. "She answers that she is never without her knife."

"Like a sculptor and his chisel," Alex said -- *a knitter and her needle.*

"Here Ibsen gets a bit morbid: Irene alludes to having killed every lover and child since Arnold, including the unborn babies in her womb."

Maia's sound became louder and angrier.

"I forgot my earplugs. I don't like loud venues anymore. But, no, this is lovely, haunting," Nora said.

*Earplugs and Casuarina seeds. Abortion? The inner voice of a crying infant?* Alex thought.

"Arnold is pleading for his life. He suggests they live life together despite both being dead inside. Irene encourages him to climb to the top of the mountain with her. Oh, this is so exciting, Alex, they couldn't have planned it better! The stormy weather is perfect for the next scene."

"They hardly need to hope or plan for bad weather here, do they?" Alex said, shivering.

"They are going to unite at the top of the mountain – eternally together."

"Beautiful," Alex said, wanting it to end.

"In death," Nora added.

"What?"

Maia appeared on stage with a white sheet and threw it over the two lovers. The urgency of her song matched the oncoming storm. Alex feared the wind would take her. Nora finally clapped, followed by the rest of the audience.

"An avalanche has taken them to their death."

"Lovely," Alex said. "Are we dismissed? I'm freezing."

As they walked back to the lodge, Alex took a moment to make a note on sound.

*We cannot hear silence as it only exists in death.*

*Death is the only silence.*

*In death the hum of breathing ceases, the beating of a heart ceases, the fluttering and blinking of eyes ceases, the rhythm of tapping feet ceases. The voices in one's head cease to exist.*

*A death rattle in the lungs precedes a natural death. Like a faulty muffler coming to a halt, so ceases a life well worn.*

*In life, silence does not truly exist. We are never devoid of sound. Roger is eternally silent. Or is he?* Alex typed.

*Voices in the head, unblocked, drive one mad be it by tinnitus, auditory hallucinations or constant squirrels. I'm feeling squirrelly.*

*A mental breakdown whether loud or dead silent, severs our tether to language, which in turn binds us to society. Norwegians enter my world through English, but without Norwegian I have no place in theirs. In Arabic, absurdity is an inability to hear. In Latin Surd means Deaf or nonverbal. Beckett's characters hum in theater of the absurd when their tether to the world is severed. The Greek logos, denotes speechlessness and irrationality and here I always thought logos was the world. Ibsen...humming...hmmm?*

"I thought the Norwegian breakfast buffets were Valhalla, but I was wrong," Alex said taking in the sight of the never-ending dinner buffet: roast reindeer, reindeer stew, lamb chops, crab legs and whale. "They need a vegan trigger warning at the door. Every local animal from whale to deer is splayed, split and spun on the buffet."

"No frog legs. The Austefjorden, which we passed on our way to the spa has a bridge for frogs. Imagine? The municipality of Volda re-routed an entire road to protect the crossing frogs," Nora told them.

"You Norwegians are full of contradictions," said Alex.

"Who isn't?" asked Nora.

They took their seats at a table near the window.

The waiter attempted to take their drinks order, but they were far more interested in observing the commotion coming from the lobby.

"Tourists," Nora guessed, "Norwegians are quiet."

"It's the police," the waiter whispered, "They're here to make an arrest. Drinks?"

Astrid was ordering a white wine when the police approached their table.

Alex felt sick.

"Astrid Andersen?" The officer asked.

"Ja?" Astrid replied. She sounded as officious as the police.

"... Roger Adams ...the night of March 31ˢᵗ..."

"Why her?" Alex blurted out, before she was fully sure of what they were accusing Astrid of.

"This is confidential -- we apologize for interrupting your dinner," the officer replied in English

Astrid handed her car keys to Nora.

"Please help yourselves to the dinner buffet," the waiter said and left.

# Fieldnotes: Frogs in the Fjord

The Fjord follows us in a game of hide and seek through tunnels from Loen toward Volda, and eventually, Oslo. Darkness is rare in spring -- my luck has us driving through the most majestic and stunning scenery in the world in the only hours of dark. Nora, understandably, is keen to return to Oslo to help Astrid. So, we drive in the dark, Nora listening to a Norwegian Noir in Norwegian, while I journal.

In the darkest of night, water stays alongside us, below us, raining down from above us. It chases us tunnel to tunnel, as we emerge from dark into light, and light into dark. In one long tunnel a laser light project keeps drivers alert. Another example of Norway's dedication to funding public works with art while keeping people alive. Funding artists a living wage and making everything pedestrian and utilitarian beautiful and interesting. This is what differentiates a civilized society from one no longer pretending to be civilized or democratic or cultured. Otherwise, the dark landscape is as haunting as Ibsen's play. To understand, to feel Ibsen, is to walk beneath these dark clouds, to feel the cold, humid Norwegian spring and biting winter snow. Otherwise, you risk missing the crisp, clean, sharp texture of Ibsen's writing.

Why Astrid? Doing ethnographic fieldwork is like doing detective work, moving from clue to clue, from interview to interview, building a picture leading to a discovery, whether of a new cultural phenomenon or a killer. Nothing led me to suspect Astrid. Anthropology is a science which does not preclude it also being a collection of coincidences. I draw conclusions from coincidences and see patterns no one else sees. Picking up on the oddities in conversations, unspoken expressions, glances. Paying attention to inconsistencies in people's stories through participant observation. Making material objects speak. Will thinks I solved the murder in Bozeman not because of my linear training in anthropological inquiry, but because I jump all over the place. Will ~~believes~~ believed in me, why don't I? What am I missing? My dream returns to me in snippets: Seeds, knitting needles, headsets...humming. Does humming have a fingerprint, a signature?

I've finished my literature review. I've researched sound, visited RITMO, learned about the headsets and rhythm. I interviewed everyone I could related to Roger.

I'll draw a kinship chart. Included will be material objects and how they relate to everyone on the chart. A kinship chart of objects.

Thorvald: seeds, knitting needle, sound (sings but does he hum?)

Anders: sound, headset, *Silent Singles*

Peder: keys, cat

Astrid: knitting needles, sound, headset...

This is stupid. I've never met the murderer. Why did they try to kill me? We've met, but I was ... wait for it: I was distracted.

We remember what is unique and what affects us emotionally. Like the color of a bully's sweater on the playground – because we were looking at it as their words struck an emotional blow. Extraordinary, (out of the ordinary), events are better imprinted as nothing competes with them for our attention. Anders stole my attention at Kulturkirken Jakob. His blue eyes, his black hat, his smile. What was I not imprinting in my memory that I should have?

Memory presents as fact -- highly susceptible to distortion. Memory is not a replaying, but a rewriting.

Ibsen's *Ghosts* -- a painter, fallen women, alcoholic husbands, alcoholic fathers and a baby.

*I am frightened of a thing in me that is ghostlike and that I cannot escape...*

A baby.

Why did Roger ghost Ibsen? *When We Dead Awaken* begins with silence. Ibsen was *the* most obvious theme for a *Silent Singles* event. And yet, Roger ghosts him. Why? Is there a connection between Munch, Ibsen and the murderer? And, no, I promise you, it's not because they're the only Norwegian artists I know. Ibsen's *When We Dead Awaken*: Irene kills all her unborn babies. All her undone lovers. In a later lithograph Munch adds a fetus embryo. After the fall: Adam and Eve. Smoldering tree. Loving woman who becomes a Madonna. Baby Jesus. The Kulturkirken Jakob mural. A baby. Ecstasy, despair, anxiety – alcoholism.

A deep, grave chill cuts through the breathtaking Norwegian landscape. It's lush and green and foggy ...like Japan. No, not the sublime; terror has no place in this story. There is however an element of beauty in human nature's terror.

Ibsen was in conversation with Munch. It's all over his diaries.

Maia's song – a knife -- previous lovers -- murdered child – seeds block crying – the mountains.

Ibsen: *There is a riddle behind everything that you say, Irene, every word is whispered into my ear.*

The riddle is being answered, the silence is being broken.

*Perhaps only I understand you.*

Dried seeds – death that leads to life. Munch's Frieze of Life starts with *The Voice*, in a series called *Love*.

Christian Krohg, a critic contemporary to Munch wrote: *Self-portrait under the Mask of a Woman* has such a musical expression Munch should be awarded a composer's pension.

Ibsen loved Munch's *Three Women*. Munch told him that the dark one standing in the tree trunk could be a nun or a woman's shadow -- sorrow and death. *When We Dead* Awaken ends with a nun and a song. A nun with the last word. A stage set for a savior's birth. A crying infant...the ghost of God? Mary, theater, pretending, singing, humming. Ane Brun! *Take Hold of Me.*

A brick hits my head, and someone hums *Take Hold of Me* Roger was killed as the DJ spun *Take Hold of Me.* Ane Brun. Why?

Take Hold of me.

Protect me?

Never let me go,

Don't drop me.

Ane Brun sang a killer song.

Take Hold of me. Don't drop me.

Anders, strong, silent Anders protected by a tattoo of Huldra, the siren who lures men to their deaths with her song. The siren with a killer song. The sorrow, the dark hidden in a tree trunk. A Japanese woman calling the name of her dead child.

I never forget a voice. Out of tune, rhythmic, melodic, wrong pitch -- I memorize it like a face. Grunting, singing, humming, talking; a voice, if you know how to listen, has a print as unique as the swirls on a finger. Would I know this voice singing, humming, or grunting? Had I paid attention and listened – then, yes, I would. And now I have.

We will meet in the shadow of the tree. But not just yet.

# Chapter 23

## *Cat on a Cold Norwegian Roof*

Alex woke with *Silent Night* in her head. Months away from Christmas music overload season and her subconscious was agreeing with her. She was on the right track. Alex's phone rang.

"No way," Liv said without a hello, "I got your message. I'm allergic to cats. You will not get me to adopt a cat."

Liv, in Alex's estimation, was the quintessential cat woman.

"Please come with me. I need a lookout."

"What for? Nope. Not going into a dead man's apartment. You are breaking a law; I am a law-abiding Norwegian citizen."

"Fine, I'll go alone," Alex said and hung up.

Alex called Anders.

"I'm not a cat or a dog person. I am a person who travels for work. A fish is asking too much of me," he told her.

"Please?"

Alex launched into all the reasons Anders should take a cat.

The scratching sounds and stolen cat food in Peder's knapsack convinced Alex that a cat needed rescuing. Peder had kept Roger's keys or a duplicate set. *Peder is up to no good.* What else had he stolen from Roger?

Alex entered the vacant lobby and took the stairs to Roger's apartment.

She could hear the cat purring the minute she stepped into the bedroom. She came prepared. She crouched down on the floor and stuck her head under the bed.

"Here kitty," she said, reaching out her hand with the offer of a liver treat.

"Leave the cat," a voice said behind her.

Alex startled and hit her head on the bed frame.

"Or else?" She asked.

"Or else I call the police."

"Why would you call the police? You're the one who shouldn't be here," Alex crawled out from under the bed and stood to face Peder. She was acting far more brazen than she felt.

"It's my cat."

"What do you mean it's your cat?"

"I live here."

"How can you live here? This is Roger's apartment."

"I'm squatting, for God's sake! Anders said you were smart, quick."

"I thought Norwegians were law-abiding?"

"We are also socialist, and this apartment is going to be vacant for the next six months while they wrap up this case and the next of kin have shown no interest in coming here...the books will be packed and sent off in the mail and as I need a place to stay–"

"So, what, you get to stay here until then?" Alex demanded, feeling she owed it to Roger. *Six months?* She said to herself.

"I've decided to stay here until then."

"So, this is your cat? You were feeding her?"

"Yes."

"Were you and Roger friends?" Alex asked.

"Not really."

"Meaning?"

"He let me stay here when he was away on research trips. He was kind and would not mind my being here now."

"No one else thought he was a nice guy."

"No one else knew his secret."

"Secret?" Alex asked.

"Why he started a *Silent Singles* group."

"You knew about the group?" Alex asked.

"He was hard of hearing, and he refused to get hearing aids. He was stubborn and it made life difficult for him."

"You might've mentioned this before."

"Why would I? To what end? What's the point? He didn't want anyone to know while he was alive. It's not my business to tell people after his death. And besides..."

"Let me guess, no one asked," Alex said.

"Exactly. Why do you care?"

"I'm trying to solve his murder, and it's a major characteristic—"

"Why?"

"Not hearing, because—"

"No, why are you trying to solve Roger's murder?" Peder asked.

"I'm a possible suspect, and I want to go home."

"You wouldn't be telling me this if you thought I was guilty," he pointed out. "If you didn't trust me," he added for good measure.

*True, I don't need to like him to trust him*, thought Alex. Confusing the two got her into trouble, especially where men were concerned. *Or had it?* She needed to think it through.

"It's about sound and silence and... something is speaking," Alex muttered, and looked around.

"Are you hearing voices in your head? It's stress. I heard them too until I went on medication."

"No, I'm not hearing voices. But it's interesting Roger wasn't hearing voices. It explains why he set up *Silent Singles*. He didn't want to mishear and respond awkwardly. He didn't want the social responsibility of listening. Nor did he desire being alone with his silence," Alex thought aloud.

"Yeah, I get it. It makes sense. You are smart, Anders was right," Peder said. "*Silent Singles* saved him from responding inappropriately or not at all to people. I can tell you it caused trouble in his relationship with Siri."

"I wonder..."

"Yes?"

"I wonder if he didn't hear his assailant," Alex said.

"Would it have made a difference? Would he have gotten out of the way in time?"

"Who knows?"

"Or the killer knew he was hard of hearing. They knew they could sneak up on him," Peder suggested. "Like a ghost."

"Yeah, maybe...It doesn't make sense. I'm not sure why. The murderer had an excess of passion and wanted Roger to know he was being punished. This was not a silent killer. Why else pick a quiet venue? Also, why not ensure he was dead before leaving the scene?" Alex asked.

"Right. The killer was interrupted?" Peder suggested.

"Why aren't you staying with family?" Alex asked.

"I need to be in Oslo for work and I'm from the West."

"I thought you went to high school with Anders?" Alex asked.

"I did, at a folk high school in the West, in the mountains."

"Oh. Look, I'm sorry I barged in like this. The key belongs to Siri. I should give it back to her. Don't worry, she is not going to use it anytime soon."

"Yeah, OK, thanks. And for what it's worth... yeah, you and Anders, not bad. You're more interesting than the other women he's picked."

"Other women?"

"He's a sensitive soul. But he chooses intense women, and it's not the right choice for him."

"Are you saying I'm not intense?"

"No, I mean, you're light. It's a good thing. We Norwegians appreciate humor. It's the Swedes who want everything dark."

"Is there anything you guys like about the Danes or the Swedes?" Alex asked.

"Should there be?"

Alex chuckled, "You're not so bad yourself, Peder. Let me know if you need me to watch your cat, I've never owned a pet before, it might be fun."

"No pets, ever?"

"I've had a transient lifestyle myself." Alex said.

# Fieldnotes: Not so Silent Scooter

A tourist on a scooter clipped me as I crossed the Europa Hotel Tram stop. I admonished him for being on the sidewalk. When he didn't respond, I yelled: "Did you hear me?"

He shook his head. "Hei at least pretend you can't hear me!" I yelled. And then I got it! Shaking his head meant he heard me but chose to ignore me. Just like Roger. It wasn't what he heard, but what he *didn't* hear. Roger died because he ignored his assailant. The murderer called to him, and he didn't respond because he did not hear the call. Had Roger's killer known him, they'd have known he was hard of hearing. Instead, they assumed Roger was ignoring them, which angered them. Roger didn't hear his killer come up behind him. That's it! The murderer called out to him, and he didn't respond. The killer got angry and stabbed him in the back. Is this theory a total stab in the dark?

ALEX

I'm mourning a cat I never lost. I'm mourning the lost opportunity to have had a pet. I imagined it so much the past few days at one point I jumped back thinking I had accidentally stepped on her tail. I keep thinking I need to feed or walk her. Am I losing it?

KIT

Walk a cat? You haven't a clue, woman. A pet would be good for you. Start with a goldfish. A buddy to talk to.

ALEX

The silent feed? A friend who won't talk back. Are you saying I need to dominate a conversation? Silence too is communication.

KIT

Your point?

ALEX

Will. No word – nothing. Anders is easy. I get him.

KIT

Opposites attract.

ALEX

Will's perfectionism, his persistent planning drives me nuts. Why are squirrels and nuts used as a metaphor for insanity?

KIT

Can you imagine living with you? You'd go crazy. You're misreading Will.

ALEX

There's nothing to read.

KIT

Not true. You are stellar at reading people and patterns.

ALEX

He's sending me every kind of signal short of using the alphabet. His silence is communicating a choice.

KIT

No one's ever accused that man of talking too much, I must say.

People say I talk too much. It hurts; it's like they're saying *I'm* too much. I'm excessive, excess, unwanted. My brain is always firing, especially when I'm stressed, and it's either talk or write and... tinnitus, of all things. Will joked that being with me is like having tinnitus. How hurtful. Wait.... Tinnitus? Yes! That's it. That's why. The humming, the voices, the crying, the lack of silence. The inability to tolerate silence. A person suffering with tinnitus would never join a silent singles group, ever.

As Will is teaching me: silence is a form of communication. Roger's death is about silence as much as it is about love. Silence and sound and the beams of endurance. Some cannot endure sound, others can't endure silence, and all of us according to William Blake can barely endure love. If I am tinnitus for Will, then Roger was the sad song in someone's head. A song too loud and repetitive -- a bad earworm, or case of tinnitus. An infant wailing. Which is worse: listening to someone else's pain without being able to help, or your own? Is this why we scream? To get it out?

Screaming for help. Screaming for catharsis. Screaming to be heard. Does screaming release pent-up anger and depression? Is it the ultimate way to blow off steam? Must we vocalize pain to release it? Screaming at a child is as damaging as hitting them.

If the force of vocalization is equal in volume -- does it count as communication, or as violence? Violence is communication.

Voices, sounds in the head. Will I hear the sound of shooting by looking at bullet holes? Will I feel pain or a slap across the face when I look at Munch's Scream?

Who is screaming for help? What can't I hear?

Can screaming decrease pain? Does it help in childbirth? Why block the ears? And why at a silent disco, where at any moment a witness might remove a headset? This was an impulsive act. The confrontation may have been planned, but not the stab. Which may explain why the killer used a knitting needle. Like my lipstick, it was laying around and on hand.

In the jungle weapons are noiseless. A blow pipe – an organ. No guns, no shots fired. No sound was emitted from a cozy cabin like in Munch's case, or a cozy suburban home in Janet Cardiff's diorama. No noise, no sound, no sonorous evidence. Silence is evidence. The killer underestimated this. Don't look at what is there, but what isn't. Always look in negative spaces. Look for what is missing. I come back to it all the time, Bernice Regan Johnson. The unwritten history, the unspoken, silent narrative, is the more powerful part of the story. Anthropology is about unearthing silence. Ethnography gives voice to stories. It offers sound and attention to the silenced. Magic is a trick of attention. The killer knew about my ADHD. Here's the story--

My bad -- I was not paying attention. The seeds are to block the dead mom's ears from the crying infant as she passes to the next life. Initially I misunderstood it as a dead infant. Why? Because I accidentally understood what happened. My synapses misfired and inadvertently led me to the real story. I was listening to everything everyone told me, but not paying attention.

An unborn baby dies. A mother continues to hear the cries. The doctors call it tinnitus; she calls it unbearable grief. She tries to block the sound but cannot. She journeys to a faraway land to forget. When she returns, she sees the man who killed her baby. She is lost in a trance of rage, the crying gets louder and louder until she takes the weapon at hand, and she calls to him. She demands that he turn and face her. But he ignores her, and she stabs him. The shock of blood makes her realize what she has done, and she runs, leaving him to die. She hides in a place she knows to go. She is lucky, no one looks for her there.

I found her by following a trail of sorrow, seeds and song.

Here's a question: does music disappear the moment it's sung?

The jungle. You would never willingly block sound from your ears in the jungle. It would be too dangerous. Noise-cancelling headphones or earplugs get you killed in the jungle. Refusing to wear hearing aids is like wearing noise canceling headphones in the jungle. Like taking off your glasses and walking to the edge of a cliff.

Nothing was planned. But as the murderer will learn, planning is underrated. Ask Miss Jane Marple.

Hercule Poirot, an older man, was believable to a 1930s audience when he solved a case with his little gray cells. Whereas Miss Marple, an old woman with Poirot's mental acuity, was not given the same respect. Hercule had the luxury of leaning on a fireplace and espousing a convoluted theory that fell nicely into place and ended with a confession. Lucy Worsley posits as a woman in those days Ms. Jane Marple was not considered a reliable narrator and thus had to prove her theory -- by which she set a trap. I'd argue it was not because she was a woman that she set the trap, but because she was using her dyslexic, nonlinear reasoning strengths, the same skills as her dyslexic author, Agatha Christie, where the answer comes first, followed by the proof. Like math geniuses who arrive at an answer without mapping out every step to get there. Poirot had a detailed roadmap, Marple had a hunch. I have more in common with Marple than Hercule Poirot, and so, if I am to prove my hunch, a trap it will be. I will be the bait. I will wait. I will listen for witchcraft in the jungle.

ALEX

Hei Hei. They've arrested Roger's murderer!!! It's all over. There is a final Silent Singles event, a memorial, Silent Sculpture tomorrow, sunset, Ekeberg Park. Meet you there?

UNKNOWN

See you there.

Game on.

# Chapter 24

## *The Silent Siren*

"There's an incline," a woman coming down the path warned Alex who asked if this alternative route into Ekeberg Sculpture Park was arduous.

"The pulse pumping kind," the woman added a warning.

"Is it an *oh my God I'm going to die* pulse or a *I'm exerting myself* pulse?" Alex asked.

"I would say, exerting," the woman answered definitively. She looked-up at the sky and added, "Bad timing for a walk in the park."

"Thank you," Alex said, looking at the path ahead of her.

Her pulse climbed less from exertion than fear, as she transitioned from walking to running -- a trot to a canter. A flying lead change? She had no idea what it meant but liked the sound of it.

The pine trees, the boulders, the paths all looked the same. The forests were walking – coming at her, enclosing her in their shadow.

"Where am I? Did I overshoot it?" she muttered to the empty space. North, southwest or East. Was she moving in circles? Had she climbed up and then down? Her phone's lost signal indicated an unfamiliar territory.

She came upon the remains of a bunker, an ancillary exhibit, a site/sight, to behold and to read about –in Norwegian. No time for translation.

The bench overlooking the reflecting pool called to her, and she wished she were meeting a friend to chat with and not entrapping a killer. Time was barely on her side. *Needs must*, she thought, and pushed on.

She hoped the killer was better at directions. She needed to catch Roger's killer *in situ*.

She finally found Huldra and laid the trap at her feet. Small speakers, for pumping sound; small recorders, for recoding sound. She created art on art.

*Thank you, Jane Marple*, thought Alex. Miss Marple excelled at reading tone having listened to conversations her whole life – while knitting. How ironic. Reading tone comes easy for those of us who have spent half our lives struggling to read text. A gift of dyslexia. *I never liked the murderer's tone*, thought Alex. She took a last look at her notes and trashed her script.

Huldra threw a dark shadow across the barely melted snow.

*Being early might be the death of me*, Alex thought, as the temperature plummeted, and a light drizzle began. The rush of the wind obscured the sound of footsteps, her own breathing, a scream, should she avail it.

Alex's phone pinged:

UNKNOWN

Where are you? No one is here.

ALEX

Sorry, I got the time wrong. Everyone is gone. Lost my new beau, want you to meet him! He's looking for the silent siren – no clue what he meant. Do you? I'm freezing, he's not responding to my texts, where is the siren?

No reply.

.   .   .

Had she scared off the killer? The answer arrived as a tattoo of heavy steps crunching snow and headed her way: 1,2,1,2... perfect rhythm, perfect symmetry. Humming: Ane Brun's *Take hold of Me* -- urgent, unhappy and off. A desperate attempt by a killer stay to calm. *Stay calm.*

"Is it not strange we four should meet here in the middle of the wild mountains?" Alex called out Maia's last line from Ibsen's *When We Dead Awaken.*

"Where are you? I thought you were lost. Is this a game? Where is he?" a familiar voice called out.

Alex stepped out from behind Huldra.

"I was right? Huldra was the talisman?" Alex said.

"What talisman?"

"The silent siren of the mountains who lured men to their death with her song," Alex said.

"Everyone knows Huldra. She's a part of our mythology."

"A siren. Like you," Alex said.

"What do you mean?" The voice was sharp.

"You're always humming--"

"I've hardly lured any men."

"This *is* she?" Alex pointed at the sculpture.

"So, we've established. Let's go, it's freezing." The figure moved toward Alex.

"The drawing on the bathroom mirror was of Huldra," Alex did not move.

The game had begun.


"What are you talking about?"

"Don't be coy," Alex ventured. "It was well-rendered."

"Are you mad?" The figure moved closer to Alex.

"No. Are you?" Alex toyed.

"*This* is mad."

"You're mad at men -- or at one man in particular."

"Because I don't date?"

"Because you plunged a knitting needle into a man's heart." Alex's heart raced.

"I didn't know Roger."

"Which explains your shock when I said his name. You thought you stabbed Anders. They were wearing the same hat. The hat was *the* detail I imprinted but forgot. You called to him; you hummed a bar of a familiar song. When he did not turn, you assumed he was ignoring you. How dare he? You lashed out, planned or not and stabbed him with a knitting needle."

The figure passed Huldra the way a cloud covered the last of the sun. They were one – Huldra and the murderer -- a sculpture and its shadow.

"I stabbed a stranger with a knitting needle? You're insane. Your desperation to find a culprit, or a scapegoat and go home is making you crazy."

"Is it? I mean, yes, it is." Alex played Ane Brun's *Take Hold of Me* on her phone. "But he didn't hold you, did he? He dropped you."

"You have no idea."

"Then tell me, aren't we friends?" Alex insisted, she needed a recorded confession.

"Friends? You befriended the monster who killed my baby."

"Anders--" Alex began.

"Don't say his name."

"While we were meeting on the stairs, you were downstairs killing Roger."

Liv let out a cry.

"I saw Anders--," Liv started.

Alex's heart raced. She was admitting her crime.

"He was coming up the stairs and you were going to stab him when I appeared. You hid in the bathroom before I saw you. You drew Huldra while Anders and I spoke on the stairs. When you came out, you saw Roger leaving the coatroom and assumed he was Anders. He had his back to you and was wearing the same black cap Anders wore."

Liv lunged at Alex. Blood streamed down Alex's cheek. She stood her ground. She needed a confession.

"What caught my attention--" Alex started.

"Let me guess, the seeds. You're *planting* this on me because of seeds. Plant...seeds. You like puns. *Please*, I am a botanist, too easy," Liv chortled.

"You said the seeds were found in his ears. They found them on his chest. They slipped from his ears and fell into the blood," Alex informed her.

"So what? It hardly implicates me. You're an anthropologist not a detective," Liv reminded her.

"For Anthropologists, the field is our mystery – we go into the field and follow clues just as detectives do. We observe as a world system emerges from people's motivations and values. What we call culture is a multi-faceted web of love and lies. Anthropology is about asking the right questions. Why does Liv want to kill Anders? That's why you're here, no? To try again?" Alex goaded her.

"Drama queen," Liv retorted.

"Drama. Exactly. Ibsen's play brought it all together. Your famous folk school was a theater school, wasn't it? Anders went to a theater folk school where he dropped a fellow dancer -- by accident." Alex knew this could put Liv over the edge.

"Accident?"

"She disappeared completely from Norway soon after." Alex watched Liv.

Liv was silent.

"Like a ghost, a revenant, she returned," Alex continued.

"I thought you couldn't read?"

"That's the beauty of theater. I *watched* the play. I'm an observer, Liv. The flipside of my inability to *connect* the right letters is my ability to *connect* ideas and clues that others would never put together. Like you and theater. Or your aversion to dance. The lady doth protest too much, I thought to myself. It's extreme for someone surrounded by music. When I hear music, I see movement," Alex said.

"Because you're strange. Forget ethnography, you should write fiction. This is absurd."

"The seeds, the humming, you can't shut off the voices, can you? Music is seeds in your ears. It blocks the negative angry voices. Below us is the former site of the sanatorium where Munch's sister was committed. On a quiet night you can hear her scream."

"It's the wind."

"Ibsen would say it's the revenants. *You* are the revenant. You returned from England to haunt Anders."

"Ridiculous."

"I couldn't understand why you so adamantly denied having met Thorvald at the Botanical Gardens."

"So what?" Liv said, her hand with the knife was dangling limply at her side while she listened.

"He told you the story of the seeds. He's a consummate teacher, he did it without thinking, without remembering," Alex said.

"He explained why the organ meat, cow hearts and liver, were placed in the gardens," Liv corrected her.

"Exactly, he explained the importance of the rituals."

"Your point?" Liv snapped.

"They were offerings for a dead child. Like the tiny hat you were knitting," Alex said carefully, watching the knife as she did so.

"All hats start small," Liv insisted.

"As does all life," Alex said. Her fingers were freezing, the blood on her cheek burned, she needed a confession. She continued, "The seeds were for Anders. He should have been the one haunted by a dead baby. Right? After all, it was his fault. When Anders dropped you, you dropped the baby. The baby's cries never cease. Headphones, music and humming are your seeds --"

"Stop!" Liv yelled and covered her ears. The knife braised her cheek, and she was bleeding.

"When you discovered you had killed the wrong man, you set out to kill Anders with a stronger vengeance. You thought he was a member of Roger's group. You shadowed him at the Munch Museum and then hoped to see him in the sauna. Clever – locking yourself in the sauna to deflect attention from yourself as a suspect. At Frogner, you aimed the brick at Anders but missed and hit me."

"I'll take better aim this time," Liv raised her hand – the knife gleamed in the last wink of the sun. "You should pen novels. I suggest murder mysteries -- way more lucrative than academic books," Liv laughed.

"Poor Roger. Had he not been wearing the same hat. Poor Roger, had he not been hard of hearing, had he only agreed to wear a hearing aid. *Silent Singles* was his hack to socialize without being misinterpreted or saying the wrong thing."

"Stop!"

"You snuck up behind Roger. You called to him. You said: *Anders.* And when he didn't respond, you stabbed him in the back with a knitting needle and placed the seeds from behind. You ran to the alcove. You knew Kulturkirken Jakob well as you'd been there for knitting. You knew where to find and replace the knitting needle."

"Pure fantasy," Liv clapped. "Great storytelling."

"You registered surprise when I told you the victim was an American named Roger. Your reaction seemed odd, and I wondered why you would care about the man's nationality, unless, of course, you expected him to be Norwegian. Was it planned?"

"I wanted him to die dancing. Doing what he did when he killed my baby," Liv said.

"You murdered an innocent man."

"Innocent? He devastated me. I left school. I left Norway. I went to England and changed my accent and switched to my middle name."

"Revenant. The ghost of your former self returned to pierce a hole in his heart."

"I'm the one who had a hole in my heart. The seeds were for me; they were in my ears. They fell out as I bent over him, I ... I was going to save him before I heard you again..." Liv said.

"When did you start hearing voices? It is voices you hear. You called them squirrels. It's not tinnitus, it's grief."

"Are you calling me insane?" Liv stepped toward Alex. They were both shaking.

"Stabbing a man with a knitting needle isn't exactly sane behavior. Why frame me?"

"The lipstick was a gift from the universe. It took the attention off me and placed it squarely where it belonged: on a suspect foreigner, a Botanical Garden worker and traitor."

"Traitor?"

"You danced with him."

"I had just met him."

"I only wanted to confront him," Liv said, coming closer. Alex stepped back, glancing at the tree trunk. *Where was the blinking red light. Had the battery died?*

"I wanted an apology. My knitting bag was a decoy, my excuse for being there. The silent disco was sold out – more good luck, as I would have been on the suspect list. There was no premeditation. I planned to confront him in a crowded setting where he couldn't escape and where no one could hear us."

"Your decoy became your weapon," Alex fidgeted with her iPhone, she needed the confession and could not be sure the camera was still recording.

"Yes."

"And now," Alex fumbled and dropped her phone. She kept her eyes on Liv and squatted to retrieve it.

"Leave it," Liv demanded. "The time for talking ended with Roger's death. Frankly, I'm done talking with you. You're always in the way."

The sun descended behind them as Liv lunged at Alex.

Alex sidestepped her.

"I wouldn't if I were you, we both know I'd make a spectacular ghost. And I would haunt you forever."

"You can't prove any of this. It's your word against mine. No one's going to believe you. You're jealous, frustrated and desperate to find a culprit so you can go home. You have been in my way at every turn. But it worked to my advantage. I've outsmarted you, Alex. I don't want to kill you. I like you. We don't have the death penalty here in Norway. Our prisons are quite nice. You may request a pet."

"What?" Alex asked.

"I will find him, I will kill him, and I will further implicate you. No one will be the wiser."

"Perfect -- you implicate me. And I run," Alex backed up.

"Wait," Liv turned, suspicious. Alex had been too eager. "Things can change on a dime. One day I woke-up and suddenly stopped wanting to kill myself. My English therapist was thrilled. She thought getting in touch with my anger at Anders and wanting to 'kill him' was therapeutic progress rather than a plan."

"So, it *was* a plan?" Alex goaded her, praying the recorder was on.

"First Anders made me want to die, then you. As I am not suicidal, I will kill you both."

Liv hummed as she closed in on Alex. In the distance, Alex heard sirens – Huldra, the ultimate siren, had sung her song. A sign for Alex to run. And Alex ran -- changing the speed, volume and velocity of everything.

# UiO Student Newspaper Interview with Alex the Anthropologist

The most brilliant move was to livestream the confession. Why livestream?

In case the recording failed. It's like backing up to the cloud. There was no straightforward way to hide witnesses on the narrow path. The livestream saved my life.

**How?**

A friend who was watching noticed Liv was agitated, and he called the police.

**Then what?**

Sirens.

**What will life be like when you return to the US?**

I'm in deep *kimchi* with my PhD committee. Things went south when I went north. I'm an anthropologist of urban culture and yet, I keep ending up in the proverbial wild.

**What's the one trait you like most about yourself?**

My curiosity, though it gets me in trouble.

**What do you like least about yourself?**

My lack of self-confidence. I don't trust my intuition enough. We grad students suffer from imposter

SYNDROME AND IT'S WORSE WITH LEARNING DISABILITIES. I HAVE ADHD AND DYSLEXIA.

**WHAT IS YOUR GREATEST FEAR?**

BEING ALONE. NOT LIKE ON A GLACIER ALONE, BUT IN LIFE, ALONE. I WAS AN ONLY CHILD OF A SINGLE MOTHER, AND SHE DIED WHEN I WAS IN HIGH SCHOOL. I HAD TO CREATE MY OWN FAMILY. MY BEST FRIEND KIT IS LIKE A SISTER.

**WHAT MAKES YOU HAPPY?**

A GOOD MYSTERY, A COMPELLING RESEARCH QUESTION, A PROBLEM TO SOLVE. I LOVE BEING DEEP IN A PUZZLE. AND IF IT INVOLVES HUMAN BEHAVIOR, ALL THE BETTER.

**IF YOU COULD REWRITE A PART OF YOUR STORY, WHAT WOULD IT BE?**

MY LOVE LIFE. IT'S DOOMED TO FAILURE. RECENTLY I WAS SENDING LOVE LETTERS WITH NO ANSWER -- IT TURNS OUT I GAVE HIM THE WRONG ADDRESS. AS I WAS LEAVING OSLO A WOMAN VISITING FROM BERGEN SHOWED UP AT MY DOOR WITH A BUNDLE OF LETTERS ADDRESSED TO ME. A WORLD OF POSSIBILITY AND LOSS EXISTS BETWEEN REJECTED AND WRONG ADDRESS.

**HOW DID SHE FIND YOU?**

EVERYONE KNOWS EVERYONE IN NORWAY!

**WHO WOULD YOU LOVE TO TRADE PLACES WITH IF YOU COULD AND WHY?**

KIT. SHE IS INTELLIGENT, GLAMOROUS, FUNNY, HAS A GREAT FAMILY AND IS KIND. SHE ALWAYS CHOOSES COLLABORATION OVER COMPETITION. KIT IS A COMMUNITY BUILDER. WE NEED COMMUNITY AND CREATIVITY MORE THAN EVER.

**WHAT'S NEXT FOR YOU?**

A WARM CLIMATE. AN EXTREMELY HOT DESERT WOULD BE IDEAL.

**DO YOUR LEARNING DISABILITIES GET IN THE WAY OF SOLVING MURDERS?**

MY DYSLEXIA AND ADHD CAN BE A REAL PAIN IN THE ASS. I WORK TWICE AS HARD AS ANYONE ELSE. BUT THE PAYOFF

IS GREATER. I AM LIKE A DOG WITH A BONE WHEN I HYPER FOCUS – THE H IN ADHD. MY DISTRACTIBILITY HAS ME JUMPING AROUND AND MAKING CONNECTIONS OTHER PEOPLE WOULD NOT. I NOTICE RANDOM DETAILS AND MAKE ODD CONNECTIONS OTHERS DON'T. IT'S NOT THAT I DON'T PAY ATTENTION -- I DO IT DIFFERENTLY.

**How so?**

FOR ONE, I AM NATURALLY UNDERCOVER AS PEOPLE TEND TO UNDERESTIMATE ME. LIKE MISS MARPLE, SITTING IN THE CORNER WITH HER KNITTING NEEDLES, PEOPLE ASSUME I'M NOT PAYING ATTENTION AND LET THINGS SLIP. ONLY MY KNITTING IS NOT AS STEALTH AS OLD JANE MARPLE, WHO SURELY HAD A MEAN CROSS-STITCH (IS THAT WHAT IT'S CALLED?). I EXIST IN A DIFFERENT TIME ZONE FROM NEUROTYPICAL FRIENDS: I GET DELAYED, I HYPERFOCUS, I EITHER SPEND TOO MUCH TIME, OR AM IN A RUSH. MY BAD TIMING CAN BE USEFUL.

**TELL ME AN INSTANCE WHERE IT WAS HELPFUL?**

SHOWING UP ON THE WRONG DAY AND CATCHING SOMEONE OUT. DISSECTING A CONVERSATION HOURS LATER AND UNEARTHING A SUPERFLUOUS DETAIL THAT SEEMED MINOR AT THE TIME BUT ENDED UP BEING INTEGRAL. IT'S A STRENGTH AND A WEAKNESS TO ENGAGE A PLETHORA OF TOPICS AT ONCE. I ALSO HAVE THE GIFT OF DIFFUSED ATTENTION –I CAN PAY ATTENTION TO A NUMBER OF THINGS AT ONCE. THE PROBLEM IS THAT NOT EVERYTHING HOLDS MY ATTENTION.

**How is being a detective like being an anthropologist?**

ANTHROPOLOGY IS ABOUT FOLLOWING ONE'S CURIOSITY. A MURDER MYSTERY IS THE PERFECT FORM OF ANTHROPOLOGY. LIKE A DETECTIVE, AN ANTHROPOLOGIST SOLVES A PUZZLE THROUGH CLUES BASED ON HUMAN BEHAVIOR. AGATHA CHRISTIE WAS A PSYCHOLOGIST AT HEART. WE LEARN ABOUT PEOPLE AND WHAT MOTIVATES THEM THROUGH THEIR ACTIONS. MOST MOTIVATIONS ARE UNIVERSAL: GREED, LOVE,

SEX, LUST, DESIRE, POWER. ALL CULTURES HAVE THEM, BUT THE WAY THEY PLAY OUT DEPENDS ON LOCAL RITUALS AND MYTHS OR WHAT WE CALL ETHNOGRAPHIC SPECIFICITY. AT THE END OF THE DAY, NO SOCIETY OR CULTURE IS MORE PRONE TO MURDER, AND NO HUMAN IS ABOVE IT. ALL OF US HAVE BLINDERS, ARE SUSCEPTIBLE TO DENIAL, AND FIND WAYS TO HIDE OR EXPLAIN AWAY WHAT IS UNSAVORY OR UNKNOWABLE. DETECTION AND ANTHROPOLOGY SHARE THE NECESSITY OF COINCIDENCE AND LUCK. BEING AT THE RIGHT PLACE AT THE RIGHT TIME, MAKING CONNECTIONS AND FOLLOWING THREADS -- GOING DOWN RABBIT HOLES.

**ALEX, IT SOUNDS LIKE YOU LOVE BEING AN ANTHROPOLOGIST.**

*MAYBE I WON'T QUIT AFTER ALL.*

THE END

ANTHROPOLOGIST ROXANNE VARZI SAYS ETHNOGRAPHIES DO NOT HAVE ENDINGS.

*TO BE CONTINUED.*

# Acknowledgments

*Tusen Takk*

My experience of Norway was nothing like a Nordic Noir, which is why it is the perfect place for a Cozy (*hygge*) mystery and why there are so many Norwegians to thank.

First, I am indebted to my dear friend and colleague Thorgeir Kolshus, or in Etic terms, Head of Department, Social Anthropology, University of Oslo, who graciously hosted me as a visiting researcher in his department.

Thorgeir (and his lovely parents) introduced me to *hytte* culture, the *dugnad* (along with his lovely family), which I thought was the ultimate insider invite, until I was handed a pair of work gloves. And inadvertently (thank you Mathias) to the Silent Disco concept.

The Department of Social Anthropology at UiO was another *hygge* environment with its Friday quiz, and many lively lunch conversations with colleagues that entailed everything from the latest anthropology research to the best ways to dispose of a body in Oslo.

Erik Hillestad and Marianne Lystrup introduced me to Oslo's musical culture. It was as Erik showed me around Kulturkirken Jakob, an organization he founded and ran for thirty years, that I discovered my crime scene.

And, my dear friends, Marit Ulvund and Stein Helge Solstad's hospitality in Oslo and especially Volda gifted me the book's primary setting by the Munch Museum and its final setting amidst the green, foggy, gorgeous Nordfjord.

Norway would not be Norway, without a Dane wondering about– and I was lucky to meet the kindest, cleverest Danish anthropologist, Astrid Oberborbeck Andersen, my Danish sister. When we weren't typing away as visiting researchers at the UiO, Astrid and I were fighting off the fear of flesh-eating bacteria in the Fjord (a myth), sweating in a sauna, eating shrimps on a nearby Island and attending an Ibsen play with Astrid's equally fun friend Solvei Grimen Fosse.

Serendipitous meetings profoundly influence any mystery, and this one had many such meetings.

Alexander Refsum Jensenius, director of RITMO and his colleagues Ann-Kristin Solbakk, Drew Johnson and Kyle Devine.

Artist-extraordinaire, Terje Nicholson, whom I met through a mis-identified portrait.

Thomas Hylland Eriksen, who intrigued to hear I was writing an anthropology mystery, shared with me his unpublished essay on detectives and anthropologists. His recent passing is a great loss to Norwegian anthropology, and it is with the kind permission of his wife Kari Spjeldnæs, that a quote from that essay appears at the beginning of this book, alongside Agatha Christie -- because anthropologists and detectives do at times belong on the same page.

Nick Seavers, who as a PhD student at UCI attended the gallery opening of my very first sound installation, now a professor, shared his article on sound. Torstein Parelius took me on a deep dive into Death Metal and Ugo Nanni into the arctic.

Many organizations hosted my Armchair Anthropology book talks, including but not limited to, the New School for Social Research, Hunter College High School, Chapman University (Disability Studies), The University of California Trust in London and especially, Greta Paa-Kerner, the UC Humanities Center, especially Judy Wu and Julia Lupton, and the Center for Medical Humanities, which hosted my discussion with Jonathon Mooney – a dyslexia-ADHD hero of mine and author of *Normal Sucks*.

Dyslexia warriors: Kate Power and Kathy Iwanczak Forsyth, Dr.'s Sally and Bennet Shaywitz, (founders of the *Yale Center for*

*Dyslexia and Creativity*), Dr.'s Fernette and Brock Eide, (authors of *The Dyslexic Advantage* and inventors of the online Dyslexia Screener). Dr. Helen Taylor's research not only pops up in the storyline, but she also popped up on stage to discuss dyslexia and ADHD with me in London at the University of East London. Mathew Bellringer and I dove deep into dyslexia, Danes and the rule of Jante. And my dear friend Sam Oscar George who is *the* most dedicated champion of twice exceptional students (especially dyslexia and ADHD), but an early reader and supporter.

Scottish mystery writer, Olga Wojtas, whose books I love, generously read my manuscript. And my Scottish *Sisters in Crime* mentor, Wendy H Jones, encouraged me to throw stones at Alex once I had her up a tree.

The Newport Beach Public Library Media Lab, especially Greg Johnson and his colleagues at the amazing Sound Lab provided a *hygge* recording studio for the audiobook version of the Armchair books. Please support public libraries!

Thorgeir Kolshus, Astrid Oberborbeck Andersen, Sean Stratton, Carolyn McAuliffe, Krista Nicholds, Charlotte Varzi, Rumi Paydavousi and Sherine Hamdy were insightful first readers. Violet and Hilla in London, and Sahba and Ali in New York City, for their generous hospitality. Brandi Williamson for walks and talks.

My friendship with Emil Madsen Brandt who emailed me twenty years ago after reading my book *Warring Souls* while studying art at Copenhagen Art Academy is a testament to the friendships books enable. This author loves to hear from readers, please reach out!

And Stephanie Takaragawa, (and Ethnographic Terminalia) for being an enthusiastic early adopter of ethnographic innovations – and one of my first Armchair Anthropologist readers.

My fellow writers and colleagues at *UCI Write*, especially Olga, Ilana and Nina for much needed writing retreats. My Romania Retreat buddies – I won't name them as one of them with a name ending in *A* may be the next murderer!

*What are the chances,* thought Alex, *I mean really, is it statistically probable that on a writing retreat with eight anthropologists from all over the world 7 of them would have names ending in an A -- one of them ending in a silent A??*

Thank you to all of my wonderful colleagues at the University of California, Irvine.

Thank you to all of the librarians, researchers, teachers, artists and parents who work so hard to advocate for students with neurodifferences.

This book was written for my students past and present, in Irvine and elsewhere – thank you for trusting the process and for keeping me teachable.

For family members and friends of anthropologists everywhere who have no idea what we really do or how we do it (including at times our own students). And for the person sitting next to me on every flight, and at every party, who upon hearing that I am an anthropologist tells me they wished they had taken more anthropology courses – this is for you.

And Kasra, the man who always fills my dance card – thank you for the beautiful cover, book design, editing, and for always